NEW ORDER

BO BLACKMAN
BOOK TWO

HELEN HARPER

For Lizzy, Symond, Marcus, Leah and Boosh

CHAPTER I

FINGERTIPS & FROLICS

The rain has made the cobbles slick and wet. They glisten in the faint moonlight, as if awash with blood. I could swear they're tinged with red but it's probably just my overactive imagination. I shiver, though not because of the cold. I've not felt cold since I gulped down a pint of O negative six weeks ago. I'm not sure if that makes me more warm blooded than when I was human or if it just serves as a reminder that I'm a freak of nature. A bloodguzzling monster surrounded by a family of bloodier criminals. I zip up my leather jacket anyway; the mundane act makes me feel more normal.

Up ahead, the shadows at the doorway to Fingertips and Frolics elongate as the latest customer exits. I squint at the figure. He went in too quickly for me to get much of a read on him but now that he's pausing outside I can tell, even from my concealed position, that he's a white witch. The tattoo shimmering on his left cheek is a dead giveaway. I can't make out the particular brand but white witches are inked on the left, black witches on the right. I feel slightly more relaxed now that I know he's on the paler side of magic users. I'm not naïve enough to believe that makes him 'good' per se, but an establishment that deals with the whites is more likely to help me out. My old family name doesn't endear me to black witches and even though I've theoretically abandoned the title of Blackman for Montserrat, I know they won't register the difference.

The press recently dredged up the old political correctness argument about witches. It's clearly a series of planted articles, paid for by the magic lobbyists, but it's of interest nonetheless. The ethnic human communities point out that to use the terms 'white' and 'black' to describe different forms of magic is racism by implication, especially when most of the population believe that black magic is inherently evil and white magic is pure and natural. Indeed, etymologically speaking, the word 'necromancer', which falls firmly in the category of black magic and sends a shiver down the spine of any tabloid-pages-swallowing human, derives from 'nigromancer', a term coined around the 1500s. That's 'niger', the Latin for black, and 'manteia', the Greek for divination. White witches are more than happy to agree with the sentiment and suggest we use the terms 'high' and 'low' magic instead. Naturally, white magic would be 'high'. This sets black magicians howling in self-righteous indignation. They argue that if the words are changed, they should be altered to 'non-binding' and 'binding'. The white witches counter that those terms are too unwieldy and will never catch on. The rest of the country watches with interest, and continues to stick to the universally understood 'black' and 'white' – at least for now.

The truth of the matter is that the words and their respective witch factions have nothing to do with skin colour and nothing to do with either good or evil. They're just different ways of doing things, I guess like Protestants and Catholics, although admittedly witches are given little choice in the matter. They're born, not made. You'd think that with a name like Blackman, my human family would be viewed favourably by black witches, but the dealings my grandfather had with them in the sixties and seventies damned our name forever among them. Whoever said that we should look forward and not back has never met a black witch. But it means that Fingertips and Frolics will be more likely to be amenable to my request. A white witch would never frequent a black magic shop.

Satisfied that the store is empty, I emerge from my shadowy hiding place. O'Shea put me onto this place and, while I still don't entirely trust the daemon's motives, I'm willing to try anything. The window, backlit with a soft orange glow, contains an artful display of carefully arranged bottles of different colours and hues, as well as numerous pieces of magic paraphernalia. I'm pleased see that there's nothing showily fake; as far as I can tell, all the contents are the real thing. My confidence is slightly buoyed. The last place I visited – again on O'Shea's recommendation – was purely for tourists. I don't think there was anything in that shop beyond daft tricks.

I take a deep breath and push open the door. I've barely stepped over the threshold, however, when there's the sound of a clanging siren. I curse: it must be a vampire alert. Businesses, unlike homes, don't benefit from the triber-based laws of physics which state that, unless invited, a vampire can't enter. As a result, many of the less bloodguzzler-friendly joints set up simple spells to alert them when a vampire crosses into their triber premises. Frankly, until recently humans have been more welcoming to vampires than the rest of the tribers put together. And if you think about it, that's completely ridiculous because the only species that vampires feed off are humans. Triber blood just doesn't taste nice. So I'm told.

Rather than moving further inside, I wait to avoid causing

more alarm to whoever is manning the store. The last thing I need is some anti-vampire spell thrown in my face. It won't kill me, but it'll damn well hurt. As a newly fledged bloodguzzler, I'm more vulnerable than most of my older Family members.

'I come in peace!' I yell, feeling faintly ridiculous as the words leave my mouth. I'm a run-of-the-mill bloodguzzler, not a goddamn alien. Still, it seems to work because a head bobs up from behind a stack of towering books and raises a speculative eyebrow in my direction.

'You're a vampire.'

I avoid rolling my eyes at this less than profound statement. 'Yes,' I nod, holding my palms up as if in surrender.

'Which Family?'

'Montserrat.' At least I have that on my side. The Montserrat Family is considered the least belligerent or dangerous of the five Families. They do, however, have far-reaching fingers in many pies so tribers tend to treat them with more respect than other vampires. Of course, I'm not here with Montserrat approval but the shopkeeper doesn't need to know that.

My interrogator's eyes blink owlishly. 'You're new.'

I'm impressed she can tell. 'Yes,' I agree. 'Only six weeks.'

She comes out from behind the stack, curiosity getting the better of her. 'I thought they didn't allow newbies out for years.'

They don't. I shrug and offer a faint grin. 'I'm special.'

'Hmm.' The woman is in her late forties and impeccably dressed. Her face is blemish-free so she's not a witch, but there's still an aura of magic clinging to her that makes me pause. 'Neo-druid?' I guess. It's a shot in the dark but I have a gut feeling that I'm right.

Her lips purse. 'A fledgling vampire who actually knows something. Interesting. What can I do for you?'

I relax slightly. 'It's knowledge I'm after,' I say softly. 'Vam-piric. I've been told you might be able to help.'

A knowing expression crosses her face. 'Let me guess. You've made a terrible mistake in being recruited and you're looking for a way to reverse it.'

It's my turn to be surprised. None of the other people I quizzed worked that out before I told them. Then again, none of them realised that I was a new vampire. My thoughts must be obvious because she gives a knowing smile that doesn't quite reach her eyes. 'Why else would such a young bloodguzzler be here?'

'You've had others?' I ask hopefully.

She shakes her head, although her expression softens. 'No.'

My delight dissipates. I don't bother with any further preamble. 'Can it be done?'

'I don't expect so. But,' she adds, holding up her index finger in the air as my shoulders sag, 'it's not something I've ever had to look into before.'

I regard her thoughtfully. 'And if I asked you to look into it now?'

The woman starts re-arranging some semi-precious stones on a shelf. She picks up an amethyst and frowns at it, before returning it carefully to its original place. I bite my tongue to avoid snapping impatiently at her.

Finally, she looks at me. 'Why would I want to do that?'

'I'll pay you. Whatever your price.'

There's a flash of greed on her face; sadly, however, her words don't match her emotions. 'Supposing there is something out there, some long-forgotten spell that can undo the transformation brought about by the recruitment process. If it exists, it's buried deep. It could take months to locate and there's no guarantee that – even if such a spell exists – it would work.'

'I can wait.'

She exhales loudly. 'You have all the time in the world. At

least another two hundred years, assuming you don't get knocked off by wandering around the streets asking stupid questions when you're as weak as kitten. I don't have so much time.'

I grit my teeth. 'I will compensate you for your time.'

'My husband would have told you that money won't help me when I'm six feet under. He was an idealist.'

'But...'

'Look. You seem nice, but look at it from my perspective. I spend time and energy finding this spell, which is so elusive no-one has ever heard of it. If I find it and use it to turn you back into whatever manner of human you were, what do you think happens next?' I frown. 'I'll tell you what happens. I have the five Families after my head. I would probably last about five minutes. So think about it. Why would I want to jeopardise my short, mortal lifespan getting on the wrong side of just about every vampire in the country?'

'They might be happy about a reversion spell,' I protest weakly.

She shoots me a droll look. 'Really? How do they benefit from such a spell?'

'People make mistakes! They should be able to change their minds.'

'What happens if the Families start using it as a weapon against each other? Medici decides he doesn't like Lord Gully so he returns him to a human state in order to be able to kill him with a flick of his wrist. How do you think that would play out?'

'They wouldn't do that. There are laws...'

'Vampire laws to protect vampires.' She cocks her head. 'It would be a different story if they were human.'

'I understand your argument,' I say, attempting to reason with her. 'But the government would go nuts if the Families started killing humans whenever they wanted to.'

She throws back her head and laughs. 'Do you really think anyone outside of the Families would care if an ex-bloodguzzler ended up dead?'

I stare at her dumbly.

'Besides, even if that wasn't a problem, do you honestly think you're the first new vampire to have regrets? It probably happens all the time. I doubt anyone would be happy to see a bunch of criminals abruptly returned to the streets. And I don't think any of the Family seniors, not even the Montserrats, want a headache like that to deal with. All that effort during recruitment for it to suddenly vanish?' She clicks her fingers and a puff of white smoke rises up to the ceiling. 'No. If I came across a reversion spell, they'd kill me without a second thought.'

I step forward, then realise that might be considered threatening, so I move back again. The fact that this woman knows the Families have a strong criminal element means she's not just blowing smoke up my arse. Literally or figuratively. Sensing any sliver of opportunity I might have is slipping away, I make a last-ditch effort. 'We wouldn't have to tell anyone.'

She looks at me steadily. I bow my head, unwilling to acknowledge defeat. 'Do you know anyone else who might be prepared to look for a reversion spell?'

'I hope that you're not encouraging me to put any of my acquaintances in danger.'

'Please. There has to be something...' My desperation is obvious.

She is stone-faced: utterly, implacably immoveable. 'There's not.'

Dead-ended, I turn to go. 'Thanks for your time,' I murmur.

'Whoa!' She grabs my arm. Reflexively, I throw her off and send her spinning backwards. Her body slams into the nearest wall then crumples to the floor. I wince. Damn it. I keep forgetting I'm a lot stronger than I used to be. I rush to help her up but she scowls at me and struggles to her feet on her own.

'I was going to tell you,' she says rubbing her arm where it had banged into the wall, 'that if you don't want me repeating this conversation to anyone such as a senior Family member, you will compensate me for the time I've just wasted and buy something from the shop. After that little act, you can buy two things.'

'What?' I blink at her. 'That's mercenary. You can't do that!'

'You just attacked me,' she points out calmly. 'Imagine if word got out that the Montserrat Family is allowing dangerous new vampires onto the street where they are harming innocent bystanders. After the murders a couple of months ago, there's enough concern about your lot as it is.'

Unbelievable. I shake my head and curse then, without looking, scoop up two random objects from the display to my left. 'Fine,' I mutter. 'I'll take these.'

'Too cheap,' she scoffs. 'Someone of your calibre can surely afford to spend a little more.'

I'm tempted to smack her hard on the head and walk out. Instead I grit my teeth. 'Can you make any recommendations?'

She smiles. 'I thought you'd never ask.' She picks up the amethyst she was frowning at earlier and passes it over. 'This. And...' pursing her lips she examines the shelves then hands me a bright green feather '...this.'

I stare down at the price tags. 'You have got to be kidding me.'

'They're very good value.'

'Fifty quid? For a feather?'

Her eyes sparkle. 'It's a very special feather.'

Gods above. I dig into one of my pockets and pull out some crumpled notes. Thank goodness I tapped Arzo for some cash the last time I saw him. He wasn't happy about it but given the mess his machinations got me into, I didn't give him much choice.

I thrust the notes at her. 'Here.'

'It's been a pleasure doing business with you. Wait here while I ring it up.'

'Don't bother.'

'Oh, you must have a receipt. Rules are rules.'

I give her a dirty look. 'Does that mean I can return the items later?'

Her smile is more patronising than friendly. I mutter a curse under my breath that would have my grandfather gasping in horror at my unladylike language. Then I leave, stupid feather, sparkly stone and bloody receipt clutched in my hand. She didn't even give me a bag.

I shove the amethyst into a side pocket. With nothing better to do with the feather, I stick it behind my ear. Then I pull out my phone. I shouldn't have it; fledgling vampires are meant to stay well away from the real world to ease their transition into their new life. This, however, is another helpful 'gift' from Arzo.

'That was a total bust,' I say as soon as O'Shea answers.

'Really?' I don't believe he's as surprised as he sounds. 'I'd heard she might be amenable if the price was right. I guess my sources were wrong.'

'It's a legit shop, O'Shea, and the owner is far from stupid. She's not going to go against the Families.' I'm trying not to sound accusatory because he got my hopes up - but it's not easy.

'It's not for the Families. It's for you,' he answers pragmatically.

I sigh. 'You know and I know – and she most definitely knows – that they wouldn't like it.'

O'Shea takes a deep breath. 'You could always leave.'

'Leave?'

'Leave the Family. Strike out on your own. Be independent.'

I snort. 'Yeah, right. Like that'll work out well. What I really need is for you to speak to your shadier contacts and see if there's anyone with a grudge against the vampires who might be willing to help.'

There's a moment of silence before he speaks. 'Sure. Except...'

'What?'

'I've already spoken to everyone I can think of, Bo. Nobody wants to get involved.'

'Try harder,' I growl, walking back down the cobbled alley-way. 'It's not like you're doing much of anything else right now.' One positive side effect of the recent events that saw me trans-formed into a vampire is that O'Shea is now being kept on a short leash. He takes almost every opportunity to complain about it but, secretly, I think he likes the attention.

'That's mean,' he whines. 'I'm doing my best.'

My fingers curl into fists. The trouble is that I believe him. 'There's got to be something else you can do,' I tell him briskly.

'Bo...'

A well-dressed man suddenly appears at the end of the street, silhouetted against the street lights. Bugger it.

'I have to go.' Without waiting for a response, I hang up and stuff the phone into my pocket. It's probably too late to hope that the man's not seen it yet, but maybe I'll get lucky. I straighten my shoulders defiantly.

'My Lord,' I say, when I reach him. 'Out for a stroll?'

Michael Montserrat glares at me. 'This is the third time in a week.' His tone conveys his mood. 'Don't you think I've got better things to do than run around after one bloody recruit?'

'Technically,' I tell him coolly, 'I'm not a recruit, I'm a fully-fledged vampire.' Although I have to admit I'm surprised that he's out here. It's usually great, hulking Ursus who deals with newbie issues. I may not have been with the Montserrat Family for long but even I know that Lord Montserrat rarely bothers his arse with fledglings' problems.

He rubs his hand across his close-cropped hair. 'Like I don't know it. Bo,' he sighs. 'What are you doing here?'

'I needed some air. I was tired of feeling cooped up.'

He glances at the lit window of Fingertips and Frolics. 'I know you don't like this,' he says, 'but you can't change it. There's no way back. It's time you stopped trying to find an escape route and started facing facts.'

I look him in the eye. 'That's easy for you to say. I never wanted this.'

'Do you think I don't know that?' he snaps. A muscle throbs in his jaw. 'I'm sorry. There are only so many times I can say that, though. What's done is done. Sooner or later you'll realise that being a vampire isn't so bad.'

'I doubt that,' I scoff.

'Bo,' his voice softens, 'I'll do whatever I can to help you. I feel responsible for what happened to you.'

'You *are* responsible.'

He sighs. 'Fine. I'm responsible. Feel free to blame me as much as you want. But you can't keep leaving the mansion. The rules are in place for a reason. Right now, you're still too vulnerable to be outside.'

I don't want to keep arguing with him but I just can't help it. This is too important. 'I wasn't doing anything dangerous.'

'How do you know? Anything could have happened! Anyone could have been in that shop!' Frustration crosses his face. 'I don't want to see you getting hurt.'

Despite feeling oddly warmed by his words, I don't veer off track. 'I can look after myself,' I tell him.

'You're part of the Montserrat Family now. That makes you my responsibility.'

'I'm not a child.'

He looks at me steadily, then gives a short, sharp laugh. 'No. You're definitely not that.'

There's something in his eyes that makes my stomach squirm. I tell myself that we have a special connection because he's the one who turned me. In these modern times, would-be recruits are usually injected directly into their veins with a combination of vampire blood. To make it easier for me to not drink for the full lunar month following my initial turning, so that I could become Sanguine and be more human than blood-guzzler, I drank Michael's blood directly. Clearly, it didn't make much difference in the end.

I put my hand on his arm. 'I'm sorry. I'm not trying to make your life more difficult. I'm really not. I just...' My voice trails away.

'Bo,' he sighs again. 'I get it. I do. But you can't do this.' He reaches out and pulls the feather away from my ear, twirling it in the palm of his hand. Then he changes the subject. 'This is pretty.'

'Not pretty enough to warrant the cost.'

His eyes narrow for the briefest second. 'Where did you get money from?' He holds up his hands. 'On second thoughts, I don't want to know. The last thing I need is to have to disci-pline someone else.' He tucks the feather back behind my ear, his fingers brushing against my skin. 'How about a compromise?'

I stare at him warily. 'Go on.'

'You're not going to find a cure. If such a thing existed we would already know about it.' I open my mouth to speak but he places a finger against my lips. 'However,' he continues, 'your case is a special one. Because you didn't want to be recruited and you agreed at my urging, I can afford to treat you differently without receiving too much flack.'

I find it hard to imagine anyone giving Michael Montserrat flack for anything.

'If you promise not to sneak out again, I'll take you out once a week.'

I have a sudden vision of us dating. Dinner, dancing, bowling. I shake my head to rid myself of the images. Far too weird. That can't be what he means.

He looks amused, as if he knows what I'm thinking. 'I'll show you how far you can push yourself. What skills you have now that you're one of us.' His eyes gleam at me in the darkness. 'I can show you your real potential.'

One-on-one vampire lessons with the Head of the Montserrat Family? I don't want to know what amazing skills I have now or what my potential is, but that's still a hell of an offer.

'Of course,' he adds, 'if you don't agree, then the only alternative is to lock you up in your room until you see the light. We've got plenty of time and I can be a very patient man.'

I'm fairly certain he's telling the truth – he'd have absolutely no qualms about sealing me inside my tiny bedroom back at the Montserrat mansion until I choose to drink the Kool-Aid and give in.

I push down my rising anger and chew my lip. I know that O'Shea has exhausted every possibility he can think of. My next plan was to visit my grandfather. He has a wealth of knowledge in that crafty head of his. The trouble is, I'm not sure how he'll react to me not making it to Sanguine. That's the main reason I've put off going to see him up till now. I don't want to have to deal with his censure as well as my own. I'm scared to think what the look in his eyes in will be. The last conversation I had with him suggested that he understood what I was doing, but that was when there was the chance I could avoid being a real vampire. He bloody well sent Beth after me to help with that.

Promising Michael that I'll stay within the fold might give my grandfather time to come around to what I am now. And it'll give me time to become brave enough to face him.

I'm not giving up on the chance of finding a cure but I can put it on hold for a while. Just because I'll be a virtual prisoner doesn't mean that O'Shea will be. Besides, Michael's not mentioned my illicit possession of a phone so I'm sure I managed to hide it before he saw it. That means I can contact Rogu3 as well. Perhaps playing docile little fledgling for a while will be a good thing.

Michael's arms are folded as watches me. 'Okay,' I say cautiously, 'I can promise that for now.'

His mouth tightens, but I swear there's a sparkle in his eyes. 'For now?'

I shrug. 'Best I can do.'

'Then it's a deal. I'll throw in a sweetener and even let you keep that damn phone.'

Before I can say anything, he sticks out his hand and I shake it. His grip tightens until I can't pull away and my fingers start to feel crushed. He leans in towards me. 'Don't break your word, Bo,' he whispers into my ear. 'There's no telling what I'll do.'

He releases me and I yank back my hand, pain shooting through my fingers. I stare back at him, remembering that he's not the Head of the Montserrat Family because he's a nice cuddly guy with good looks and a pretty smile. He's bloody scary.

CHAPTER 2

ROOFTOPS

Beth and I are lounging on the sofa in companionable silence when Ursus appears. He gives a good impression of a snarl. With a lazy yawn, she gazes at him. 'Hi Ursus.'

'You are supposed to be meeting Ria to go through your latest evaluation.'

Beth checks her watch, an old battered Timex that she never takes off. 'Oh smeg. Yeah, okay.' Slowly clambering to her feet, she yawns and stretches her arms high above her head.

'Get a bloody wriggle on!' Ursus curses, his expression growing more irate when she takes her time over finding the stilettos that she insists on wearing. Eventually she manages to put them on and flashes him a brilliant smile. 'Thanks for the reminder, boss!' she trills, before sauntering away.

I hide my smirk, not moving from my position on the sofa. He jabs a finger in my direction. 'This is all your fault!'

I blink, a picture of innocence. 'I didn't know she had a meeting. I don't see how it's my fault.'

'It's your attitude,' he hisses. 'It rubs off on all the others.'

'Hmm. My attitude, you say? I'm never late for a meeting.'

It's true. I can't abide it when people aren't punctual so I make a point of always being on time. Or if not on time then early. I just don't think my time is more valuable than anyone else's. But that didn't stop me from enjoying Beth's little show.

Ursus glares at me. Since the time he and Ria attacked me in the garden of the Montserrat mansion – followed swiftly by me saving the day from psychopathic Nicky – we have fallen into an uneasy truce. I have a bit of a soft spot for the big bear. He tolerates me; I think he's wary of the fact that I seem to have a good relationship with Michael and is worried that I'll blurt out what he did to me. I wouldn't do that but it's fun watching him tiptoe around. For all that vampires are supposed to live exciting, glamorous lives, it does get rather dull hanging around the Montserrat mansion as a fledgling. I need to invent my own entertainment if I'm not going to go completely stir crazy. It already feels as if the walls are closing in on me and I've barely been here for six weeks. And that's with sneaking out several times too. Goodness knows how bad things will get when I can't enjoy any solitary freedom in the outside world.

'You need to drink before you go out.'

The humour leaches from my face. 'I'm not hungry.'

'You've not had any blood today.'

I gesture towards a bowl of salt and vinegar kettle chips. 'I've been nibbling.'

'You didn't drink yesterday either.'

My stomach grumbles, loudly betraying me. Ursus raises his eyebrows but doesn't say anything.

'I'll grab a blood bag on the way out,' I say, getting up. I try to face up against him but he's almost two feet taller than I am and considerably wider. Even I know my posturing looks ridiculous.

He shakes his head. 'That's not going to cut it, Bo. To have full strength, you need to drink from the vein. You know that. I have no idea why you insist on having this conversation at least once a week.'

He does have an idea – more than an idea. Michael told me that he got together all the Family seniors who are in London to tell them exactly who I was, how I'd ended up as a recruit and what I'd done as a result. Sympathy isn't exactly Ursus's thing, though. I prefer it that way: I'm not going to get anywhere by crying on his shoulder. He barks a lot at me for a reason; I do need to drink – I just don't want to.

'Fine,' I grumble, stalking out with him at my heels. 'You don't need to come with me though,' I tell him without bothering to turn round.

'I wouldn't want you to get lost on the way.'

I'd laugh but I had tried that a couple of weeks ago. I told Ursus I was going to drink, then somehow got caught up chatting to a few others along the way. He was not impressed when I almost collapsed a few hours later during his latest PowerPoint presentation.

I give in and let him catch up. We trail down the huge staircase and into the one room in the mansion that really gives me the heebie-jeebies. My feet freeze to the floor before I enter. It's not a conscious act and I hate myself for it. Ursus nudges me in the small of my back and propels me forward. Matt is already there, his blond head curved round the neck of a pale-skinned woman. His minder is by his side, double checking that he doesn't go too far with his guzzling. Unfortunately Matt doesn't go anywhere these days without an experienced vampire by his side.

A red-headed guy bounces toward me. He looks impossibly young and my stomach turns. 'You can have me!' he says, with far more enthusiasm than should be allowed. He pulls down the collar of his T-shirt to expose his jugular. I shudder.

'Actually,' I mutter, 'your wrist would be better.' Most

vampires go for the jugular; it's nearer the heart so the blood tastes sweeter. It's also much more convenient but I hate the intimacy of it. I eye my willing victim. 'How old are you?'

'Twenty-two.'

I'm still suspicious. It's not unheard of for teenagers looking for kicks to pretend to be older than they are so they can become vampettes. The Family is pretty good at sorting out the fake IDs but no system is perfect. 'Are you sure?'

He blinks, suddenly nervous at my tone. 'Yeah.'

Ursus lays a hand on my shoulder. 'Connor is one of our regulars, Bo. He knows what he's doing.'

I'm not about to give in so easily. 'Why?' I ask him, trying to ignore the faint outline of blue veins under his freckled skin. 'Why do you do this?'

'I want to.' He shrugs and looks at me archly. 'I don't come here normally – I tend to hang around the vampire watering holes. They're quite friendly and it's a good way to meet people.'

I can think of easier ways to make friends. Connor is starting to realise I'm more scared than he is and his nerves are disappearing in favour of a bit of attitude. That's better than fear, I guess.

'Bo...' Ursus warns.

'Okay, okay,' I snap. I glance at Connor as I bring his wrist to my mouth. 'I'm sorry about this.'

A dreamy smile crosses his face. 'I told you. I want to do it.'

The familiar ache rises in my teeth as my fangs elongate. Nell tells me repeatedly that it's my gums which hurt as the tooth enamel shifts. I don't care. The pain feels like it's in my teeth so that's what I'm going with. Maybe I should get someone to bring me some Bonjela, in case she's right. I take a deep breath, push down the nausea rising up from the pit of my stomach then slowly and very, very carefully, sink my teeth into Connor's flesh.

It's the initial piercing of the skin that's the worst. I'm not sure if it's psychological or not but the sensation of ripping someone apart, even gently, always makes me feel ill. Once I find the vein, however, and the warm sweet blood fills my mouth, everything else starts to fade away. I can't quite bring myself to suck; instead I just let the blood gush down my throat. It means I don't drink as much as I probably should before the healing properties of my bloodguzzling saliva close up the wound but I get enough.

When Connor's blood slows to a trickle, I pull away. I concentrate on not stepping backwards and throwing up. If this young bloke is going to offer himself as a vampette for my delectation then I'm not going to waste any of his precious blood. It would be insulting to him and – worse – Ursus would make me drink all over again. I breathe deeply, then paste on a smile. 'Thank you, Connor.'

He opens his eyes. 'That was great. You were very gentle.'

I scan his face. He seems to be telling the truth. I'll never understand what drives people like him to wander off the street to donate blood to vampires but I have to respect his choice. I bob my head in acknowledgment then, slowly and without too many jerky movements, leave.

Michael is outside, standing next to two others. His head is inclined towards a female vampire who looks about twenty but who I know for a fact is closer to the ripe old age of ninety-five. She smiles briefly in my direction and departs. Then he turns to me.

'This is Patrick Jones.' He gestures at his remaining companion. I realise with surprise that he's an Agathos daemon. 'He's a barrister who occasionally helps us out.'

I'm puzzled. I thought the Montserrat Family had in-house lawyers. I give Patrick a quick smile in greeting.

'Nice to meet you. I've heard a lot about you,' he says.

Michael stiffens, making me wonder what's been said. My eyes narrow.

The lawyer hands me a card, shiny and embossed with gold letters: *Patrick Jones. Employment Law. Vampire Recruitment Law. Advocate with the Agathos courts.* There's a phone number. 'Thanks,' I mutter, stuffing it in my back pocket.

Patrick bows in my direction then shakes Michael's hand before going to speak to Ursus. I wonder why he's here. There's a lot going on in the underbelly of the Montserrat Family that we fledglings aren't party to.

'You're looking, um, casual,' I say, turning to Michael. He's wearing a pair of jogging bottoms and a tight-fitting T-shirt in the midnight blue colour that signifies Montserrat. I try not to notice how well it clings to his body.

I receive a grin in return. 'We're going to do some exercise.'

'Oh. Okay.'

'It'll help you work out some of that tension.'

'I'm perfectly relaxed,' I lie.

'If you say so.' He glances towards the large oak front doors. 'The sun went down about an hour ago so we're good to go.'

Michael walks out and I trail after him. I wish I was strong enough to go out during the day; I'm sure some sun would help me feel better. Unfortunately, I won't be in a position to do that for at least another year and a half, maybe longer. The thought is incredibly depressing. Still, as soon as I'm outside in the brisk night air, I suck a deep breath far into my lungs. It's good to be allowed out without having to keep looking over my shoulder, even if I'm under escort.

'I hear you like feeling power between your thighs?'

I blink. 'Er, what?'

Michael grins and gestures in front of him. Ursus's gleaming motorbike sits at the edge of the road. I can't help smiling.

'Here,' he says, throwing me a helmet.

I catch it and look down, frowning. Michael is already clambering on the bike.

'Why don't you have a helmet?'

'Because I'm a stronger and older vampire whose skull won't be bashed in if we crash,' he replies patiently.

I open my mouth to retort, then think better of it and jam on the helmet. So far, I've yet to come across any advantages to being a bloodguzzler.

'Can't I drive?'

'You don't know where we're going.'

I can't argue with that. Maybe I should stop being so truculent. If I continue to bicker about every little thing, he may rescind my little bit of freedom. I need to be smarter and pick my battles.

I climb on behind him. It's a long time since I've ridden pillion and being this close to the Lord of all the Montserrat vampires makes me nervous. Rather than putting my arms round his waist, I grab the handholds behind my hips. Michael tuts and pulls my hands around his middle. 'Don't play coy,' he tells me, 'it doesn't suit you.'

Before I can reply, he guns the engine and takes off, accelerating down the long street with the large houses on one side and the leafy shadows of Hyde Park on the other. He's a remarkably adept driver. It's still fairly early and we're in central London so there's a fair amount of traffic but Michael weaves in and out of the cars with ease and speed. It turns out that Lord Montserrat is actually a bit of an adrenaline junkie. As I gain confidence in his skills, I relax against him and pay attention to where we're going.

We whizz past shop fronts and streets packed with revellers out to enjoy the evening. The few times we pause at traffic lights, I realise that nearby pedestrians are shooting us curious looks. A few recognise Michael and point him out to their friends. One or two turn away in open disgust. I frown. Another drawback to being able to venture outside only when he's with me is that I lose my anonymity. Fortunately, it's not long before he pulls up outside a nondescript building about eight storeys high. He turns off the engine. I get off, freeing myself from the confines of the helmet, then I look around. The area is full of offices. I'm confused.

Without a word, Michael walks to one of the buildings and leaps upwards, his fingers grabbing the windowsill on the second floor. With no apparent effort, he brings up his feet then springs over four feet to the next sill. He continues upwards. I merely gape.

He's almost at the top when I realise that I'm supposed to follow him. I lick my lips. Didn't he just say something about not bashing in my skull? Falling twenty feet onto a hard pavement might have the same result. I'm determined not to appear weak, though. I focus on the first windowsill then I squeeze my eyes shut and jump.

I'm so surprised I make it that I almost let go and fall back down. Clinging on with my fingertips, I heave myself up and brace my arms against the walls surrounding the glass. The office inside is dark but I can still make out the desks and chairs. It reminds me abruptly of Dire Straits so, before I dwell too much on that thought, I jump quickly to the next window, copying Michael's movements. The higher I go, the more confident I become and I'm at the second to last storey when I catch myself grinning. Okay, maybe this is kind of fun.

I'm about to leap up to the roof when something feels wrong. There's an odd sound of cracking then, half a second later, my right foot falls and I slip. My stomach flies up to my heart as I scrabble for purchase and only just grab what remains of the crumbling stone edge with my left hand. My body swings slightly in the air and I curse. I dig my feet into the side of the building, willing myself to hang on, then swap hands so I can manoeuvre across to the window on the right-hand side instead. There's a light inside and, throwing myself towards it before I lose my grip, I hope I don't surprise some poor cleaner going about their night shift.

Fortunately the bricks on this side are better maintained and I pull myself back up. Inside the brightly lit office, a couple is sprawled across a desk. They stare at me, frozen in horror. The woman, who's on top, is wearing nothing more than a lacy bra. When they shake themselves from their rabbit-in-headlights inaction and spring up to find their clothes to protect their modesty, I catch the glint of a wedding ring on the man's finger. Old instincts die hard, and I check the woman's hands as she scoops up her discarded blouse. Her fingers are bare. It would be pretty damn easy to be a private investigator spying on cheating spouses with these kind of Spiderman skills. I give them a friendly wave and push off from my toes to make the final jump. Then I'm on top of the flat roof, rolling onto my back, limbs akimbo and breathing hard.

Michael bends down. 'Are you alright?' There's a distinct lack of concern in his voice.

'Yes.' I sit up. 'I almost fell though. I didn't notice you rushing to catch me.'

The corner of his mouth crooks upwards. 'There's a difference between taking foolhardy risks and challenging yourself to your limits so you learn.'

I clamber to my feet, irritated. 'I wouldn't learn much if I plummeted seven storeys to the ground.'

'You weren't going to do that.'

I wipe my palms across my thighs and eye him suspiciously. 'I was following you step for step. You knew the bricks around that window weren't sound. You did that deliberately.' I can tell from the look in his eyes that I'm right.

He shrugs. 'How do you feel?'

'Exhausted! Scared! And bloody annoyed!'

He shakes his head. 'No. How do you *really* feel?'

I pause. I'm covered in goosebumps. I didn't realise that was possible for a vampire. My pulse is fast, but not frantic. I feel ... alive. I stare at him dumbly, not answering his question. He grins. I give him the tiniest smile back and his grin widens.

'The next part will be even more fun,' he promises. He points north in the direction of the London skyline. 'Do you see that flag?'

'Huh?' I draw my eyes away from the familiar silhouette of the Gherkin and scan round. Eventually I spot a flagpole. It's so far away that I can't make out what is draped from it. 'Yes,' I say slowly.

'I'll race you it. And because you're just a little fledgling, I'll give you a twenty-second head start.'

'I can't reach that!'

'Eighteen seconds.'

Wanker. I focus on the next building. The gap doesn't seem too wide – for freaking Superman.

'Fifteen seconds.'

I snarl under my breath then start running. It takes me a few seconds to pick up speed then I'm at the edge of the roof. Without stopping, I keep my eyes on the next rooftop which, thankfully, is a few feet lower. I leap, sailing over the gap and letting out a loud gasp of relief when I register that I'm going to clear it easily. I land and my knees bend slightly but a fraction of a second later I'm moving forward again.

'Ten seconds,' he shouts from behind me. I ignore him. Handicap, my arse. I'll beat him.

I sprint faster, staying on my toes. The next gap is both higher and wider but there's a drainpipe on the side of the building which I jump over to and catch. I bounce up and keep running. The wind whips my face and I feel pure exhilaration. I knew vampires were stronger and faster but I'd never had any opportunity until now to test how much. I'm Usain Bolt, Michael Jordan and Nadia Comaneci all rolled into one. On steroids. I laugh aloud, the sound ripping away from me and into the dark sky. I'm...

Shit. Michael Montserrat passes me. I put my head down, willing myself to go even faster but his lithe form draws away and, no matter how much I push myself, he outpaces me. I don't give up but it's clear who's going to win this race. My feet pound across various rooftops and I spring over various gaps as if I'm flying. When I finally reach the flagpole, however, he's already leaning against it with his arms folded and his cheeks dimpled.

I bend double, gasping. I gave that everything I had and Lord sodding Montserrat looks as if he's done nothing more than go for a short stroll.

'Could have been worse, I suppose,' he drawls.

I rest my palms on my thighs and cock my head up at him. 'Piss off.'

He smirks. 'Do you need some help? You look breathless. I understand it can be difficult for women to maintain their equilibrium around me.'

My mouth drops open. Did he really just say that? I straighten up, itching to give him a slap when, abruptly, there's a loud scream from somewhere far below.

Michael's eyes snap to mine. 'Stay here,' he grounds out, before vanishing over the edge of the building. I peer down after him. It's a long drop but he manages it easily, reaching one lower rooftop by jumping down, then skimming down the sloping edges of several tiered skylights until he's close enough to reach the ground in one knee-juddering leap. I see what appears to be the shape of a woman lying on the ground. As he kneels next to her, something – or rather someone – catches my eye on the street opposite. The person is running as fast as possible away from the fallen woman.

Keeping the fleeing figure in sight, I leap to the same rooftop that Michael did. Instead of following him down to the street, however, I sprint after the runner. He's clearly no vampire and it's not long before I'm keeping pace. He may be on the other side of the road but I can still make out his clothing – baggy jeans, flapping T-shirt and a scarf wound round his face as a makeshift disguise. As far as I can tell, he's no more than a teenager.

He reaches the intersection and peels off to the right, away from me. I search for a way down, eventually spotting an awning jutting out not too far away. Making sure it's directly under me, I twist round and drop until only my fingers are curving round the edge of the roof. Then I let go. Unfortunately for me, the awning is not very sturdy and the material rips under my weight. I land painfully on the pavement and, when I try to get up, the awning's thick fabric catches on one of the zips on my jacket. I heave myself upwards, pulling free. Tingles of pain are shooting through my legs although I do my best to ignore them. I'm moving more slowly now, but it's not long before I catch sight of him again. He obviously thinks he's free and clear because he slows to a walk. I smile humourlessly. Sucker. I force my legs to keep going. I'm barely five feet away when he turns his head. His eyes widen as he clocks me.

I bare my teeth. He tries to run but it's already too late. I leap up in the air, grab his collar, I slam him against the wall and yank down his scarf. As I expect, he still has the acne pocks and spiteful eyes of someone barely old enough to drink beer.

'Hello,' I coo into his face.

He flinches. Michael, appearing out of nowhere, snarls in his direction.

'How's the woman?' I ask.

'Shaken but otherwise alive.'

'Good.' I keep my hands on the kid. 'Now I'm *really* having some fucking fun.'

CHAPTER 3

FRIENDS AND FOES

We haul the mugger back to the alleyway where Michael left the woman, but she's nowhere in sight. He frowns. 'I told her to wait here so we could get her to a hospital to be checked over.'

'And of course everyone always does what you tell them to,' I mutter under my breath. Unfortunately, he hears every word.

'Yes, they usually do. In fact, once upon a time I remember you telling me that you were going to be as good as gold and do what you were told, too.'

'A lot has happened since then,' I inform him coolly.

The kid squirms in my grip, apparently tired of the byplay between his captors. 'No victim, no crime! You've gotta let me go!'

'No chance, buster,' I tell him.

Michael quirks an eyebrow in my direction. '"No chance, buster?" Have missed your calling as an actor in a Hollywood B-movie?'

I wink at him, flipping back my hair.

'Do you feel lucky, punk?' Michael says to the kid with an affected American accent.

I can't help myself. I shake my prisoner. 'Well?' I ask. 'Do ya?'

The kid looks from Michael to me, baffled. 'What the fuck is wrong with you two?'

Michael tuts. 'The youth of today.'

I shake him again. 'And don't swear.'

'You did,' he flips back.

'Yeah? Who do you think is in charge right now?' For good measure, I allow my fangs to grow ever so slightly and lick my lips very deliberately.

The kid grows pale and there's the stench of urine. I look down to see a growing patch of wet across the groin of his jeans. Maybe I should feel sorry for him. But I don't.

Michael takes the kid's arm and throws me a set of keys. 'You get your wish,' he says. 'You can drive. Get the bike and meet me at the nearest police station. I think it's…'

'Two blocks down on the right.'

He stares at me impassively. 'Sometimes there's more to you than meets the eye.'

I give him a little curtsey in return then, without waiting to see his reaction, I start jogging in the direction of the parked bike. My legs are still killing me but I'm damned if I'm going to let the pain show. By the time I reach the police station, Michael is already inside and the kid is being cuffed.

'Did he take anything from the victim?' a uniformed copper asks, directing his question at Michael.

'Didn't take nuthin',' the kid mutters.

A look passes between us. The policeman starts patting him down and pulls out a small lump of hash from one pocket. He raises an eyebrow at the boy.

'S'not mine,' he sniffs.

'Right. You're just holding it for a friend, are you? Well, you can think about that in one of our cells for a few hours and then we'll have another chat.' He marches him towards a keypad-locked door. As if by magic, it opens and a plain-clothed copper wanders out, giving a curious glance in our direction. Suddenly he stops in his tracks as if he's forgotten something and heads back inside.

'You can't do this!' the struggling mugger yells. 'I've got rights!'

I roll my eyes and am about to turn away when I catch sight of something. 'Wait!'

They pause. I lift the edge of the kid's T-shirt. He stiffens. 'This is harassment! She can't do that!'

I ignore him, staring instead at the object sticking up from the back pocket of the jeans which hang precariously halfway down his arse. I'm not surprised the policeman missed it, but I'm baffled as to what it means.

'Isn't that...?' Michael asks.

I nod distractedly. It's a bright green feather, the same as the one the woman in Fingertips and Frolics made me buy. I pull it out and hold it up. The kid twists his head round. When he sees me grasping it between my thumb and finger, its garish colour enhanced by the harsh lighting, his face blanches.

'This is what you stole, isn't it?'

The policeman takes the feather from me and gives me a warning glare, no doubt for touching the suspect. I'm too preoccupied by the feather to pay much attention.

'Why?' I round on the boy, demanding answers. 'Why did you take this?'

He hawks up phlegm and spits in my direction. Fortunately for him, my reflexes are improving by the day and I dodge. Annoyed with himself for missing, he looks away from me and fixes on the policeman. 'Wanna lawyer.'

The policeman shrugs at me. 'Thanks for your help. We'll be in touch later about a statement.'

'But…'

Michael places a hand under my elbow. 'You're welcome,' he says firmly. Then he guides me out. Pissed off, I yank my arm away and stalk sullenly back to the street.

Once we're outside, I scowl up at him. 'You're Lord Montserrat. You could have used your influence to find out what that thing was and why he bloody well nicked it from that woman.'

'He knew who I was. You need to learn the art of diplomacy,' he chides. 'It can be a much more satisfactory way to gain information. We have to come back here in the next day or two to give a statement. By that time the police will have questioned him, according to human laws, and will have more useful details to tell us. You interrogating him in the middle of the police station is not going to gain us any favours.' His voice softens. 'We have to be careful how we approach the police. We're vampires, Bo.'

As if I could forget. My good humour entirely gone, I walk back to the bike. Before Michael can say any more, I shove the helmet back on my head and start the engine. I wait for him to demand driving privileges but he gets on behind me. I feel the pressure of his arms round my waist and briefly close my eyes. Then I rev up and we veer off into the inky night.

I SLEEP BADLY and my limbs feel as if they're made from lead, but the next day I force myself to rise when the sun is still high in the sky. Of course, I can't see it from my windowless bedroom but I instinctively know it's daytime without padding downstairs to the glass-topped, UV-protected atrium. I'm also used to waking early – or late - it depends how you look at it. When we arrived back from the police station, I mumbled something to Michael about being tired and came straight up to my room. I was aware of his gaze following me but I couldn't bring myself to talk to him. He's tried hard to make me see at least the physical benefits of vampiredom and it was starting to work – which more than slightly terrifies me. The conclusion to our night, however, brought me crashing back to earth. I'm still a fucking vampire and there's still nothing I can do about it.

The rest of my floor is quiet; no doubt everyone else is taking the sensible option for a fledgling and staying asleep during the day. I take a cold shower to rouse myself, then towel off and get dressed. Usually at this time, I pace around the mansion from room to room, aimlessly walking until my fellow fledglings wake up and I have something to do. It's not like I have a job; until we can stand the sun we remain under training, which means endless PowerPoints on all manner of vampiric details and a range of physical workouts. After last night's activities, I realise how gentle those workouts are.

A week or two ago, Nell came across me when I was already on my third circuit. She said I looked like a polar bear trapped in a zoo, pacing endlessly up and down its enclosure. Her words didn't help. For once I don't want to play out my caged-animal routine so I stay where I am and find my own feather on the shelf of my sparse belongings. No matter how closely I examine it, I can't see anything to suggest it's more than a goddamn feather.

I give up and turn on my phone. After texting O'Shea to get his arse to Fingertips and Frolics and call me as soon as he arrives, I call Rogu3. Using our long-established code, I let it ring twice before hanging up. The third time, he answers.

'Yes?' The caution in his voice is evident.

'Hi.'

There's a moment of silence. It fills the line and expands, making me feel even more uncomfortable.

'Rogu3?' I prompt.

'I'm not sure we should do this now, Bo.'

'I might have guessed that you'd track me and realise what happened.'

'You're a vampire.' It's not a question.

As much as I'd like to evade his statement, I owe him more than that. 'Yes.' I take a deep breath. 'I'm still me though.'

'Do you drink blood?'

I realise to my alarm that my eyes are welling up and, frustrated, I rub them hard with the edge of my sleeve. 'I have to. I'm trying to find a cure...'

'There is none.'

He's so matter of fact that it hurts. I clench my teeth. 'How are things with you?'

'Okay, I guess. My maths teacher is making me take my GCSE exam early.'

'That's good.'

'My parents are making me fucking study all the time.'

'Don't swear,' I say automatically, echoing my words to the mugger from the night before.

He laughs slightly. 'Maybe you've not changed that much after all.'

A ghost of a smile traces across my lips.

'I got your money, by the way.'

For a moment I'm confused. Then I remember that because of my recruitment into the Montserrat Family, I didn't have time to pay him for his services. My grandfather must have done as he promised and deposited the money into Rogu3's bank account. I'm surprised and suffused with unexpected gratitude.

'Good.'

'The lawyer seems straight up. He has some dodgy clients but he seems trustworthy. For a lawyer.'

Harry D'Argneau. It seems like a lifetime ago that I asked Rogu3 to check up on him. In a way it is. 'I'd forgotten all about him, to be honest.'

'So you're not calling about him and I guess you're not calling to ask how my maths is going.'

I bite my lip. 'No. I need something else. If you don't want to help though, I understand.'

The silence stretches out again. I wonder if he's hung up and I've not realised when he blurts out suddenly, 'Confederate.'

'Word of the week?'

'Yeah. It means ally or friend.'

'Oh.' I know it's inane but to say anything else is beyond me right now.

'I'll have to charge you more. Special rates for bloodgu... I mean, vampires.'

I smile; he's ever the entrepreneur. 'Okay. I don't have any cash of my own right now because the Family takes care of everything.'

'That sounds like one of those weird cults you get in the middle of nowhere in America.'

He's not far off the truth. 'I will get you it as soon as I can.'

'No problem,' he tells me, suddenly cheerful. 'I'll just charge you interest in the meantime. My rates are very good.'

'And with all that maths studying you're doing, I imagine you're a dab hand at the calculations.'

Rogu3 laughs. It's a joyous sound. 'What do you need?'

'Find out everything you can about a shop called Fingertips and Frolics. It's on Carnavon Close in Shoreditch.'

'Magic place?' he guesses.

'Yes.'

'Done. I'll contact you when I've got something. And Bo?'

'Yes?'

His voice is quiet. 'I'm glad you called.'

I choke slightly and hang up before I start crying again. Good grief. It must be a vampire hormone thing. At times like this, only one thing is going to work. I pick myself up and head to the large kitchen on the ground floor. Hopefully I'll be able find some chocolate there.

I'm almost at the bottom of the stairs, lost in thought, when I spot an unkempt man hovering close to the front doors. I squint at him. It's unusual, although not unheard of, for a human to wander inside without a Montserrat escort but there's a desperate air, about this guy that gives me pause. It's not just the shadow of stubble around his jaw or the slightly sour, unwashed smell drifting from his crumpled clothes. It has to be something else. I glance around. No one else is in the vicinity so, curiosity getting the better of me, I walk over to him.

'Can I help?'

He jumps about a foot backwards in fright. I'm close enough to tell that his heart rate, which was already abnormally fast, has abruptly increased. I'm not sure if he's about to turn and run out of the door or vomit all over the gleaming marble floor.

'Are you a vampire?'

I point to my eyes. 'I have a red dot in my pupils. When you see that, you know you're talking to a bloodguzzler.'

If he's surprised by my use of the less than complimentary term, he doesn't show it. Instead he swallows hard. 'I'm looking for someone.'

I wait. When he doesn't say anything else, I sigh, starting to wonder if I'm dealing with a traumatised family member of one of my fellow recruits. My own experiences aside, we're not meant to have any contact with anyone from our former lives. Worse, it could be a former victim of one of them. As I discovered not too long ago, a number of my fellow vampires are reformed criminals.

'Who?' I finally prompt.

'Gelzman,' he says. 'Arzo Gelzman.'

I blink. 'Arzo?'

I don't know his last name but it seems unlikely that there is more than one Montserrat member called Arzo. Although I'm not sure whether he can actually be classified as a genuine member of the Montserrat Family or not. Arzo is Sanguine. He didn't drink blood for the entire lunar month after his initial turning so he didn't become a full vampire; technically speaking, he's still human. As is Peter, the nervy older man who was recruited at the same time as I was. I'm not bloody Sanguine, I'm a freaking fully-fledged vampire. I snarl, making the man back away. He almost trips over his own feet in his haste to get away. Bugger it.

'Sorry,' I apologise. 'I'm having a bad day. That wasn't directed at you.'

He doesn't look comforted. I should send him to one of the more senior bloodguzzlers. There are several in the mansion who are tasked with managing human–vampire relations. I feel guilty for terrifying this man, though, and I want to redeem myself.

I attempt a smile. 'Arzo's not here. Perhaps I can pass on a message?'

'I'm happy to wait.'

The last thing he looks is happy. I try again. 'He doesn't actually stay here.' Without knowing who he is or what's going on, I don't want to give away too much information. My private investigator senses are trickling slowly to the fore. I glance down at his shoes and register that they look expensive. Interesting.

'Where can I find him?' The man's desperation is rising.

'Tell me what you need and give me your contact details,' I say, 'and I'll make sure Arzo gets in touch.'

'It's Dahlia,' he blurts out. I frown. I've heard that name before. 'She's missing.'

I scan his face. He looks to be in his early forties, around the same age as Arzo. It fits. Arzo told me before that the reason he came knocking on the Montserrat door was because his fiancée – Dahlia – had disappeared and his best friend told him he thought she'd been recruited. In truth, they ran off together and wanted Arzo out of the way. It was a heartbreakingly callous thing to do. Anger rises and my fingers bunch into fists.

'You were his friend,' I hiss. I take a step towards him. 'His best friend.'

He pales. 'You know about that?'

'How dare you?' I'm outraged on Arzo's behalf. 'How dare you come here? Do you think she's here too? That she changed her mind and came back to hook up with Arzo? Because,' I jab a finger in his direction, 'I can tell you that Arzo is a damn sight more honourable than you. He wouldn't waste a minute of his day on her again.'

I'm half-expecting him to turn round and run away, a gibbering wreck, but he stands his ground. 'No,' he says quietly. 'I know she's not here. But I heard Arzo was working as a private investigator and I thought he might help me look for her.'

I stare at him. I didn't know Arzo very well before the majority of our colleagues at our old firm, Dire Straits, were brutally slaughtered. I still don't know him very well but I'm fairly certain that if he discovers his old love is missing, he'll move hell and high water to find her. The trouble is that, whatever the end result, he'll still lose. Either she's dead and he'll be devastated, or she's alive and he'll save her and she'll go back to playing happy families with this bozo. My life might have fallen apart at the seams; it doesn't mean other people's have to.

I make a quick decision. 'Arzo is away on business. He won't be back for at least a month.'

'Do you have a phone number for him?'

'He's in Antarctica, investigating the effects of twenty-four sunshine on vampire physiology. The place is very remote and there's no direct communication.' That's so ridiculous it sounds almost plausible.

The man frowns. 'But satellites...'

Damn. 'It's cold. The technology doesn't work very well on the ground.'

Disappointment clouds his face. 'Alright then. Thank you for your time.'

'Wait. I'm Arzo's assistant. I'm tasked to deal with his jobs while he's away. I worked with him at Dire Straits.'

He peers at me. There's a sudden flicker of recognition. For once, having my face plastered across London for a few days when I was being treated as a mass murder suspect might come in useful.

'So,' I continue briskly, 'I will help you find Dahlia. When did she go missing?'

'I don't know.'

I gaze at him impassively. 'That's not very helpful.'

He sighs and runs a hand through his salt-and-pepper hair. I'm pleased to note that the salt is winning; I don't think Arzo is grey at all. 'I was away on business,' he explains. 'I left last Saturday.'

I've lost track of the days. It takes me a moment to work out that today is Friday.

'When did you get back?'

'Wednesday evening. Our house had been turned over. There's furniture upside down, photos smashed. There's even a broken window.' A flicker of pride crosses his face. 'Dahlia fought hard.'

'And this could have happened any time between Saturday and Wednesday?'

He shakes his head. 'I spoke to her on Sunday night on the phone. She sounded fine. I rang again on Tuesday but there was no answer.'

'Have you contacted the police?'

'They came round and asked me some questions and dusted for fingerprints. But they've not found anything. I don't think they're even trying.'

I grimace like I'm taking him seriously. 'And is there anyone who would want to hurt her – or you? Anyone you've upset who might be looking for revenge?' Other than Arzo, you smug, two-faced, treacherous bastard.

'No.'

I find that difficult to believe. 'I need the details of every business transaction you've done over the last six months.'

'I'm an accountant. I work for Ross and Ross. It's one of the largest firms in London. I deal with dozens of clients!'

'You'd better start on the list as soon as you leave here, then. And I'll need details of all the friends and family members you've spoken to in that time frame as well.' When he doesn't answer, I raise an eyebrow. 'You do want to find her, right?'

He nods vigorously.

'Well, then. Do you have a phone?'

He pulls one out of his pocket. I take it from him and jab in my own number, give myself a missed call, then pass it back.

'Where's your house?'

He gives me an address in an affluent part of London. Accountancy must pay well.

'Invite me.'

'Huh?'

'Invite me to enter.'

He looks panicked. 'You're invited to come into my house.'

'Great.' I keep my tone even. 'I'll get started right away. I'll call you tomorrow about those details I asked for. And don't come here again. It's…' I search for a reason to keep him away. 'It's getting close to Halloween and everyone's a bit on edge.' I run my tongue very obviously round my teeth for good measure. It must work because he shudders visibly and glances nervously around the foyer.

'Okay.' He jerks his head in agreement.

'What's your name?' I ask, realising I still don't know it.

'Stephen. Stephen Templeton.'

'I'm Bo.'

He sticks his hand out for me to shake. I eye it for a moment, then look up.

'Sorry,' I say. 'I'm really hungry right now so I can't.' He whips his hand back. I almost smile. 'You'd better go now,' I tell him.

ONCE I'M sure that Stephen Templeton has gone, I continue to the kitchen in even more desperate need of chocolate. I find a huge bar of cooking chocolate inside a cupboard and make a mental note to tell Ursus that he should get in some proper stuff. I might not need 'real' food in order to survive physically in my new life as a vampire, but nobody eats chocolate for that reason anyway. Ideas should be clear, blood should be freely given and iron-rich – and chocolate should damn well be thick and creamy. Still, in a pinch this will do. I snap off a large corner and cram it into my mouth.

'There you are!'

I turn round, my mouth full, and see Nell. Unable to speak, I give her a little wave.

'Your friend is here.'

Using my teeth to break the chocolate into more manageable chunks, I look at her questioningly. She takes the bar of chocolate from me, sensibly eating only a small piece.

'The Sanguine one. Arzo?'

My eyes widen in alarm. The chocolate goes down the wrong way and I start choking and coughing. Nell thumps me hard on the back – another person who still isn't fully aware of her new vampire strength – and the remaining chocolate comes flying out of my mouth. It spatters against the pristine floor and cupboards in an unpleasant facsimile of a Jackson Pollock painting.

'Where is he?' I spit out, once I regain control of all my faculties.

'In the foyer,' she answers. 'I think he only just arrived.'

CHAPTER 4
TRAUMA

I try not to run through the corridors. It seems inconceivable that Arzo missed his ex-friend leaving the doors of the Montserrat mansion. It's equally inconceivable that he'll blithely accept my meddling in his affairs. I don't want to lose his respect and I definitely don't want to lose his friendship.

I slow down as I approach him. He's facing away from me but, despite being trapped in a wheelchair, his large muscular body is unmistakable. Even before I knew he was Sanguine, I was vaguely aware that there was something triber about him. He's friendly and charming but he also possesses an air of dangerous implacability. For a while I even wondered if there was a touch of Kakos daemon in his lineage, as impossible as that sounds.

I swallow and walk up to him. He wheels round towards me. There's an odd look in his eyes that I try – and fail – to decipher.

'Bo,' he says, 'how are you?'

I stare at him mutely. For an opening salvo, this seems rather benign.

His brow furrows slightly. 'Why don't we head out towards the garden for some air? The sun is almost down.'

I find my voice. 'Okay.' It comes out as little more than a squeak and the crease in Arzo's forehead deepens. 'Did you just get here?' I ask.

'Pretty much.'

'Are you here to see Michael? I mean, Lord Montserrat?'

He flicks me a glance. 'No. Actually I'm here to see you.'

Shit. Shit. I lick my lips. 'Oh.'

We head slowly through the house, passing an odd vampire or two. As we go through the atrium, I wince at the weak rays of sunlight still floating down from the sky. I know they can't hurt me here but I still feel prickles of discomfort on my skin. Arzo's silence isn't helping much either.

When we reach the doors that lead out to the garden, I look anxiously at him. Is he going to demand that I go outside? It's still not dusk and the remaining rays of the sun will be enough to scorch my weak-arse, fledgling vampire skin. Perhaps that's his plan. I straighten my shoulders in preparation but he merely leans backs in his chair and gazes out for a moment. Then he turns and fixes me with a steely stare.

'This isn't working very well for you, is it?'

I meet his gaze and tell myself to get a grip. 'What do you mean?'

'Jeez, Bo, look at you! You're pale and shaking. I know you probably only just woke up but have you drunk anything yet?'

I finally register that this has nothing to do with Stephen Templeton.

He reaches up and grabs my hands. 'You have to drink blood. Every day.'

'I know.'

'So why the hell don't you?'

Suddenly I feel like a five year old being told off for not eating my vegetables.

He continues. 'Lord Montserrat tells me you're acting aggressive. That you take every opportunity to argue with him or the other senior members of the Family.' His eyes harden. 'Ursus tells me that your sullen manner is rubbing off on the others. This is hard for them too, you know. Just because your recruitment was unusual doesn't mean you're the only one who's finding it hard to adjust.'

'I'm not responsible for what the other fledglings do!' I protest, as something snaps inside me. 'And I don't argue all the time.'

'You're arguing now,' he points out calmly. 'This isn't you. You're normally the thoughtful, nice one. Instead you have every Montserrat vampire in the vicinity tiptoeing on eggshells around you.' He shakes his head. 'I gave you money and a phone because I thought you might use them sensibly. Now I find out you're using them to find a cure that doesn't exist.'

'Just because you've not heard of a cure doesn't mean it's not out there. Besides, what did you think I was going to do with the money? Buy myself a new pair of shoes? Did you think I'd use the phone to call up my old colleagues and tell them what a great life I've got as a prisoner in the Montserrat house? Oh wait,' I say, my voice rising, 'I can't do that because most of them were slaughtered two months ago.'

Arzo squeezes my hands. 'Have you heard of PTSD?'

I blink. 'Post-traumatic stress disorder? I don't have that.'

'How are you sleeping?'

'Fine.' He gazes at me speculatively and I bristle. 'I don't want to be a damn vampire, alright? That's all.'

'We have doctors,' he begins.

'Goddamnit! Do I look traumatised to you? I said it already – I'm fine.'

'No, Bo. You're not fine.'

I glare at him malevolently and slam open the door to the garden without checking first to see whether dusk has fallen. I stalk out, taking several long steps. My skin warms but the sun has already sunk too far to do any real damage. I don't have PTSD. I may have snapped at Michael a few times the previous night but we still joked around a bit. I've been friendly with Beth and Nell. I even managed to smile at Arzo's very own sodding nemesis. I'm not ill, I just don't want to be a freak of nature. That's all. There's nothing more sinister to it.

'It's not anything to be ashamed of,' Arzo says from behind me.

I whip round. 'I know that! But I told you...'

'You're fine.'

I nod. 'Yes.'

He sighs. 'Alright. But think about what I've said. And call me if you need to talk or you need help or if anything untoward happens.'

You mean like your best friend who betrayed you showing up at our door, I think. Aloud, I say, 'Of course.'

He smiles grimly, then twists round and leaves me standing alone in the growing shadows of the garden.

I'M STILL in the garden, staring into nothing, when my phone rings, shaking me out of my reverie. I pull it out from my pocket and answer. 'Hello.'

'I'm not your slave, you know,' O'Shea says cheerfully. 'I have a life. I've got other things to do than run around and meet your every whim.'

'Jesus!' I explode. 'It's not like I'm asking you to lay your sodding life on the line. It'll take you less than an hour to go to the shop for me. It's not like I can just wander out of this stupid building whenever I want. The least you can do is this one little favour.'

For a moment, O'Shea doesn't speak. I rub my forehead tiredly. 'Sorry. I didn't mean…'

'Don't worry about it.' His voice is distant. 'I'm at Fingertips and Frolics.'

'Oh. Well, good. I need you to go inside and speak to the woman there about the feather she gave me.'

'I can't.'

I force myself to stay calm. 'She's friendly enough, O'Shea. And she's a neo-druid. They get on all right with daemons, don't they?'

'It's closed.'

'Oh.' I'm confused. As it's a nocturnal store, I'd expect it to be open once twilight hit. 'Is there anything on the door? Does it say what time it opens?'

'It's boarded up, Bo. There is a sign but it says the shop's shut until further notice.'

That doesn't make sense. I was only there a few days ago. 'Are you sure you have the right place?'

'I'm not an idiot.'

'I wasn't suggesting…' I sigh. 'Sorry. Again.'

'Are you okay?'

I nod, then remember I'm on the phone. 'Yeah. I'm fine.'

'I can break in,' O'Shea says helpfully. 'Have a look around, see if there any clues. I always wanted to be Sherlock Holmes.'

'Watson.'

'Huh?'

'You're Watson. I'm Holmes.'

'That's not fair! I'm the one doing something. You're lolling around a mansion while I get down and dirty.'

'Exactly,' I tell him. 'That's because you're Watson.'

He exhales loudly. 'So?'

'So what?'

'Do you want me to break in?'

I consider the ramifications. Tam, my old boss at Dire Straits, always made it clear that we were never, ever to break the law, no matter what the circumstances were. But Tam's dead.

'Do it.'

'Sure thing, boss. I'll call you back.' He clicks off.

I wander deeper into the garden, eventually sitting down on an uncomfortable stone bench. It's not been twenty-four hours and I'm already regretting my promise to Michael to stay inside the walls of the Montserrat mansion unless he's with me. Goodness only knows how I'll manage to get to the Templetons' house tomorrow. I'm half-tempted to forget about that entirely but if I do, Stephen Templeton will come back. As annoyed as I am at Arzo, I know he's concerned about me and I don't want him upset by ghosts from his past.

The phone rings again. I answer quickly. 'O'Shea?'

'I'm in.'

'That was fast.'

'Yeah. It doesn't make any sense. Any magic shop worth its salt would have a perimeter spell. This place isn't even alarmed.'

I think about the vampire alert that went off when I entered. He's right. It shouldn't have been that easy.

'What can you see?'

'Nothing. The place has been completely emptied.'

I hiss softly through my teeth. What in the hell is going on?

'Do you want me to hang around? Maybe someone will come back.'

'No, don't worry about it. You can get back to your real life.' I try not to sound too bitter. 'Thank you, Devlin,' I say quietly. The least I can do is remember my manners.

'You're welcome.'

I tuck the phone away and stare up the brightly lit mansion. A babble of voices floats down from one of the open windows, punctuated by laughter. I draw my knees up to my chest and hug them, then sigh. I'm surrounded by people, many of whom I count as friends, and I've never felt more lonely in my life.

EVENTUALLY, deciding that I need to stop wallowing, I pick myself up and head for Michael's office. The mystery surrounding the strange green feathers and the abrupt closure of Fingertips and Frolics, not to mention the promise I made to Stephen Templeton to investigate Dahlia's disappearance, give me something to focus on besides my own situation. If I bury myself in work, maybe I'll forget everything else. It's apparent, however, that if I'm to manage that I will need to re-negotiate the terms of my imprisonment. Michael's been reasonable enough so far. I just need to keep my temper and come across like the balanced person I apparently used to be and I'm sure I can get him to agree.

I knock on his door and wait to be summoned. I glance down, scuffing the edge of the carpet with my toe. There are two indented trails leading away from Michael's door. They're perfectly even, swerving in from the same direction I came from, then leading away in the opposite one. They must be from Arzo's wheelchair; I guess that after speaking to me, he made his way here to report back. It occurs to me that if I had agreed to see one of the Montserrat doctors, as Arzo had suggested, anything I said would have been passed on. Nothing's private.

There's a muffled 'come in' so I cautiously open the door

and peer inside. Michael is seated behind his desk, a tall pile of papers in front of him.

'Do you have a few minutes?' I try hard to keep my tone polite and non-aggressive. He looks really busy and I don't want to wait to talk to him.

'Sure.'

I heave a silent sigh of relief and walk in, closing the door behind me.

He smiles at me, dimples appearing in his cheeks. 'What can I do for you, Bo?'

I twist my hands nervously. 'That promise I made…'

The smile disappears instantly, as if someone has pressed delete. 'Yesterday,' he says flatly. 'The promise you made yesterday.'

'Well, the thing is, I kind of need to go out. I'd rather not see him right now but I'm sure my grandfather might be able to shed some light on the green feathers and their significance. Plus Arzo…'

Michael stands up, folding his arms and glowering down at me. I feel very small. 'The vampire laws regarding recruitment have been in place for hundreds of years. Some people say they're archaic, but the law is the law.'

'Yes, but…'

'When you join any one of the five Families, you renounce your previous life. You stay within the confines of your new Family's domain so you can adjust and learn. Until you are strong enough to withstand the sun, you cut all ties to your biological family.' His expression is flinty. 'You've already broken several of our laws and I've bent other ones on your behalf. Your recruitment was unconventional, I know, and you expected to turn Sanguine. However, you still signed the contract, Bo. I'm helping you as much as I can but you need to give me something in return. There's only so much rule breaking I can allow.' His eyes travel the length of my body and back up again. I flush. 'No matter who is doing the asking.'

'I understand all that. I do. I wouldn't ask if I didn't think it was important. Besides, I'm no weaker than I was when I was a human. I'm much stronger, in fact. And I managed to wander around on my own then without too many problems.'

'You weren't part of the Montserrat Family then, were you? You have to accept that things are different now. You've already had more leeway than any other fledgling has ever had. The other Family Heads were impressed with your actions at Big Ben but they won't accept you being out on the streets while you remain under the Montserrat name. It's not just for your benefit, Bo. There's a strong risk that you'll be overwhelmed by bloodlust. We can't afford any more accidents.'

'I think I've shown I can go without blood when I need to,' I respond stiffly.

'You almost killed someone once.'

'When I was a recruit. Not now.'

'What happens if you spend too much time away and don't drink? We've already proved that you need to be forced into taking the blood you need.'

'I'll control it. I won't let that happen.'

'No.' He shakes his head. 'This is getting ridiculous and I can't allow it to continue. I was wrong to let you have more freedom than the others. All it's done is make you crave more liberty. It won't stop until I stop it first. You're a vampire. Accept it.'

'The feather...'

'If you're that bothered by the feather, then give it to me and I'll pass it to Arzo to investigate. You can give me the phone and any money you have left at the same time. Enough is enough.' His face softens for a moment. 'I know it sounds harsh, Bo. But, believe me, it'll be better in the long run. I'm being cruel to be kind.'

The walls around me are awash with red. I step over and slam both my palms down on Michael's desk. 'It's not just the fucking feather! There was someone here earlier about Arzo. He needs help and I promised I'd provide it. I...'

I blink. Tam's body writhes between my hands. He tries to speak but he can't because there's a gaping hole where his throat used to be. There's a strange sound behind me and I spin round, ready to lash out. It's Tansy, the receptionist from Dire Straits. She's holding a nail file to her wrist and slashing it across her skin. There's an inarticulate scream. For a second I don't know where it's coming from then I realise it's coming from me.

'Bo!' Michael reaches out, his hand curving round my arm. I fling him off, sending him flying into a nearby wall. He looks stunned.

'What's going on?' I mutter. 'What the fuck is going on?'

Michael moves towards me again. I feel my fangs growing, jutting out from my mouth and I snarl at him. He grabs something from the desk and hurls it in my direction. I throw up my hands in alarm, attempting to shield myself, but I'm too late. I'm drenched in water and spluttering. I rub my eyes with the back of my hand.

'What...?' I say again.

Michael's arms reach round me again and he pulls me to his chest. 'Shhh,' he says. 'It's alright, Bo. You're alright.'

My body is shaking. He smoothes my hair, continuing to murmur. I feel like I'm going to throw up. I pull away and stare at him, wide-eyed.

'I have to go to the bathroom.'

'Bo...'

'I have to go *now*.'

I turn, yanking opening his office door. Outside I see Nell, looking alarmed. I want to smile at her reassuringly but I can't. I push past her and dash to the toilet, locking the door behind me then bending over the bowl and retching over and over again. Nothing but bile comes up.

I lean my hot forehead against the wall and screw my eyes shut. I feel the panic of claustrophobia seeping out of every pore. It's not because of the bathroom – it's this whole goddamn place. Arzo was right when he said this wasn't working for me. I can't do it; I can't stay here any more. I pull out my phone and search for directory inquiries. There's a knock and I hear Michael ask if I'm alright. He sounds concerned. I know he could break down the door with his little finger if he so desired, so I tell him I just need a few minutes. Then I get the number I need and call it.

IT TAKES LESS time than I thought it would. I'm sitting outside again in the garden with Nell on one side and Beth on the other. I know that Michael is hovering around as well, but I avoid his gaze. I'm terrified about how he's going to react.

It's Ria who appears to make the announcement. She looks at me nervously and turns to Michael. She is trying to avoid his eyes as well. 'Uh, Lord Montserrat, there's someone here to see Bo.'

'What?' His brows snap together. 'Tell them to get lost.'

She licks her lips. 'He wants to see you too.'

I stand up. 'I asked him to come.' My voice rings out with surprising clarity.

Michael looks at me for a second, his expression unfathomable. Then he focuses back on Ria. 'Who is it?'

'He's a barrister. A human barrister. We've had a few dealings with him in the past.'

Michael looks at me again, this time for much longer. I wish I knew what he was thinking.

'His name is Harry D'Argneau,' Ria adds helpfully.

A shadow passes across Michael's face. 'What does he want, Bo?' His voice is soft but there's an underlying steel that makes me shiver.

'I'm sorry,' I say for about the umpteenth time today. 'I have to get out of here.'

A muscle jerks in his cheek, then he strides away. Next to me, Beth is tense. 'What have you smegging done, Bo?' she breathes.

I swallow and give her a tremulous smile. 'What I have to.' Then I get up and follow the Head of the Montserrat vampires.

I have to hand it to D'Argneau. At this time of night and based on what I already know about him, I'd expected to see him looking somewhat more dishevelled. But he's immaculately dressed – every inch the professional. This is probably a very dangerous thing for him to do but I guess the allure of knowing more about the inner workings of the Families is too great. He hands some papers to Michael, who looms over him.

'I'm here to secure the release of Bo Blackman,' D'Argneau says, as if he's cheerfully announcing the start of a holiday. If Butlin's are recruiting any time soon, I reckon he'd be a shoo-in.

There are several sharp intakes of breath.

'You can't do that.'

'The law states clearly that anyone recruited to be a vampire must do so independently and of their own free will.' He smiles benignly at Michael and gives him a brief bow. 'My Lord, did you approach Ms Blackman to join you?'

I don't think I've ever seen Michael look so angry. The skin around his mouth is white and his shoulders are hunched. 'You need to get the hell out of my house,' he growls.

'I'll take that as a yes,' D'Argneau says. 'You placed undue pressure on Ms Blackman to be recruited. Not only that, but you implied that she would not have to be a bloodguzzler.' He allows himself a small smile. 'Pardon me. A vampire. You made it quite clear that she could be Sanguine. A term, I believe, for someone who possesses some vampire characteristics but who has not completed the turning process and is more human than vampire. Ms Blackman is not Sanguine, is she?'

Michael doesn't answer. I get the impression that he's barely holding himself back from snapping D'Argneau's neck right here in front of everyone. I'm confused as to why his anger is directed at the lawyer. After all, I'm the one who asked him here. I'm the one who's going to break the Family law and leave.

D'Argneau continues. 'In which case, Ms Blackman's contract is null and void.'

Everyone is so quiet, I swear I can hear Michael's teeth grinding. He turns to me. 'What is this about, Bo? That bloody feather?'

I shake my head. 'No.' I step up to him until he's so close I can inhale his masculine scent. 'It's about me,' I say quietly. 'These walls are closing in on me. I can't do this. Not for the time it'll take to become used to the sun.' I look down for a moment, take a deep breath and raise my eyes. 'I know you've tried to help me. You've done far more for me than anyone could have expected. But you're right. You can't break the rules for me. It's not fair on anyone else. And I can't stay here like a prisoner. It's not just the trauma from what happened before. If I stay, this Jekyll and Hyde stuff I've been pulling isn't going to get any better. I didn't choose this life, Michael. What happened just now in your office...'

'Was nothing to do with being a vampire or being here.'

'I know,' I answer quietly. 'But being here makes it worse. If there was any other way...' My voice trails off.

'I understand,' interrupts D'Argneau, 'that the circumstances surrounding Ms Blackman's recruitment were unique. In every situation, your recruits – and those recruits from the other Families – make the initial approach. Therefore for them, there is no case to answer. That means there will be no repercussions from this for any other vampires. And there should be no repercussions for Ms Blackman.'

'You're still a vampire,' Michael says to me, ignoring D'Argneau. 'Nothing's changed.'

'I know.'

'You still need to drink.'

'I know.'

'Bo, you won't manage this on your own.' His face is a mask; I can't tell whether he's angry or worried.

Instinctively I reach a hand up to touch his cheek, think better of it and withdraw before I connect. 'I will.' I look at the door then glance back at Michael. 'I really am sorry.'

Then D'Argneau and I walk out.

CHAPTER 5

CRIME SCENE

When I wake up, I'm completely disorientated. I can't remember where, or even who, I am for a few seconds. My disturbed dreams keep playing out in some nightmarish loop. That's another thing Arzo was right about: I need professional help if I'm going to prove I can do this on my own. I sit up, running my hands through my hair and doing my best to ignore their visible tremor. Then I check my reflection in the rear view mirror and grimace. Even if vampires aren't really undead, I certainly look like I am. I pinch my cheeks to get some colour into them but all I succeed in doing is making my skin blotchy and sore.

Giving up on my appearance, I push open the car door so I can stretch my aching muscles. D'Argneau offered me a bed but, as I wasn't sure it didn't come with strings attached and I needed some time alone, I declined politely and got him to drop me off a few miles away. I had to put some of my old evasion skills into practice to make sure I wasn't followed. I suppose that sort of thing is a bit like riding a bike: you never really forget it.

If I'd hoped that Michael would send someone after me, I

was disappointed. As far as I could tell, I really was on my own. There was the option of my grandfather, of course, but spending the night in my rusty old car was more appealing than facing him. Even if I had to rip out the front passenger seat first; it was still caked with O'Shea's dried blood from weeks ago and the smell was horrific. I'm not sure whether my nose has simply got used to it or whether it dissipated after I removed the offending seat.

The lock-up is dark but there's the faintest chink of light coming in from under the door. Thanks to that, I'll know when I can venture safely outside. I try not to think about Michael's expression if he knew I'd spent the day here. The trouble is, the harder you try to not think about something, the more you end up dwelling on it. And thinking about Michael enhances my feelings of guilt. I have done what no other vampire has dared to do. It's simply not the done thing to leave your Family. I imagine if anyone else tried, they'd be executed before they got more than five steps from the door. I'm still very much alive, so D'Argneau's legal loophole must be offering me enough protection. It doesn't change the fact that I betrayed the Family, though.

I trace a shape on the dust covering the body of the car: the Montserrat logo. Then, scowling to myself, I rub it away and dust off my hands. I'm still wearing my Montserrat jumpsuit under my leather jacket. I'll need to find something new to wear. I briefly consider driving to The Steam Team so I can 'borrow' another abandoned outfit from Rebecca but I'm not convinced that I can trust myself these days, so it's probably not a good idea.

My stomach growls. Something else to worry about.

I should focus on myself first. I'm homeless and hungry – and apparently hallucinating from time to time. But I promised Stephen Templeton that I'd be in touch today and I can't afford to wait too long. He's hardly going to be nocturnal like me. It would be easy to dismiss him, now that I'm probably *persona non grata* with Arzo but my reason for finding the errant Dahlia hasn't changed: it's not something that Arzo should be concerning himself with. So, as soon as I'm positive that night has fallen, I pull up the garage door and reverse out, heading for the Templetons' house.

Unfortunately it's on the other side of the city so it takes a long time to get there. When I arrive on their quiet residential street, however, I find the house quickly. That's because it's the one plastered in *Do Not Cross* crime-scene tape. Bugger. The tape looks undisturbed, meaning that Templeton, the devious bastard, is living somewhere else for the time being. It should have occurred to me before. I take my phone out to call him, noticing that the battery is almost dead. I ignore two missed calls from O'Shea. I'll have to find a charger before I worry about him.

'Ms Montserrat!' Templeton says before I can utter a word. 'Have you found anything? Have you found Dahlia?'

I'm about to snap that it's been bloody daytime so I couldn't go outside when I think better of it. He has no reason to know that I'm a fledgling and not strong enough to face sunlight yet. If I tell him, he might go back to the Montserrat mansion to find someone more experienced. Then he may discover that Arzo's not swanning around the icy wastes of Antarctica after all.

'I've had other things to do,' I say tersely. 'But I'm at your house now. Come and meet me with that list.'

'It'll take me a while to...'

'I'll wait. And don't call me Ms Montserrat. It's Blackman. Bo Blackman.'

He's puzzled. 'I thought all vampires took on their Family name.'

'I'm different.' I hang up before he can say anything else. I probably should have gone along with the Montserrat nomenclature but I couldn't bring myself to do it.

I duck under the tape and try the door. Unsurprisingly, it's locked. I examine it carefully. The lock itself is sturdy and unscratched. Whoever disturbed the Templetons' perfect lives didn't break in this way. I'm probably strong enough to kick the door open but I don't need nosy neighbours calling the police because there's been a second break-in. I've been in enough trouble in the past with the police thinking that I'm a criminal, I don't need it now. Vampires aren't subject to human laws; all punishment is meted out via the Families. Now I'm without a Family, goodness knows where I stand.

I skirt round the large house, setting off various motion-activated lights. Their presence gives me pause. It seems unlikely, although not impossible, that Dahlia's kidnapping – or murder – took place in broad daylight. But these lights would put off any night-time burglar. Were the Templetons specifically targeted? If they treat other people the way they treated Arzo, then I wouldn't be surprised.

There's a broken window but it's on the second storey. After my rooftop lesson with Michael, I know that I can reach it easily but I don't see how a human would be able to without a ladder. It's covered by an opaque sheet of plastic, rippling in the faint breeze.

I'm proud to say that when I worked for Dire Straits I never once *technically* broke into anyone's property. As a private investigator, that kind of thing can lead you into a whole heap of trouble. More often than not I did my surveillance from outside or had the owner's permission to go inside. When it came to cheating spouses, however, I might have the husband's permission but not the wife's, or vice-versa. And if my client wanted to know exactly who their partner was having an affair with, from time to time I had to slip inside houses when the targets were 'otherwise occupied' to look for identification cards. It seems to be a mark of furtive affairs that couples feel the need to discard their clothes in every room of the house bar the bedroom. Desperation, I guess.

I only entered houses for that reason a few times. As with nasty crimes, the perpetrator (or in these cases the cuckolder) would often be someone already known to the so-called victim. I never got caught on the occasions I surreptitiously sneaked into houses although I was always prepared for that eventuality so I looked for alternative entrances to the front door. That way, it would be believed that I was a burglar and not an investigator. In the unlikely event I was apprehended and the police were called, it would take the officer on the scene one call to the station to realise I'd been given permission to enter and that the police had been informed beforehand by the legal owner about my actions.

It's a distasteful thing to do and the boundaries between right and wrong in these sorts of cases are often blurred. It could be argued that following someone, or sitting in a car outside their house and watching them, is an invasion of their privacy. But if that was against the law, private investigators wouldn't exist. Neither would a lot of journalists. Certainly, the police's abilities to solve crimes would also be severely curtailed. I hate breaking into people's houses, even though I only did so when I had property owner's legal permission. I also drew the line at setting up surveillance equipment inside. Nanny-cams and listening devices are, for me, a step too far. There are other less-scrupulous investigators who use them regularly.

The knowledge that I gained from those few experiences tiptoeing into houses will benefit me now. That's the reason I use the garage as my point of entry. It's shocking how many people – even those who are security-conscious – forget to lock it up properly. I don't have the patience to wait for Stephen Templeton and it will be easier to look around without him hovering by my shoulder. I should have asked him to tell the police what I'm doing, but according to vampiric law I'm doing nothing wrong because he's already invited me in. As long as I don't disturb the crime scene, that is.

The first garage door is locked but this is a big house and it boasts a double-door system. As I suspect, the second one is open. I lift it about a metre and duck under to get in. It closes quickly behind me and I'm left in the darkness. There's a car inside – Dahlia's, I assume – and it's locked securely. I peer through the windows; it seems spotlessly clean inside. My night vision is improving daily and the mundanity of the Templetons' lives is clearly visible: a dirty lawnmower, half-opened tins of paint and various cardboard boxes.

There's a door in the back of the garage, no doubt leading directly into the house. I walk over to it and hope for the best. The doorknob turns easily and I step inside. It's immediately obvious from the broken glass and fallen painting in front of me that something terrible happened here. There's an undertone of blood in the air but it's faint and smells old. It doesn't fit with the time frame that Stephen Templeton gave me so I can only think it's from an old minor injury.

Stepping carefully over the glass shards to avoid disturbing them, I venture further inside. Other than a wooden stool knocked to the ground, there's not much of a mess. There is, however, a wine glass sitting on top of the marble-covered island. It has a mouthful of red wine inside. I'm surprised that the police didn't take it away to brush it for fingerprints. I spot a pair of rubber gloves by the sink. They're a lurid pink but wearing them will make it easier for me to protect the integrity of the scene. I pull them on, wrinkling my nose at the rubbery smell, and move through the rest of the house.

Templeton was right about one thing: there was definitely some kind of commotion here. The living room is a mess. An overturned plant pot has sent dark earth spilling across the cream carpet, while the wide-screen television has been pulled off its bracket and lies on the floor, cracked screen facing upwards. A row of photo frames have been knocked off a mahogany side table. The table itself probably cost more than I make in a year but it's not what I'm interested in. I pick up one of the photos and frown at it. Unbelievable. Judging by the clothes of the smiling people captured within the frame, it's an old shot. Not only is a fresh-faced Stephen Templeton beaming out at me, along with a dark-haired woman who must be Dahlia, there's also the unmistakable visage of Arzo. He's a good twenty years younger than he is now, but it's definitely him. It doesn't make sense that the Templetons would display a photo of their former friend – and Dahlia's former fiancé – so prominently, considering what they did to him.

I return it carefully to its original position and go to the sofa. The bright floral cushions are in disarray. Interesting. I leave the room through a different door and locate the front entrance, then I turn and gaze speculatively round the house. If an intruder appeared from here or from the window upstairs, presumably while Dahlia was in the kitchen drinking her wine, they'd have disturbed her in that room. That's why the stool was knocked to the floor. After that, for some reason, they walked – or fought – in the living room. It's a big room and the television screen is at least four metres from the sofa. The little side table with the photos isn't close to either of them. I glance back at the inner garage door and the shattered painting. From the living room, they seem to have moved towards the garage. There's still a car there, however, and only one vacant spot.

I jog upstairs, glancing in the various rooms until I find the one Dahlia and Stephen slept in. Everything seems fairly normal. I open a few drawers. There's a diary which I flick through (apart from the first week of January, the pages are blank), some eye-drops and pieces of costume jewellery. I can't see anything else noteworthy. There's another door leading to a walk-in wardrobe which is filled with more of Dahlia's clothes than Steven's. I examine the shoes. Most of the pairs are barely worn but there's one set which seems to have been re-heeled recently. Dahlia's favourite pair, perhaps? I chew my bottom lip. This case is becoming more interesting than I'd imagined it would be.

I go to the room with the broken window. It's a small box room, obviously unoccupied. In theory, it would be a sensible entrance point, especially if the garage were the exit. How would the intruders know that, though? I lean in to inspect the remaining glass around the edges of the frame. I'd need a magnifying glass to be sure, but I'm fairly certain from the angle of the shards that this window wasn't broken into. It was broken out of – from the inside rather than the outside.

I check my watch. It's already gone 11pm. That's annoying as I really want to talk to the neighbours. None of them are going to be keen to talk to a vampire at this time of night. I'll have to come back another time. Yet again I'm stymied by my nocturnal nature.

I'm making my way downstairs when the front door opens and the pale face of Stephen Templeton appears. He looks surprised to see me.

'Hello.' He scratches his cheek. 'How did you get in?'

I see no reason to lie. 'Your garage,' I say. 'You should take care of that. It's wide open so anyone could enter.' I find my own actions considerably less important than his, however. I watch his eyes carefully. 'Mr Templeton, why did you lie and tell me you called the police?'

'Wh-what?' he stutters.

I dislike him even more for not owning up immediately but I distance myself emotionally from his reaction. The last thing I need is to get worked up and have to deal with another hallucinatory episode.

'You said the police dusted for fingerprints but there's no dust. I've yet to meet a police department that takes the time to clean up after themselves. Not only that but they would have taken Dahlia's diary, regardless of how little is written in it. They'd also have made sure that her wine glass, if indeed it is her glass, was examined.'

I lean towards him. From the look in his eyes, he's feeling intimidated. That pleases me more than it should. When I was human, my lack of height meant that the only people I intimidated without trying were very small children. In fact, thinking about my teen babysitting years, even that's not true. I've not grown at all since I turned, so it must be some indefinable vampire quality.

'The tape. The crime scene tape,' he says, with a hint of desperation.

'You put that there yourself.' His lack of reaction tells me I'm right. 'Why?'

He shifts uncomfortably and coughs. 'I didn't want the neighbours to call the police. I thought that if they believed the police were already investigating, they'd leave things alone. I got the tape from a joke shop and paid a couple of people to dress up as officers and come round. I told them it was a prank.'

'So it was you who messed up the house?'

This time he actually looks surprised. He blinks rapidly. 'What do you mean?'

'It's a set-up. And not a very good one either.'

'But...'

I sigh. 'The window's broken to make it look like someone entered upstairs. Except they could have come in the same way

I did through the open garage. And the window's been smashed from the inside. The wine and the stool indicate Dahlia was in the kitchen but the evidence of a struggle is in the living-room. The way in which the sofa cushions have been disturbed, the range of the fallen objects...' I shake my head. 'It's all too pat. You pretended the police had been here and someone else pretended there had been a fight.'

Templeton waves his hands in the air. 'No, no, no! You're suggesting Dahlia faked all this! She wouldn't do that! She...'

I hold up my hand to stop him babbling. 'I think you're probably right. I think she was taken.'

'Eh?'

'Her shoes,' I tell him. 'Unless she's been shopping recently or was barefoot, she left her favourite shoes behind.' I know enough from living in close quarters with Beth that women who are into footwear – as Dahlia seemingly is from the number of shoes she has in her closet – never let go of their best pair. The ones she had re-heeled. I shrug. 'I mean, it's not defi-nite and I may be wrong, but that's what my gut tells me.'

His shoulders sink. 'That doesn't make any sense.'

I search inside myself for a trace of sympathy. It's pretty hard. 'Why didn't you tell the police in the first place? Have you been in touch with the kidnappers? Has there been a ransom demand?'

'No.' He looks miserable. 'I didn't want... I mean, I couldn't...' He runs a hand through his hair. 'I've done some things the police might not look on too kindly. If they investi-gated and found out...'

I stare at him in disgust. 'So you staying out of prison is more important than your wife's life?'

'It's not like that!' he protests.

'I think it is very much like that.' I feel grubby just being in the same room as this pathetic excuse for a human. I put my hands on my hips. 'No wonder you were so reluctant to give me a list of your business dealings. So who have you pissed off?'

Templeton droops. 'There was the Triads,' he whispers.

I roll my eyes. Bloody hell. 'Okay. At least they're human. Give me their names and...'

'And a few white witches.'

I take a deep breath. 'Right.'

He shrinks further into himself. 'And the daemon.'

'Is that it?'

He nods.

'Then we'll assume it's one of them who's taken Dahlia,' I say briskly. 'You'll need to tell me what you actually did and who to, so I can talk to the Triads. And the witches. I have a contact who can help with whoever the Agathos daemon is.'

'No,' he moans.

I'm finally starting to lose patience. 'Look, if we're going to find her, then we need to...'

'You don't understand. It wasn't an Agathos daemon.'

My throat constricts. 'You've got to be kidding me.'

He raises up his head and looks me in the eye. 'It was a Kakos daemon.'

Sodding hell.

CHAPTER 6

PAYING FOR IT

Look up Kakos daemon in Spreitzer's *Almanac of The Triber World,* and you'll find a definition of what it means to be evil. Stories of daemons date back to the Hellenistic period and Alexander the Great. Just as black and white magic are said to be two sides of the same coin, so are Agathos and Kakos daemons. It is widely accepted that Agathos daemons are generally 'good'; Kakos daemons, meanwhile, are an entirely different story. Unfortunately for the rest of us, they're at the very top of the food chain.

They don't often show themselves to other tribers. I've heard that this is because they consider the rest of the world not worth bothering with. Whatever their reasons are, it's a good thing. Being in the same room as a Kakos daemon is enough to drive someone entirely and irrevocably insane. And that's assuming the daemons don't eat your heart out first. Apparently hearts are a delicacy. At least vampires sip arterial blood because they need it to survive; Kakos daemons munch on body parts just for the hell of it.

I've never come close to one. I can confidently state that even my grandfather, who has an encyclopaedic knowledge of the triber world and has had more dealings with its different denizens than almost any other human, has never met a Kakos daemon face to face. And now Stephen Templeton, wanker extraordinaire, is telling me he's involved with one. I don't think he's lying, but also I don't think it's true. It has to be some idiot posing as Kakos. God help whoever it is when the real daemons finally catch up with him. I desperately want to call Michael and ask him what he thinks. Of course that's completely out of the question.

Whoever has taken backstabbing Dahlia obviously has their reasons. There's been no ransom demand and, while it's true that missing persons are more likely to be rescued safe and sound if they're discovered within the first twenty-four to forty-eight hours, she's already been gone for several days. Perhaps I'd have more of a sense of urgency if that wasn't the case. Regardless, I'll look for her – and not just because of Arzo. Before I left, Stephen Templeton thrust a wad of money in my direction and begged me to continue investigating. I don't trust him an inch – let's face it, even his own wife can't trust him not to place his safety over hers. But the money will solve my immediate problems. I have to push away my distaste at being employed by someone who harmed a man I genuinely respect. Fortunately, for the moment, our needs converge.

The streets are quieter now so I make good time getting back to the police station where the feather mugger is being held. There's no parking nearby and, tempted as I am to pull up wherever I can and damn the consequences, I'm wary of getting into more trouble. I end up leaving the car a long distance away before trudging back to the station.

The desk sergeant is a different guy. When I tell him I'm here to make a statement about the McGuire Street mugging, his face blanches. He picks up a phone and mutters something into it, then asks me to wait. It's barely twenty seconds before a plain-clothed officer appears and directs me into an interview room.

'You made a citizen's arrest of the suspect, along with Lord Montserrat, is that correct?'

I nod, carefully describing all the events and everything the kid said. The officer transcribes it all. His manner is distant and unfriendly but I don't think that's because of me or my vampire status. There's something else going on.

'Sign here,' he instructs.

I do as he requests, then look up. 'Is he still here?'

Deliberately obtuse, the officer asks, 'Who?'

I settle back in my chair, cock my head and don't reply. Eventually the policeman fills the silence. 'There was an incident.' His eyes flick nervously to the door. 'The suspect's interrogation was scheduled for the following morning when the next duty officer was in. As per protocol, we checked on him every hour.'

I'm getting an idea where this is heading. 'He's dead, isn't he?'

I receive a nod and my stomach sinks. He may have been a little shit but he didn't deserve to die.

'What happened?' I keep my voice soft and unthreatening but I can feel my pulse starting to pick up.

'We're awaiting the results of the post-mortem.'

No doubt they'll be putting a rush job on it. It never looks good when someone dies suddenly in police custody. I'm not in the mood to wait any length of time, though.

'But you have an idea,' I probe.

'We're not releasing...'

'Off the record.'

He sighs. 'All I know is there is a hex on the wall of his cell.'

'Black or white?'

'White.'

'Can I see it?'

He glances at the door again. 'No.'

I frown. 'But...'

'Thank you for your time.' He stands up. 'If you remember anything else, I'd appreciate it if you get in touch. Here's my card.' He pulls out a small white oblong and scribbles something on the back. 'My direct line is there.'

I take the card and flip it over. Instead of a number, he's hastily drawn an intricate shape on the back. The hex. I look up and smile. 'Thank you.'

'We always welcome the support of the Families. Please convey our gratitude to Lord Montserrat.'

I try not to wince. So that's why he's being so helpful. Michael brought the mugger in and they're hoping that Michael will absolve them of any wrongdoing. Unfortunately he's passing on that message to pretty much the worst person in the world. I'm lucky that news of the first-ever vampire abdication hasn't yet reached human ears.

'I don't suppose you've had time to examine the feather he stole?' I ask casually. 'Lord Montserrat is keen to understand its significance.'

The officer swallows. 'It's gone,' he says quietly. 'It vanished from the evidence locker around the time the suspect died.'

Curiouser and curiouser. The police aren't incompetent and they're well aware of the various triber abilities that might impede real investigations. Unlike vampires, witches aren't immune from the full weight of human prosecution – a fact that undoubtedly sticks in their magical craws – but after the highly publicised case of Thomas Argyll, a white Romany witch who charmed sprigs of white heather to cause a number of deaths and who also managed to spirit away all the evidence against him from right under the investigating officers' eyes, the government paid vast amounts of money to ensure all police departments are heavily protected from similar magic invasions. It's a powerful witch indeed who could break through those enchantments.

I'm careful not to pass judgment. 'I see,' I murmur. 'And has the suspect's name been released to the press?'

'Samuel Lewis.' Then more quietly, 'He's also known as Slick. He lived at 5D Easthouse Road.'

I give the policeman a tiny smile of thanks and leave, shoving my hands into the pockets of my leather jacket. My efforts at looking serious and tough fail me entirely, however, when I see the flashy stretch limousine waiting on the street outside and two vampire goons looming on the pavement. All coherent thought flees and I'm convinced I'm about to be cut down right here on the steps of the sodding police station. I finally register that the colours they're displaying are Medici Red, not Montserrat Blue. I have no idea whether that makes my situation better or worse. The car door swings soundlessly open and both goons point towards it.

I glance up and down the street, searching for an escape route. I know it's a futile gesture. I'm not even two months old yet, in vampiric terms, and only just starting to control my abilities. If I run, these two will mow me down in a heartbeat. I'd rather scratch together some dignity and go out with my head held high than act like terrified prey, so I paste on a smile and nod like I was expecting them. Then I get inside.

It's Lord Medici himself. I swallow my growing terror when the car door shuts and we glide smoothly down the street. Of course. Even though the vampires won't get into trouble for ending my short, miserable life, it makes more sense not to taunt the police by doing it in front of their eyes.

Medici bares his teeth in the semblance of a smile and fixes me with his pale aquamarine eyes. They're entirely incongruous with his olive skin.

'So,' he says, drawing out the word, 'we meet again, Ms Blackman.'

The fact that he's using my real name speaks volumes. 'I would say it's good to see you, but I'd be lying,' I tell him, with considerably more courage than I feel.

He barks out a laugh. 'There's no need to be afraid.' He reaches out and trails a finger down my face. Despite my best intentions, I flinch. The amusement in his eyes grows. 'I'm not here to hurt you,' he says. 'Quite the contrary.'

'Oh?' I squeak.

'You've left the Montserrat Family. I'm here to offer you a position with us instead.'

I stare at him, not quite sure I heard him correctly. Is he looking for all-out war between the Families? Poaching other vampires is an absolute no-no.

'I can assure you that I'm not breaking any rules,' he says, as if he can tell what I'm thinking. 'You are no longer of Montserrat.'

The hackles on my spine are fully raised. 'I didn't leave because of Montserrat. I left because of me.'

'You want freedom. I can give you that under the protection of my Family. You can live where you want, do what you want. You'll just do it in the name of Medici, with our full blessing and with the benefit of all our resources.'

I swallow down rage. This has nothing to do with me: it's about getting one over on Montserrat. I've always known that relations between the Families are never more than icily cordial but Medici is over-stepping the line. There's no way I'm going to become a pawn in a game of vampire one-upmanship. And there's definitely no way I'm letting Medici do anything to make Montserrat appear weak.

'That's a really nice offer,' I say with saccharine sweetness. I think I've overdone it but Medici smiles.

'Excellent.' He pulls out a one-page contract. 'Just sign here and you're safe. You'll be one of us.'

I take it from him and scan it. Actually, the terms are generous. Not that it makes any difference. 'Unfortunately, you've approached me,' I tell him, layering on disappointment. 'And you've done it publicly.'

His smile vanishes. 'So?'

'That's the reason I used for leaving Montserrat. That by approaching me, rather than the other way around, my contract with them was null and void. If I join you in the same way, my lawyer assures me the original legal loophole will be closed. I'll still be bound to Montserrat.' D'Argneau had said nothing of the sort. I have no idea whether it's true or not, but it sounds pretty good.

Medici's eyes narrow. 'Are you hungry, Ms Blackman?'

'Um...'

'How long has it been? At least twenty-four hours, I imagine. It's difficult when you're still a fledgling. I remember once, when I was still very new myself, I came across a young girl in a park. She'd fallen over and was bleeding.' His eyes gleam. 'Not much, you understand, but then it only takes a drop of rich, salty blood for the scent to overwhelm. She was so young and so pure.'

I feel sick and wonder whether he killed her outright. He certainly seems to be implying that he did. 'That's a nice memory,' I force out.

He licks his lips and presses a button on the armrest. 'William, park the car and come in here.'

We come to a smooth stop almost immediately and I start to worry about who William is. The passenger door is open and a man – William, I presume – climbs inside.

'I prefer females,' Medici says emotionlessly. 'I think it's because the act of drinking is so closely related to that of sexual intercourse.' He turns in my direction and I see that his fangs are already in evidence, their brilliant white glaring against his dark skin. 'William will happily provide that service too. If you so desire.'

My nausea is growing. Medici nods in William's direction and he begins to undo his shirt, revealing the skin underneath. I see the throb of his blood and almost forget to breathe. With one swift movement, Medici curves his head towards William's neck. There's a hiss of breath. At this point, I'm not sure whether it comes from the hapless human or from me. Medici drinks for a few seconds before pulling away. He dabs delicately at the corner of his mouth with a handkerchief thoughtfully provided by his own victim. I stare at the trickle of blood running down from the two small puncture wounds in William's neck. Medici gestures towards him.

'He's all yours.'

I need to drink. I know I need to drink. But I'd rather be dead than accept this offer. It's somehow tied to his desire to sign me up to his Family. I think Lord Medici is expecting me to fall ravenously upon his driver with an uncontrollable thirst, but I haven't really lost control since I was a recruit. I feel a twinge of self-satisfaction that Montserrat is managing to keep some secrets, namely that drinking blood might fulfil my physical needs but I hate doing it. That little titbit was openly discussed among the Montserrat vampires and I had to endure several strangers offering me advice on how to deal with my aversion. The fact that Medici doesn't know as much as he thinks he does means there's no leak, or disloyal spy, within the Montserrat camp. Michael himself must have declared to the other Family Heads that I had decamped.

'Thank you but no,' I say with enough conviction to surprise myself.

There's a flash of rage in Medici's eyes, although he masks it quickly enough. 'So be it. Expect consequences.'

I think this is going to be the moment when I meet my Maker but he snaps his fingers and the door next to me opens. I look at him, then out at the pavement and the promise of freedom.

'You may go,' Medici says, dismissing me. 'You can tell your Lord Montserrat that it won't work. The humans won't fall for it.'

For a moment I'm frozen, wondering what on earth he's talking about and whether this is some elaborate trick.

'Unless you'd like to change your mind,' Medici adds blandly.

I almost trip over in my haste to get out. The door slams shut after me, although there's no sign of Medici's goons. William escapes from the other side and, without a glance in my direction, gets back into the driver's seat. The engine starts and the car speeds off, leaving me staring after it. My stomach growls and I shush it loudly.

'Soon,' I tell it. 'I promise.' My list of urgent things to attend to is growing.

I WALK BACK SLOWLY towards the police station and my car. It's just my bad luck that Medici drove in the opposite direction to where I parked – now I have even further to travel. I could run but I can't seem to muster up the energy. I still want to head to Fingertips and Frolics and check it out for myself. It's not that I don't trust O'Shea but until I get my phone charged, I have no means of contacting Rogu3 and getting any other leads on where the shopkeeper might be. I estimate that I only have a couple of hours until the sun rises. I have to prioritise.

I debate as I walk, then finally make a decision. There's a reason why airlines tell you to fit the oxygen mask over your own face before you attend to anyone else. I'll do no good if I pass out from lack of sustenance. Fledgling vampires are a bit like babies: they need to drink often. Medici's driver reminded me of how hungry I was while Medici himself underestimated how long it was since I last downed some blood. It's been more than a day. If I drink now, I can go without tomorrow.

Connor, the willing human victim I drank from last, mentioned there were bars where vampettes hung out in the hope of being selected as snacks. I'd heard of these bars before and I think I went inside one or two in my former life. I don't understand why some humans want to be food but at least I know that the vampettes are doing it voluntarily. I need to find one of these clubs.

Rather than walk in front of the police station, I take a shortcut and skirt through some quiet side streets. As soon as I reach the car, I head for Soho. It seems the likeliest area. Yet again, I'm forced to park some distance away. Perhaps I should use Templeton's money to buy myself an old motorbike – it'd certainly make life a lot easier.

My head is beginning to pound and I feel over-tired. The thought of squashing into a loud, crowded bar doesn't appeal. I need to get this over and done with as soon as I can.

I achieve my goal faster than I expected. I'm barely past the first of the sex shops when someone steps out in front of me. 'Vampire,' she purrs.

I glance up and down. It's a woman, probably in her mid-thirties but trying to look younger. She's wearing too much make-up and too few clothes.

'Thanks,' I say, 'but I'm not looking for sex. Besides, I swing the other way.'

She stretches out her neck and licks her lips. I can see faint bruises on her skin where her pulse is. Oh.

'I taste good.' She winks at me.

I don't know how to react. Beth was a prostitute for many years and, while we've never really spoken about it, I'd never judge her for it. Live and let live. As I discovered when I worked at Dire Straits, if you treat people fairly, they can be very helpful. I got some good tips in the past from working girls; they spend a lot of time on the streets and they see more than people think. I paid them for their help, of course, and tried not to dwell on the immorality of their lifestyle.

'It's your first time, innit?'

My thoughts must be plastered all over my face.

'Look, love. You can go into a club and have one of those daft vampettes. I'll get other business. I do alright. But I'm here now, I'm clean – and you don't have to buy me a drink first.'

It's wrong, a voice screams inside me. This is so wrong.

She smiles at me, her face softening. 'You're not taking advantage, love. Five minutes for some blood is a damn sight easier than lying on my back with my legs in the air.'

It seems so easy; it even makes a kind of sense. I need blood, she's got plenty. Pass her some money in return and everyone wins. Despite my nausea, I can feel myself weakening.

'I usually charge a hundred but as you're so nice and pretty, I'll give you a discount and call it eighty.' Her eyes move behind me and I turn to see what she's looking at. It's a bald-headed man in a shiny suit who's leaning against a car. Illegally parked, I might add. He's watching me carefully. I realise it's her pimp.

'I'm sorry. I can't.' I don't even continue on to the bars and clubs, I just spin round and start running in the opposite direction, while her laughter rings out after me.

CHAPTER 7

REALITY TV

There's still about thirty minutes to go before dawn when I pull up outside Fingertips and Frolics. This time I don't give a sod where I park the stupid car. I'm hungry and tired and I have to spend the next fourteen hours cooped up indoors in case the stupid sun turns me into a pile of smoking ash. I am definitely not happy.

O'Shea was right about the emptiness of the shop. The window display which I'd previously admired has completely vanished. All that remains are the silk drapes. I note that the wood around the Yale lock is splintered. I roll my eyes – O'Shea's doing, no doubt. I'm sure that if he'd tried harder, he could have found a way inside that didn't involve battering down the door. Still, I take advantage of his efforts and enter from the front seeing as the door is now open. This time no alarm announces my presence.

All that remains inside are bare shelves. The shop was jam-packed with items last week. It doesn't look like the shop owner had to leave in a hurry in some kind of sudden midnight flit; this was planned. My suspicions are confirmed when feel something sticky underfoot. I glance down: it's a piece of brown tape, the sort you use to seal boxes. It's been neatly cut with a pair of scissors, not ripped off its spool by anxious teeth. I purse my lips.

With no time to go anywhere else, I walk round the counter and hunker down against the wall. I can sleep here until night falls again. In the unlikely event that someone opens the front door, the counter will protect me from any sun rays that filter in. I close my eyes and try to relax. Then I hear the ringing.

Frowning, I dig inside my leather jacket for my phone. It's completely dead. I stand up and cock my head, trying to work out the direction of the sound. It's coming from underneath the counter. I duck back down and spot an old-fashioned telephone at the back of a dusty shelf. I watch it ring for a moment, then I shrug and answer.

'Hello?'

'I thought for a minute that you weren't going to pick up. Where have you been, Bo? I've been trying to reach you for ages.'

I'm puzzled. 'Rogu3?'

'How many other top-grade hackers do you know? Wave for the camera.'

'Huh?' I look around, finally spotting a small surveillance camera set in the ceiling. 'You've hacked into the shop's system?'

'Only because it's already transmitting elsewhere. So, yes, I can see you but it means whoever it's transmitting to can see you as well. And no, before you ask, I've not found out where the signal is going. The security on *that* is much more elaborate than the shop's system. I'll break it but it'll take me a few days. To be honest, you're lucky I spotted you. I got up early because I've got this rad programme running that's looking for ways into my school's exam board intranet. I wanted to see if it was finished. I still had the camera into the shop running on a different monitor.'

I scrunch up my face. 'You're not trying to cheat, are you?'

'No.' He sounds affronted. 'I want to make sure that no one else can cheat! I'm testing their system for cracks so I can tell the exam board how to fix them. If I have to sit this stupid exam, I want to make sure it's fair.'

'Uh, okay.' I guess I believe him. 'Did you find anything else useful about the shop? Other than the surveillance?'

I hear him smack his mouth on the other end of the line. 'Sorry,' he mumbles. 'Early breakfast. Let me find my notes.' There's the shuffling of paper then he comes back. 'So, the shop's been around for about twenty years. Two joint owners. The first one, Fingertip, died a few years ago, not long after the September 11th attacks in the States. His partner, Frolic, has been running the place since.'

It hadn't occurred to me that the name of the shop would be the same as the name of the owners. I suppose it was Frolic herself that I met the other day. Weird name.

'She's forty-three years old, has close ties with the white witches and often pitches up to their meetings. I came across an old newspaper article where she was interviewed about the relationship between the white and the black witches. It was around the time there were those protests about the black witches digging up graves to talk to the dead. She wasn't very nice about them. Apparently her hubby was a white before he died. Old alliances, I guess.'

'Is there a home address for her?'

'Just round the corner from the shop. I tried to check it out but it's a rented flat and it's already been vacated. A property agent nearby started advertising it as available as of yesterday. You won't find anything useful inside.'

I nod. That confirms my thoughts: Frolic had been planning to skedaddle all along. I wonder why.

'How did he die?'

'Who?'

'Her partner. Fingertip. How did he die?'

'Heart attack. The post-mortem indicated it was natural.'

I'm impressed. Rogu3 has been really thorough.

'Thanks. You've been a huge help.'

'Any time, Little Bo Peep. There is one other thing, though.'

'Yes?'

'The shop's been struggling financially. That's probably why Frolic shut it down.'

It's a similar scenario with many smaller stores: the financial crisis has hit them much harder than the larger corporations. It seems sad when the economy is just starting to recover and she's clung on all this time... I sigh.

'One of the corporations, Magix, was trying to take it over. It's put lot of pressure on her, hassled her. I suppose it just got too much.'

'Right.' I'm not surprised. The big conglomerates seem to do little more than grow in size and bulldoze everyone else out of the way.

'Do you know what happened to her inventory?'

'Magix took it all. At a knockdown price.'

I wonder whether any more bright green feathers were included. It'd be worth checking out.

'I'll let you get back to your breakfast and your exam board,' I tell him. He must be about the only teenager in the world who's awake at this time of day. It's not fair of me to keep him any longer.

'No worries. I'll keep working on the surveillance. Sort your phone out so I can call you.'

'Yes, sir!'

'Three bags full?'

'Whatever,' I answer, drolly. 'Thanks again, Rogu3.'

'See ya.'

I hang up and stare at the ceiling. The camera is bugging me and I wonder who else it's sending images to. Theoretically, it's Frolic keeping an eye on her old store, but if there's nothing left inside then why would she bother? My illegal entry will already have been beamed in full Technicolor to whoever is watching so it's too late to worry about the consequences. I suppose I could argue that the shop was already open so I merely took advantage of the fact because I needed somewhere to hide while the sun goes about its daily business. It doesn't mean I want someone peering at me while I sleep, even from a distance.

I take off my leather jacket. It's too heavy for my purpose and the rest of the shop is completely bare so I'll get no joy from that quarter. For a moment I'm tempted to strip off and use my bra, but I don't want the Peeping Tom on the other side to watch so instead I dash back outside. Streaks of orange are starting to highlight the sky: I don't have long. Cursing, I look up and down the narrow street. Irritatingly, it's remarkably free of rubbish. Then my eyes fall on my car and I grin.

I wrench the door open and retrieve an old, mouldy coffee cup. Then I grab some chewing gum from the glove-box. I congratulate myself on not having cleaned up at the same time as I ripped out the seat. With a nervous glance at the sky, I scoot back indoors and shut the door before setting to work and manoeuvring one of the heavy shelves. Once I'm satisfied that it's directly underneath the camera, I point up in its direction and mouth, 'You're mine.' Then I climb up.

Fortunately for me, the shelves are strong enough to hold my weight. I stand up precariously. If I stretch, I can just about reach the camera. Good enough. I shove a wad of chewing gum in my mouth and masticate fiercely, then take it out and press it around the rim of the cup. It'll be tight but it should just fit around the camera. I push the cup up till it covers the bulbous lens and press as hard as I can. Satisfied it will stick, I lower myself back down. That's when I start to lose my balance.

The shelf rocks dramatically from side to side. I throw my arms out to stabilise myself but it's too late. The shelf and I crash down to the floor. I catch the edge of my forehead on the shelf's sharp corner as I careen downwards. The unit falls on top of me and I wince with pain. Struggling out from underneath it, I hold a hand up to my head. It comes away wet. I lick my fingers gingerly, registering the sharp, salty taste of my own blood, and smile humourlessly. If only vampires could live off vampire blood I could self-cannibalise. I shrug. At least I know I'll heal quickly.

I check the ceiling. The cup remains in place, hiding the camera from me – and me from it. Satisfied, I crawl back behind the counter. My eyelids are heavy and I stifle a yawn but I need to take advantage of the phone in front of me. I pick up the receiver and dial.

'Hello,' says the calm voice on the other end of the phone, 'my name is Jane and you have reached the Samaritans.'

I sink down further. It's not a therapist – that'll have to wait – but it's a start. Quietly, I start to talk.

THE FOLLOWING NIGHT, I think I'm ready for action. I want to use my time more wisely and make the most of the dark hours. My movements are sluggish, however, and there's a nasty taste in my mouth. I exhale into my open palm, sniff and cringe at my halitosis, wishing I'd not bothered. Ignorance is not always a bad thing. Feeling slightly dizzy, I leave the shop and head for my car. I pause when I reach it; I definitely don't feel very well. Driving is not a good idea.

Absently patting the bonnet, I leave my rusty heap where it is and wander to the main road, swaying slightly. At least I manage to flag down a taxi within a couple of minutes. If I knew where Arzo lived I'd try him but I don't, so I give the driver the only other address I can think of. I have to face my grandfather sooner or later. Perhaps he'll look more kindly on me now that I can barely stand up straight.

The radio crackles as the taxi pulls away and the tinny voice of the dispatcher fills the air. The words are incomprehensible. I check the time on the dashboard: it's almost eight o'clock so the news is about to start. It would be helpful to know if gossip about my exit from the Montserrat Family is being broadcast.

I lean forward. 'Do you mind putting the radio on?'

The driver looks at me nervously in the mirror, no doubt noting the pinprick of red in my pupils that denotes my vampire status. 'Sure,' he says, pressing a button.

A bouncy pop song is playing. It's kind of catchy, although I've never heard it before. My enforced incarceration in the Montserrat mansion kept me in a bubble of ignorance; it's clear, however, that the rest of the world has continued without me. It's an odd, albeit very selfish, realisation.

The song ends, fading into the familiar theme tune for the news. 'Good evening. Fighting has broken out again in Gaza, just hours after the last official truce ended. There have been reports of rockets fired across the border and at least eleven deaths have already been confirmed.'

I wince. What right do I have to complain about my own life with that kind of suffering going on in the world?

'The corporation Magix has announced the creation of five hundred new jobs across the country as it opens a series of new stores.' I sit up. 'Its flagship store in London will open a new wing at the weekend.' The newscaster takes a short pause. 'And there have been a number of small protests outside the Mayfair Hotel after a meeting of the Heads of the five Families. Insiders at the hotel state there was tension between Montserrat and Medici, but it is not clear whether this was as a result of growing calls for the vampires to be more open about their activities. Neither of the Heads were available for comment.'

The driver's eyes flick towards me in the rear-view mirror. I turn my head and gaze out of the window as the news ends and the music starts again. My thoughts are racing. I know that the Heads meet regularly to discuss matters that require their combined attention. I also know that there's frequently 'tension' between them. I wonder if it's egotistical of me to think that the source of the tension might be me this time. It could, of course, all be smoke and mirrors; very little real information about the Families escapes into the news. I tell myself that it's none of my business; it doesn't really work.

I'm relieved when we pull up outside my grandfather's small house. I peel off some notes and pay the driver, then get out. The tyres screech as he accelerates to get away. His fear is disturbing; I feel a trickle of guilt as it occurs to me that I probably should have done something to reassure him. I guess it's too late now.

As per usual, the cul-de-sac is quiet. My grandfather's fat ginger cat eyes me from the middle of the path and I can see its nose twitching in the air. Without warning, it arches its back and hisses. I take a half step backwards and stumble, falling to my hands and knees. The cat looks ready to launch itself at me, teeth and claws bared. Then the door opens and my grandfather mutters something. The cat flees inside.

'Stupid girl,' he mutters. Is he referring to me or the animal? 'Do get up from there, Bo. You look ridiculous.'

I grimace, pull myself to my feet and walk unsteadily to the doorstep.

'I've been waiting for you,' my grandfather says. He looks at me expectantly. Unsure if I'm doing the right thing, I kiss his cheek. When I draw back, however, I'm surprised to spot a twinkle in his eye. My grandfather is not usually the twinkly-eyed sort. I half expect him to whip out a bag of Werther's Originals from behind his back. He's not about to confound me that much, though.

'Come in,' he says. Then he turns and goes back inside.

The fact that he's invited me in must mean something. I ignore the cat that glares at me malevolently from the stairs and wobble forwards. My grandfather has picked up his telephone, a make so old fashioned it wouldn't be out of place in a museum.

'She's here,' he says into the receiver. His eyes are trained on me. I stiffen. 'No,' he continues, after a brief pause. 'Bring some food.' He hangs up.

'Well,' he says, one eyebrow raised. 'You really have got yourself into a mess this time, haven't you?'

I can't help myself. A single tear rolls down my cheek. He tuts.

'Blackmans do not weep.' He opens a cupboard door and throws me a towel. 'The smell emanating from you is quite off-putting, my dear. Go upstairs and take a bath. I'll lay out some clothes for you.'

I move towards him then stop as my knees buckle dramatically.

'On second thoughts, you should probably make that a shower. It wouldn't do to have you collapsing unconscious and drowning, would it?'

He goes into the kitchen, leaving me alone. I scowl after

him. I'm not sure if I can stay upright long enough to do his bidding.

'Who were you calling?' My voice is weak. I know he can hear me but there is no answer. I know from experience that he won't bother with me until I'm a good girl and do as I'm told. Clutching the towel with one hand and the banister with the other, I slowly climb the stairs. The cat swipes at me with one paw and spits. I don't even look at it; it would take far too much energy.

I scrub myself down. My head is swimming but I manage to towel off and put on the Laura Ashley dress my grandfather left out for me. I have no idea where he got it from. I allow myself a brief moment of humour at the thought that perhaps one of his lovers left it behind, then lurch downstairs to the kitchen. At least the sodding cat has vanished.

As soon as I enter the small room, however, my hackles rise. I tense and, for a moment, forget that I'm on the verge of collapsing. Sitting with a delicate china cup of Earl Grey that looks incongruous in his large hands, is Michael Montserrat. He gets to his feet and looks me over, his face a dark mask. For a moment my heart sings with delight at the sight of him, then I remember that I walked out on him.

I hiss at my grandfather, 'This is who you called?'

He sighs. 'Sometimes, my dear, I wonder whether you were left at the bottom of the garden by a stork. It causes me endless confusion that you can be so dim-witted.' He walks out, leaving me alone with Michael.

Michael steps towards me as, finally unable to hold my weight any longer, my legs give way. He pulls me upright and his eyes sear into mine. 'Where the hell have you been, Bo?'

I open my mouth but no words come out. He pushes my wet hair away from my face and his eyes harden. 'Who did this? Was it Medici?'

Confused, I stare at him. 'Did what?'

His fingers gently touch the side of my forehead and I wince. It's the cut from my fall. 'I thought that would have healed by now,' I mutter.

'You've not drunk since you left, have you?'

I shake my head mutely and he looks even angrier. 'You know you're more vulnerable because you're a fledgling. How could you be so stupid? You have to drink every day! You're not healing because you're not drinking. Goddamn it!'

My tongue cleaves to the roof of my mouth. I have no idea what's going on.

'Connor!' he yells.

'Not in the house,' I hear my grandfather say from the other room.

Michael grips my arm and pulls me towards the garden door. After two steps, he frowns and lets go. Before I can say or do anything, he scoops me up, carrying me against his chest. I let out a small yelp.

'Shush.' He opens the door to the small patch of well-trimmed grass behind my grandfather's house.

'Put me down,' I protest.

Gently, he allows me to escape his embrace. Embarrassingly, however, I have to lean against him or risk falling flat on my face.

I see Connor's red-haired mop in front of me. He smiles and steps up. 'Hi,' he grins, then thrusts out his forearm. 'Wrist, right?'

This time I don't even think, I just sink in my teeth. I've never tasted anything so glorious. I suck and suck and suck, dimly aware of Michael curving an arm round my waist to support me as I drink. I can feel the warm blood trickling down my throat and making its way through me. A glow spreads through my body. When I can't take any more, I pull away.

Connor opens his eyes and smiles again. 'Thank you,' he says as he leaves.

I'm the one who should be showing gratitude. I'm starting to realise how stupid my enforced starvation has been.

Michael is still at my back. His arm tightens round my waist and I feel his breath on my neck as he bends down towards me. 'Don't ever do that again, Bo Blackman,' he whispers, 'or I swear I will kill you myself.'

I stay where I am. There's an odd fluttering in my stomach – it must be because of Connor's blood. 'What are you doing here, my Lord?' I ask. 'I thought you'd be happy to wash your hands of me.'

'If you'd done what you were supposed to do and come here first, we wouldn't have had this problem,' he growls. 'Were you with the lawyer?'

I start. 'No.' I finally pull away and turn to look up at him. 'I don't understand. What do you mean do *what I was supposed to?*'

A smile flickers across his mouth. 'You really haven't worked it out yet?'

My expression must give him my answer because his grin widens. 'You weren't coping. We have this one-size-fits-all law that all fledglings have to stay within their Families' walls until they can withstand the sun. The trouble is that you're not the same size as other people.'

'You're making fun of my height?'

'No, love.'

The endearment jolts me. I search for something to say to avoid showing my surprise. 'If you knew I wasn't coping, why didn't you do something?'

'I did.'

I frown at him.

'I got the daemon to suggest you could leave.'

'O'Shea?'

'And Arzo to tell you things weren't working for you.'

I do a double take.

'Connor told you about other places where you could drink freely,' Michael continues.

'Hold on, you *told* them to say those things?'

'I even introduced you to a bloody lawyer who deals with vampire recruitment.' For a second, he scowls. 'You were supposed to call *him*, not Harry freaking D'Argneau. Why do you think I let you hang on to that phone?'

I gape. 'But you said you'd lock me in my room! You made it very clear that I wasn't to leave.'

'I'm sorry I pushed things so hard in my office. I didn't mean for you get so upset.' His eyes search mine. 'It was the red-button theory.'

'Uh?'

'If you tell someone not to push the red button, that's all they want to do. Nine times out of ten they'll push it.' He shrugs. 'It's human nature. And vampire nature.'

'You were goading me into leaving?' I step back and fold my arms.

'I told you I thought the law was archaic. I took you out to show you what you were capable of so you'd realise you were strong enough to manage.'

'Why the hell didn't you just tell me I could go?' I yell.

'It had to come from you – it's the only way the other Family Heads would accept your departure. Once you'd chosen to go, I could present it as out of my hands and offer them an acceptable alternative. You have the fact that you saved their hides a few months ago on your side.'

I try to absorb what he's telling me. 'Medici. Medici said it wouldn't work and that the humans wouldn't fall for it. Is that it? He was referring to your alternative?'

Michael's jaw tenses. 'I thought you'd come here. I didn't

have anyone follow you when you left the mansion because this seemed the logical place to come. When you didn't arrive...' He lets out a quiet snarl. 'Medici should never have approached you.'

'He tried to get me to sign up with him. That was because of this alternative,' I say, thinking aloud. 'What is it?'

Michael takes my hand, his thumb gently stroking my palm. 'The humans' antipathy towards us is growing. Ever since Nicky, there's been a movement to stop us recruiting and to strip us of our legal powers. It's a small minority for now but it's gaining momentum.'

I think of the taxi driver's reaction to me. 'So?'

'So we set up an agency. A bridge between the humans and the vampires. It will investigate complaints and deal with any issues that arise. It'll smooth over problems.'

Comprehension finally dawns. 'And you think I can be a part of this.'

'It's a good compromise, Bo. You will still have the Family's protection but you don't have to feel trapped by us. Arzo is in. Connor will be there.'

I start to protest but he stops me.

'I know how much you dislike drinking. If you stick to one donor then it won't be so hard. Connor will make a great personal assistant. Matt will join you for protection.'

'What?'

'He's a fledgling like you but he's strong and loyal.' A shadow crosses Michael's face. 'Keeping him in the mansion isn't doing him any good either.'

'Why would the humans trust a bunch of vampires to investigate vampires?'

'Because you voluntarily left the Family. Arzo is Sanguine. Connor is human. You can hire another human investigator to even things out.'

I run my hand through my hair. 'What about the other Families?'

'They're all on board.'

'Apart from Medici.'

'He was outvoted. I'll have words with him about approaching you in the way he did.'

'Don't bother,' I say absently. 'That's what he wants you to do.'

'If it works, the other Families will send representatives to join you.'

'*If* it works,' I say.

'Do you think it won't?'

'No, it's a good idea.' I look down, scuffing the grass with my toe. 'I guess my grandfather agrees too.'

'Yes.' There's a pause. 'What's wrong, Bo?'

'You manipulated me!' I burst out. 'And I didn't even twig that's what you were doing. I'm supposed to be a private investigator who can work things out and see through people and you had me dancing on strings like a puppet!'

'Bo...'

'Just like Nicky did!'

His eyes soften. 'Nicky fooled all of us and I've been around a lot longer than you. A bit more experience and a bit more training, and you'll run circles around the lot of us. Your best teacher is your last mistake.' He looks away from me, as if he's embarrassed. 'I've never met anyone I have more faith in,' he says quietly.

I swallow hard. I'm about to reach for his hand again when I hear someone approaching and turn round. My grandfather walks in and gives me a cup of tea.

'It's a new order,' he says gruffly. 'Your Lord Montserrat is smarter than he looks.'

'There's a lot that won't change, Bo,' Michael adds. 'You're still a vampire. And what Arzo say about post-traumatic...'

'Yeah,' I interrupt. 'I know. When we argued in your office, I had a hallucination.'

'I thought as much. We can get you help.'

I smile at him. 'Thank you.'

'You said something else back then. About Arzo. Is there anything I need to know?'

I really want to tell him about the Templetons. Another thought strikes me, however. 'Um, if this is going to work, it has to be independent. If we come running to you all the time then no one will trust us. If I'm going to be a credible go-between...'

Michael nods. 'I understand.' A shadow crosses his face. 'If there's any danger though...'

'I'll have you on speed-dial.'

'Charge your goddamn phone first.'

I grin.

'Well done, Bo.' There's a hint of pride in my grandfather's voice. 'This might just work after all.'

SEEMINGLY ASSURED that I'm not going to keel over again, Michael takes his leave. On his way out, he promises to finalise my new contract within the next day or two and tells me that Arzo is already looking for new premises. Apparently they have to be showy enough to merit Montserrat approval but not so intimidating that no one will dare to enter them. A week on Monday, Michael's PR team will release the details to the press.

I walk out with him, noting that he used Ursus's bike to get here. We stand together for a moment, neither of us saying anything. I wish I knew what he was thinking. The silence stretches out, then he gives a little shake, gets on the bike and goes without looking back.

I stare into the night after him, wondering what he would have done if I'd grabbed him and kissed him. I eventually decide that I'm reading too much into our relationship. His position as Head of the Montserrat Family means that he cares about all his vampires, even the half-witted ones like me. I promise that when this new firm is up and running I'll do everything I can to make it a success. Not just because I need to prove myself competent, but also because I owe it to Michael.

I go back inside and join my grandfather at the kitchen table. He raises an eyebrow but doesn't comment on how long it took me to say goodbye to Michael.

'I've lived in this house for a long time, Bo,' he tells me. 'I've never invited a vampire in during all that time.' He shakes his head.

I watch him carefully. Is he disappointed that I've turned into a full-blown bloodguzzler? I've never heard him say anything complimentary about any triber.

He grimaces and focuses on something else. 'So, shell-shock?'

I shrug. 'I guess.'

'You need to find the trigger,' he says. 'There'll be one thing that sets it off. My father – your great-grandfather – fought at the Somme. Afterwards...' His voice trails away.

I stare at him. He's never spoken about the past before. Before I can ask him to continue, he changes the subject. 'Speaking of the war, do you know the significance of white feathers?'

'Something to do with pacifism?'

He inhales. 'I told your mother she shouldn't have sent you to that comprehensive. Sometimes your education is sorely lacking.'

I bristle.

'Yes,' he continues, 'some cultures consider the white feather as a symbol of pacifism. During World War I, however, it was used for more confrontational purposes. Women, often not much younger than yourself, would present men with a white feather as an encouragement to enlist.' His face twists. 'If you received a white feather, then you were a coward. You weren't man enough to fight in a war. Those silly girls thought they were promoting bravery and patriotism. It got to the point where almost anyone out of uniform, no matter where they were or what they were doing, was given one of the damn things. Soldiers on leave and wearing civvies got them. Discharged veterans minding their own business on public transport got them.' He shakes a finger at me. 'Those suffragettes may have done a lot of good for this country but they also demonised any man who had the guts to refuse to sign up.'

I blink at his tirade. He wasn't born until a few months into the start of the World War II so it can hardly be based on personal experience. Unless...

'Great-grandfather,' I say softly.

'Yes.' He stares off into the distance. 'The Order of The White Feather has a lot to answer for.'

'They're not still around though, surely?'

'Not in that guise.' He comes back to the present. 'Your Lord Montserrat told me about your feather.'

'He's not my anything,' I say firmly. 'And besides, my feather is green. Moreover, I paid for it. I certainly wasn't given it.'

'I understood you had little choice in the matter.'

I jut out my bottom lip. 'Not much,' I finally admit.

'White is the colour of peace,' he says. 'The Order subverted it to represent cowardice. What is green the colour of?'

'Jealousy.'

'Indeed. Or in this case, being in possession of something someone else wants. The white feather was a challenge to enlist. The green feather is also a challenge.'

'A challenge for what?'

'That, my dear, is something you'll need to work out on your own.'

I curl my fingers round my cup and gaze at him. 'I was looking for a cure. Some kind of spell that might bring me back to what I was.' Hope fills my voice. 'Maybe if I meet this challenge, the neo-druid who sold me the feather will find the cure for me.'

He snorts. 'Good grief. There's no cure! If there was, don't you think I'd have heard about it? And what's this nonsense about a neo-druid? There's no such thing!'

'Ha!' I jab a finger at him. 'You don't know everything. She was impressed when I worked out what she was.'

'Bo,' he shakes his head. 'Tribers include witches, daemons, ghosts and vampires. There are no neo-druids — they're an invention, nothing more than people who want to dabble in the magic arts but don't have the ability. I have no doubt that when you told this woman you thought she was a neo-druid, she was congratulating you on realising that she's actually just a shill.'

'But I got a sense of magic from her.'

'That may be so but it doesn't change their lack of power.'

'I've been in a more than one sodding magic shop recently,' I argue. 'This one was real.'

He throws his hands up in the air. 'So she sells the genuine article. So what? It doesn't make *her* genuine.'

'She's not selling anything any more,' I say grumpily. 'She's run off.'

'Good riddance. You'll gain nothing from going further down that avenue.'

I think about the dead mugger. There's more to this than meets the eye. 'Let's say it's an avenue I *want* to go down. Where would I find someone pretending to be a neo-druid?'

'How would I know?'

I give him a look. He casts his eyes up to the heavens. 'They venerate nature so maybe you'll find her in a field somewhere in the Home Counties.'

'That's not very helpful,' I inform him.

'They also tend to conduct their important ceremonies during the eye of the sun.' His mouth twitches. 'I take it that might be a bit of a problem for you.'

'You think?'

'Sarcasm is unbecoming.' He gets to his feet. 'Anyway, I am going to embark on my own journey up the wooden hill to bed. It's late. You are welcome to stay for as long as you wish, Bo.'

'I have things to do on the other side of the city. But thank you,' I add.

'Where will you spend the day then?'

'I'll work something out.' It occurs to me that I should have discussed salary with Michael while he was still here so I could pay for somewhere to stay. My own flat was disposed of by the efficient Montserrat recruitment team as soon as I signed on the dotted line. I shrug. I guess it gives me an excuse to seek him out again in the next day or two.

'Suit yourself.' My grandfather's eyes turn serious. 'For what it's worth, I apologise.'

'For what?'

'If Elizabeth had done her job, you wouldn't be in this predicament now.'

I frown. 'Elizabeth?' Then I realise he means Beth. 'It wasn't her fault. There was nothing she could have done.' I sigh. 'There was nothing anyone could have done.'

'Not even your Lord Montserrat?'

I meet his gaze. 'No,' I say, telling the truth. 'Not even him. The only person I can blame for my vampire state is me.'

I'LL HAVE little time to sort out this Templeton mess before Arzo starts working with me and tracking my movements. He's not stupid; he'll soon realise I'm hiding something from him. I reluctantly put the enigma of neo-druids and feathers to one side and dig out Stephen Templeton's scribbled list of suspects. The most likely culprit is the fake Kakos daemon. Apparently he's the big shot behind Streets of Fire, the latest company to vie for internet domination. However, their offices encompass an entire building in the centre of the business district; they'll be heavily guarded and there's no way I can waltz up and knock on the door without preparing properly. I'll do that before sundown tomorrow. Tonight I'll focus on the Triads. Templeton told me he helped them with a money-laundering scam and skimmed cash off the top. The prat thought they wouldn't notice.

Unfortunately for me, Chinatown is located in Soho. After my humiliating trip there yesterday, the last thing I want to do is head back in that direction but it has to be done. Once I'm away from my grandfather's quiet cul-de-sac, I flag down another taxi so I can return to the city. This time the driver is much more relaxed in my presence. I clock his name on his ID and lean forward. 'Ray?'

'Yes, little miss?'

'Are you a cinema fan?'

'Sure,' he drawls. 'I don't get much chance to go, what with two little ones at home and the night shift. But I like a good action movie.'

I smile. 'Me too. Van Damme?'

'Van Damme, Seagal, The Rock. I like them all.'

'It makes a difference watching them on a big screen.'

'It sure does.'

I carefully bait my hook. 'My boss, he hates going to the cinema. Doesn't like people munching popcorn around him. He loves those martial arts films though.' I paste on a look of frustration. 'I was at home just now, chilling, when he called, wanting me to get him a movie. I don't get much time off these days. I'm always running around doing his bidding. Lord Medici is kind of demanding.'

The driver nods in agreement. 'I've heard that about him.'

'Yeah.' I lower my voice. 'Just between you and me, he can get pretty angry when he doesn't get what he wants.' I gesture towards my quickly healing forehead. The driver gapes at me in the mirror and I catch a flash of good, old-fashioned male protectiveness. 'Right now he wants to see *Sea of Blood*. I have no idea how I'm going to manage that at this time of night. I thought there might be a few shops still open in Soho.'

'Man,' he says in sympathy, 'that film's not even been released yet.'

I pretend surprise then start reeling him in. 'It's not? I am so screwed. I hope…' I drop to a whisper, 'I hope he's not going to get too mad.'

Ray stays quiet for a minute. I do my best to look scared.

'There are other places,' he says finally. 'Sometimes you can get DVDs before you're supposed to.'

'Pirated? That's against the law though.'

'Bloodguzzlers can get away with a lot.' There's just the faintest trace of rancour in his voice.

I switch tactics before he focuses on the inequality. 'I guess there's a market for those sorts of films with humans too. I wouldn't know where to start looking for that kind of place though. And it's not like I know much about the internet and can just illegally download the film.'

Ray watches me in the mirror. I look down at my hands and twist them in my lap. He sighs and presses a button on his radio. 'Where'd you get those black market DVDs from, Stace?'

'Aren't you working right now? I thought you had a customer.'

'Come on…'

'Only because it's you.' She rattles off a Soho address.

'Thank you,' I gasp. 'Thank you so much! You might have just saved my life.'

'You didn't hear it from me, right?'

I nod vigorously. 'My lips are sealed.' I press them tightly together which is a good thing because stops me smiling.

THE TAXI DRIVER drops me off in front of the aforementioned address. I tip him generously and he wishes me luck. I wait until he's disappeared then turn, ignoring the shifty man outside holding a dirty bag and thrusting the latest rom-com under my nose. I pull back my shoulders and stalk through the door. I barely make it two steps before I'm stopped.

'What do you want?'

I narrow my eyes and hiss, displaying my fangs. The bouncer is underwhelmed. 'Get lost. We don't like your kind here.'

'I'm looking for Cheung.'

'He ain't here.' His eyes move up and to the left. He's lying. I feel a flip of exultation that I've found my target so easily.

'Where is he then?'

The bouncer moves his face close to mine. 'Fuck off, girlie.'

I sense someone at my back and stiffen. Half-turning, I

register a daemon, orange eyes gleaming at me from the rough skin of his face. 'Since when did bloodguzzlers wear cute little dresses?'

Before I can stop myself, I glance down at the Laura Ashley outfit my grandfather donated. It probably does look kind of stupid with my leather jacket. I flick back my hair and widen my eyes. 'What?' I purr. 'You don't like frills?'

The daemon snorts at my attempt to flirt and flashes the bouncer a wad of cash before passing through. The bouncer moves forward, stepping deliberately on my foot. He's a heavy bastard.

'I won't say it again. Get your arse out of here.' He releases his shoe.

I hold up my palms. 'My mistake.'

'Damn right,' he growls.

I leave the building. I can already hear him laughing to a buddy about how he just scared off a bloodguzzler. The grubby DVD seller glances at me, then digs into his bag. '*Twilight?*' he asks. 'I've got the whole series.'

I snarl at him and stalk off. As soon as I'm out of view, however, I drop my shoulders and relax, then skirt round until I find an alley leading to the back of the building. From the shadows, I spot two guards so I head further back until I'm several streets away. I wait for a group of party-goers to pass, then I grab hold of the nearest window sill and start climbing. I must be getting better because within moments I'm on the roof and looking down. Running lightly across the rooftops, I jump from one roof to the other until I'm back where I need to be. The trip is much easier than the one with Michael because the buildings are packed together more densely. I don't even work up a light sweat.

The handiest thing would be a skylight but, sadly, the roof is flat-topped and covered in asphalt. I creep along the edges, peering down. Each wall has three windows. I bloody well hope Cheung is on the top floor – there's a limit to how much building-dangling I want to do when I'm wearing a dress. I play eeny-meeny-miney-mo then stroll to the left side. I twist round and step backwards, grabbing the edge of the roof. Once I'm secure, I drop again, my fingertips curling round the first window ledge. I raise my head up and glance in. Nothing: the room's completely dark. An argument starts up on the pavement beneath me. I wait, holding my breath in case the antagonists look up, but they're too occupied shoving each other. I jump over to the next window.

Once I've exhausted the possibilities on the first side of the building, I clamber back up and explore the second. This time I'm in luck. When I reach the second window and bob my head up, despite the netting covering the glass I make out a group sitting round a table. I dig my toes into the wall to get more comfortable and try to work out what's going on. The shapes are indistinct. Even if I knew what Cheung looked like, I've little hope of figuring out which shape belongs to him. I duck back down and try to listen. The voices are muffled but I think I know what's going on.

I flip back to the window on the far side and jump up to the roof again. Sitting down cross-legged, I take out my newly revived phone and call O'Shea.

'Montserrat is going nuts looking for you!' he yells.

I hold the phone away from my ear for a moment. 'He found me,' I say drily. 'Thanks for the heads-up about the secret plan to get me out of the mansion.'

'It worked?'

'Yeah, it worked. Some Watson you are, keeping me in the dark like that.'

'Bo, who do you think I find scarier, you or Lord Montserrat?' He has a point. 'I think he kind of likes you,' he adds slyly. 'Do you kind of like him?'

'Shut up, O'Shea.' I swear I can hear his grin down the line. 'I need your help.'

'Anything.'

'Get as much cash together as you can and come to Soho.'

'When you say as much cash as I can, how much are we talking about?'

I have no idea. 'I dunno. Twenty grand?'

'Twenty thousand pounds? Are you nuts?' he shrieks.

I wince. 'You'll get it back.' Maybe.

'I don't have that kind of money.'

I don't think that's true: I wouldn't be surprised if the daemon has stacks of the stuff hidden all over the place. 'Raid a few morgues,' I suggest. Another thought strikes me. Perhaps that would be a way to find out more about the unfortunate Samuel 'Slick' Lewis. I file it away and return to O'Shea. 'Please?'

'What do I get out of this?'

I smile. 'You get the opportunity to double your money, of course.'

'What do you mean?' he asks suspiciously. 'You're broke.'

I know I've got him. 'Are you any good at poker?'

CHAPTER 8

POKER FACE

It takes O'Shea a while to pitch up. I'm nervous that the game will finish before he arrives so I'm forced to keep checking what's going on. My fingertips are throbbing from clinging to inch-thick ledges. I discover that I can make life easier by swinging down headfirst with my toes over the lip of the roof to keep me stable. I'm slightly dizzy when I push myself back up and it makes me feel a little like a bat. I wonder idly if that's where the old myth about vampires turning into bats comes from. Then I remember some doctor on television stating quite categorically that vampires evolved from someone who was first bitten by a vampire bat.

I'm getting bored with waiting when I hear loud shouts from the busy street out in front. Alarmed that this is related to Cheung, I sidle over to peek. The sight is troubling: on one side of the pavement, a group of humans are holding up crude placards. *Exterminate The Guzzlers. Save Our Innocent Children. Finish Off The Families. God Doesn't Love Monsters.* My stomach drops, not just at the words but also at the hatred reflected in the protestors' eyes. They seem to be directing their chants at a bar.

It has two bouncers, burly humans who watch carefully but keep their faces frozen in emotionless masks.

There have always been factions against the various triber groups and, because of their need to drink human blood to survive, the vampires have recently come under fire more than the others. I've never seen such open vitriol before, though. The damage Nicky's brainwashed posse did a few months ago is immense. I shift position as a human couple walk up, arm in arm. Both have the tell-tale scarves of vampettes around their necks. I watch the unfolding scene in horror as the chanting gets louder. One of the protestors steps out from the group and spits at the vampettes. The potential for this to end in catastrophe is huge.

A wave of vertigo rolls through me and I'm forced to pull back. When I peer back down to the now blood-soaked street, I realise there's a body lying there. Alarmed, I grip the sides of the roof, ready to jump down and do what I can. Then the body moves. Arzo gazes up at me with pain-filled eyes, mouthing something. He's telling me no. Horror consumes me; I'm stuck up here and I can't get down and he's going to die and...

I take a deep breath. Arzo vanishes, replaced by the tarmacked road. The protestors are still chanting but there's no sign of the vampettes. I rock back on my heels and wipe my forehead. This has got to stop. I think about what my grandfather said about a trigger but I can't see any link between Michael's office and this rooftop. Regardless, my mental issues are nothing compared to the growing threat of bloodshed from people like those below me. There's even more of a need for Michael's 'bridge' than I'd realised.

My phone buzzes and I see a text from O'Shea telling me he's here. Steeling myself, I look back at the street. I spot him almost immediately, strutting arrogantly towards the building. I hope he's brought enough money.

Good, I text back. *You need get into the poker game. When you work out which player is called Cheung you can leave.*

He raises a hand to his forehead in a salute. I frown; anyone could be watching. There's a flash of lightning in the distance as if the weather is echoing my thoughts. I keep my attention on O'Shea as he disappears from sight. I'm half-expecting him to land arse-end on the pavement but a few minutes pass and there's no sign of him. His sweet talking and flash of cash must have been enough. Either that or his corpse is being dumped out the back.

I jog to the other side of the building and drop down. Bracing my palms against the rough wall, I wait. I can just make out the dim shapes of the seated players inside.

There's a rustle of movement and the quality of light inside the room alters slightly. The door must be opening. I listen hard. I needn't have bothered; O'Shea's loud voice is clearly audible even out here. 'I love a good game of cards!' he bawls out.

There's a muffled response and several shadowy figures rise up. I watch nervously. Fortunately, O'Shea shifts from loud-hailer to charm and there's some shaking of hands. A few good-natured guffaws drift up, making me wonder how much money he actually brought. It must be a fair amount to be treated so cordially.

Eventually the game resumes. There's a flutter of movement around the table as a new hand is dealt. I count the shapes. With O'Shea and the dealer, there are now ten people. It shouldn't take the daemon long to work out which one is Cheung. I know at least one of the other players is another daemon so that's, at most, only seven he has to focus on. I swing back up and massage my toes, then squat on the roof. Above the hum of traffic, I catch a rumble of thunder. A drop of rain lands on my nose, trickling down until it dangles at the end

like a small kid's snot. I rub it away with my cuff. I hope O'Shea
is quick.

~

An hour later, I'm soaked to the skin. Because my leather jacket
is on the large side, the rain has sneakily found several avenues
to slip down and not an inch of my body is dry. The collar
chafes uncomfortably against my neck and I have to blink and
rub my eyes repeatedly to clear my vision. Pools of orange light
from the lampposts reflect in the puddles far below. Between
the rat-a-tat of raindrops on the corrugated iron roof opposite
me and the booming thunder overhead, I can't hear a damn
thing. At least the sodding protestors have gone home. Bloody
O'Shea is inside, dry and probably sipping a fine malt whisky
while I pace impatiently up and down in the rain. There has to
be an easier way to identify Cheung.

I'm on my umpteenth circuit of the roof when I hear something below. I cock my head and listen harder. Then I catch it
again: voices raised loudly in anger. I sprint back to the window
and drop down headfirst.

Everyone is standing up. From what I can see from this side
of the sheer curtains, their bodies are tense and ready for a
fight. I feel a sinking sensation; I bet that this is all O'Shea's
doing. I'm trying to decide whether I should continue watching
or help out when the rain makes up my mind. The roof is slick
and wet and my toes start to lose their grip on its edge. It's only
a matter of moments before they slip off entirely and I plunge to
the ground. At the same moment, there's a roar of disapproval
from inside the room and the table is flipped over, sending a
cascade of chips and cards flying in all directions.

I take a deep breath, raise my fist and punch through the
glass. A spider's web of cracks appears. As my toes finally lose

their purchase I punch again, this time with both fists, and fling myself into the broken window, arms outstretched like an Olympic diver. It would have been a more impressive entry if I hadn't got caught up in the net curtain covering the frame. I'm struggling to free myself when an alarm squeals. Figures rush towards me and there's the crack of a gun. I yank hard to escape from the fabric and roll, grabbing the nearest person and bringing them crashing down to the floor with me. Then I spring up, manoeuvring my foot so it's over my hapless captive's neck, and sweep a death-stare across the room's occupants.

The door opens and the bouncer from downstairs appears. One of the men holds up a hand and the bouncer pauses. Something glints in my peripheral vision and I duck, just in time to avoid a knife flying into my face. It nicks the edge of my ear instead. Now it's not just water that's streaming down my face; I'm covered in cuts from the broken glass like the old Chinese punishment of *ling chi*, death by a thousand cuts. I suppose it's appropriate.

'She was here earlier,' someone spits.

I glance over and realise it's the daemon I tried feebly to flirt with to get in. His eyes are glowing bright orange, warning me of my peril. Would this fall into Michael's category of 'danger'? I wonder. It's too late to ask him for help now though. Vastly outnumbered, I look around the room. O'Shea is in the corner, bleeding from a cut in his cheek. This is hardly the sleek entrance and covert questioning I'd hoped for.

'Bloodguzzler.'

'Indeed I am.' I shake my hair, sending an impressive spray of water around the room. With little to lose, I smile at the occupants. 'Has anyone got a towel I could borrow?'

'Who are you?' A small man steps forward. While the others remain wary and on the verge of sudden – and no doubt brutal

– attack, this one is calm. He seems vaguely curious. I reckon I've found my mark.

'As the man said,' I respond, 'I'm a bloodguzzler.'

'She looks familiar,' I hear someone mutter.

I'm feel like an exhibit in a zoo but as long as they're not trying to kill me, I suppose that's a good thing.

'Which Family?' Maybe-Cheung asks.

I'm tempted to use Medici's name again. However one of them has already indicated that he might know who I am, so I tell the truth. Or at least a version of it.

'Montserrat.' I note a few shared glances. 'But I'm not here on official business.'

'Are you with him?' He jerks his head at the slumped O'Shea. The daemon does seem to have a knack for getting beaten up.

I hesitate for too long before answering, giving myself away.

'We don't like cheaters,' grinds out one man.

I stare at O'Shea. 'You tried to cheat at cards? With these guys?'

He lifts himself up unsteadily. Everyone tenses, even the guy under my foot, but no one moves. I suppose they're waiting for Cheung's order.

'I wouldn't call it cheating exactly,' O'Shea says.

Maybe-Cheung remains impassive. 'He was crimping the cards.'

I'm unfamiliar with the term but I can guess what it means. I bow slightly. 'I apologise for my colleague's over-zealousness. He will reimburse you for all costs.' I ignore O'Shea's pout. 'We're not actually here to play cards.'

Maybe-Cheung links his fingers together. 'That much I am starting to gather.'

'Boss…' starts the bouncer from the door.

'Enough,' he snaps. 'Leave us.'

Despite their anger, the others file out of the room. I receive several vicious looks and more than one unspoken promise to blow my head off the next time I'm spotted anywhere near here. O'Shea suffers a painful kick to his shin. He groans slightly but manages not to move. Maybe-Cheung coughs delicately and I remember I'm one footstep away from squashing someone's larynx. I step back and fold my arms while my victim scrambles to his feet and follows the rest.

'You have destroyed my room,' Maybe-Cheung states, keeping his eyes on mine.

I gaze directly at him. 'It was not my intention.'

'I have no desire to antagonise the Montserrat Family. I have a long memory.'

For a moment I think he's threatening me. Then I realise he's referring not to what he might do in the future but what Montserrat has done in the past. It's a troubling insight.

'As I said,' I reply calmly, 'I am not here in an official capacity.'

'Just so.' He looks away from me and glances at O'Shea. 'It is a difficult concept for outsiders to understand, but "face" is very important to us. It is akin to losing one's spirit.'

I understand what he's getting at and I don't like it very much. 'What would it take for you to retain face?'

'A hand would suffice.' He picks up a shard of broken glass and examines it thoughtfully. 'Stealing is often punished thus.'

O'Shea is intelligent enough to stay quiet. 'That doesn't work for me,' I say.

'I didn't think it would.' Maybe-Cheung tosses the glass on the floor. There's something very odd about our conversation, the polite words and dulcet tones when we are discussing dismemberment.

'Financial reparations...' I begin.

He shakes his head, interrupting me. 'Face,' he says, enunciating the word carefully, 'demands more.'

Maybe-Cheung lifts one hand and strikes me across my cheek. There's little force behind the action and it's not particularly painful. I doubt even my old human form would have felt much more than a sting. He raises his eyebrows as if waiting for something. I open my mouth and scream very, very loudly.

'There is no terror in your voice, Ms Montserrat.'

I swallow. 'Actually, to be honest, it's Blackman now.'

If he's surprised, he doesn't show it. I scream again, then add in a moan at the end for good effect. To help move things along, I bend down and pick up the glass shard he'd been fingering. I use it to slash a line along my forearm and watch as blood drips down, pooling on the floor next to my feet. He smiles. It's not very pleasant.

'Are you Cheung?' I ask, as the blood continues to fall in a steady stream.

He nods almost imperceptibly. 'Why are you really here, Ms Blackman?'

'It's about your accountant.' I'm starting to feel dizzy. I turn my arm so it's facing upwards. Connor's willing donation from earlier is a big help; the wound starts to heal almost immediately. I scan Cheung's face. A look of fleeting puzzlement crosses his eyes. Damn.

'Which one?' he asks.

'Look, Jack, you know very well which one. Stop prevaricating.'

His eyes narrow. 'Eugene.'

'Excuse me?'

'My name is Eugene.'

I blink. 'Not Jack?'

'No.'

'Is Jack your son?'

'Ms Blackman, I grow tired...'

I look at O'Shea who is watching the proceedings carefully. The only sign of tension in his face is a furrow on his forehead that trails down from his hairline. It looks as if he's been sliced in half.

'Didn't I tell you what would happen if you made another mistake?' I snap, stalking over to him.

He catches on. 'Ms Blackman, I only did what you told me to. You know I would never deliberately screw up. I admire you too much to...'

I slam a fist into his solar plexus. He collapses to the ground. 'Sucking up doesn't compensate for fucking up,' I tell his prone figure.

I pat down his body and retrieve an inch-thick bundle of money, along with three playing cards which I hastily return to their hiding spot. Turning back, I throw the money in Cheung's direction.

'Again,' I say formally, 'I apologise.'

He watches me with hooded eyes as I pick up O'Shea's body and sling his arm round my shoulder. His feet drag on the floor as we lumber out. I wait for Cheung to change his mind about letting us off so easily, but our exit is unimpeded. We are, however, watched by several pairs of eyes. I pause several times to appear as if I'm struggling with O'Shea's weight – and the pain from Cheung's 'beating'. My act seems to be good enough and, before long, we are outside with the rain thrumming down.

'You do realise,' O'Shea groans, 'that you can kill me by hitting me there?'

'I didn't hit you that hard,' I mutter. 'How could you be so stupid as to cheat at cards?'

'It was raining. I wanted to hurry things along in case you were getting wet.'

'Right,' I snort.

'You gave him all my money. That was my rainy-day fund.'

'And guess what?' I say. 'It's still bloody well raining.'

I drag him along. A car slows down. The window is wound down and a head pops out. 'Hey! Do you guys need any help?'

'No thanks!' I call out sunnily.

'Are you sure? Because you look like you do.'

I turn my head to the driver. He obviously clocks that I'm a vampire because he blanches, mutters something and drives off.

O'Shea barely blinks. 'Who's the accountant? Is it that guy with the funny coloured hair? And the weird French name? The one Montserrat doesn't like?'

I stop and stare at him. 'Do you mean D'Argneau? How do you know about him?'

'Lord Montserrat asked me to follow him around a few days last month and see what he was up to.'

I frown as another trickle of water runs down my spine. 'That guy's a lawyer,' I reply, shortly. 'Not an accountant.'

'Hey! Don't shoot the messenger!'

I let O'Shea go and he collapses onto the pavement. He scowls up at me.

'What is it with you running around doing Michael Montserrat's bidding all the time?' I ask.

'Darling, have you seen those muscles?'

I roll my eyes. He sticks a hand up in the air and waves it around. 'Help me up.'

I watch him for a moment then give in and pull him to his feet.

'D'Argneau has nothing to do with this.' I consider O'Shea speculatively. He could be a worthy sounding board for my issues with Arzo's former friend. 'How good are you keeping secrets?'

He scratches his head. 'I'll be honest, Bo, it's not really my forte.'

I laugh. 'Fair enough.'

I spy a short-skirted woman on the opposite side of the road. I can't tell whether it's the same prostitute I encountered previously but I start walking away, just in case. I have no desire to re-visit that humiliation. O'Shea follows me.

'Whatever you're looking for,' he says, 'that Cheung guy obviously isn't it.'

I sigh. 'Sadly, no.'

'He seemed alright for a human though. Except...'

'What?'

'He's obviously had dealings with Montserrat in the past. What do you think they were?'

I'm glad I'm not the only one who spotted that. I shrug. 'I've no idea.'

'Perhaps,' he murmurs, 'it was a steamy love affair. Someone as sexy as Michael Montserrat can't be completely straight. I guess it ended badly, though.'

'Why do you say that?' I ask, playing along.

O'Shea's humour vanishes. 'He was scared, Bo.'

I have nothing to say to that because O'Shea is right. Cheung may be human but he's the *de facto* leader of a large section of London's Triads. He's not someone who scares easily. We lapse into silence and keep walking, crossing several streets. The rain doesn't let up but I'm so wet it no longer bothers me; instead I find I'm rather enjoying the stroll.

After a while, O'Shea pipes up again. 'Bo?'

'Mmm?'

'Where are we going?'

I pause. 'I have no idea.'

'We're just wandering aimlessly?'

'Isn't it great?' I tilt up my face, enjoying the sensation of the rain on my skin.

He gives me a few moments, then interrupts softly. 'It's just gone four.'

I don't respond immediately.

'It'll be dawn in less than two hours.'

I give him a half smile. He grins. 'It'd be awkward for me if you burst into flames. I prefer to keep a low profile when I'm out and about on the mean streets. Do you need a place to stay?'

'That'd be great. Could we make a stop first though? I could do with some help.'

'I am at your service, Bo Blackman née Montserrat née Blackman.'

'You're an idiot.'

He smirks. 'Where is it you want to go?'

'The morgue.' I hold up a hand. 'Not to rummage through the belongings of corpses. I'm looking for someone in particular on the off-chance their spirit is still here.'

'You can communicate with them?'

'If I concentrate.'

He purses his lips and shrugs. 'Sure. Which morgue?'

I falter. I have no idea. I may know more than most about the geography of London but I've never spent time hanging around chillers full of dead people. When my father died, I said my goodbyes to him as he lay cooling in his hospital bed. Even in my role as an investigator, I only spoke to coroners a few times and most of those were over the phone to confirm cause of death in the case of contested wills. Funnily enough, the police don't take too kindly to PIs wandering in off the street and demanding to examine dead bodies. It would make sense to visit the morgue closest to the police station where Samuel Lewis breathed his last but his body may have been moved closer to where he lived to make the final arrangements easier for his family. I don't have time to traipse across half the city. Then I remember the prostitute we avoided.

'Scratch that idea,' I say. 'Do we have time to head to Crossbones?'

O'Shea shivers. 'Isn't there somewhere else you'd rather go?'

I shake my head decisively. 'No, it's perfect.'

'I bloody hate that place,' he mutters.

CHAPTER 9

MOTHER

In many ways Crossbones Graveyard is indeed a horrible patch of land. It has a long and troubled history. Technically it's not even a graveyard, it's just a space near Clink Street that covers a pit of 18,000 densely packed bodies which date back to the twelfth century. It was a paupers' cemetery, situated outside the old city walls in the shadowlands of London. John Stowe, a historian from the late 1500s, called it a 'burial ground for single women'. There's a euphemism, if ever I heard one. The truth is that nine hundred years ago, a less-than-charming man named Henry De Blois, who gained the powerful position of Bishop of Winchester, legalised prostitution in the area. Not so that he could help those downtrodden women whose only recourse against an early death from starvation was to sell their bodies, but so that he could tax the brothels that housed them. As a result, prostitution boomed in the area. When those unfortunate women died, they had to go somewhere. A consecrated burial ground was out of the question; thus Crossbones was born.

There were some benefits to De Blois' new law. Stringent rules and regulations were put into place to guard against

117

sexual slavery and more obvious examples of exploitation. However, the women were forced to wear an item of clothing that openly advertised their profession, a rule nastily akin to the yellow star in Nazi Germany. Aprons were a big no-no because they were a mark of a 'respectable' woman. Often, girls who broke the rules were subject not only to fines but to the violently distasteful cucking stool.

The authorities used ducking stools which forced suspects into water to seek out both black and white witches. If they drowned, they were innocent of witchcraft. If they survived, then they were deemed guilty and subject to even worse terrors. Witches on both sides of the spectrum cite those days as times of persecution for which they should receive reparations. At least witches didn't have to undergo cucking stools, though. The prostitutes weren't ducked into water – they were ducked in raw sewage.

One aspect of the ignominy of being laid to rest, so to speak, in Crossbones' pit, was that bodies were placed face down. I don't know what it is about that fact, but for some reason I always feel it strips the Crossbones' inhabitants of any remaining shred of dignity. Of course, it's not just prostitutes who are buried there: it was also used as a convenient place to dump the remains of plague sufferers or, later, just about anyone who couldn't afford to be buried in a churchyard. By the nineteenth century, it was surrounded by slums that reeked of disease. Even the police were afraid to set foot there. Unable to fit in any more corpses, the graveyard eventually closed. If it hadn't been for the ghosts, it would probably have been completely forgotten.

Humans, and tribers too, only use history as a reminder of an unfortunate past when they can blame someone else for the atrocities that went on. When they are responsible, it's easier to pretend it never happened. For some reason, the spectres of Crossbones took umbrage at that.

These days there's an annual pilgrimage to the site when simple rituals are held and both locals and tourists pay homage to the poor souls who remain there. Although most have passed on by now, there are still far too many who linger, their decaying spirits unable to travel any further. They can often cause an inordinate amount of trouble and the small ritual services help to appease them. Both my father and grandfather encouraged me to join in – it became a family tradition. We'd trip along and pay our respects then stop off for high tea somewhere on the journey home. After my father died, I no longer had the heart to keep up the visits and I've not attended a service for years. My lifespan, at least my human one, is a blink of an eye for most of these ghosts though. I'm banking on being remembered so at least one or two of them will be inclined to help.

Now that we have a goal in mind, O'Shea and I find my car; thankfully it's been neither clamped nor stolen. I quickly check Fingertips and Frolics before we drive off, but it seems undisturbed. Even the mouldy coffee cup I fixed over the camera is in place. I guess whoever receives the images isn't bothered by what happens now in the empty store.

With nothing more than a space where the passenger seat used to be, O'Shea is forced to sit in the back. He's being driven around, chauffeur style, in the shabbiest limousine in the city and he's not impressed. I think he's almost relieved when we pull up outside the graveyard's iron gates. Just like every other time I've been here, the surrounding streets are jam-packed with ghosts. It's rare to have so many congregate in one area; most cemeteries only have three or four hanging around, and they are usually the newly dead. Few souls linger in this world and not many people have the ability to see them; even those who possess the skill naturally need a considerable amount of training. There are even fewer people who can talk to them. Thank you, grandfather. It's been a while since I've tried communicating with the dead, but it's a bit like riding a bike: once you've learned the knack, you never forget it. As long as you remember to stay calm and respectful and avoid looking directly at them, then you're good.

I've just put my hand on the gate when I'm approached.

'Good day, Bo.'

I turn and see a young girl and I'm both surprised and upset. I met her the first time I came here.

Before that first visit I was bloody terrified and begged to stay at home. I think my father would have given in but grandfather, of course, was having none of it. I was dragged the entire way, kicking and screaming. Once we arrived, however, I fell into a terrified silence. I wasn't as good at seeing the different ghosts as I am now, but I saw enough to make me want to run for the hills. I remember one sour-faced woman in particular who had a suckling baby attached to her breast. She wouldn't leave me alone no matter what I did. The panic that I felt then is similar to the way I've felt during my recent hallucinations. Of course, I recognise now that desperate tragedy must have befallen the woman and her child for them to end up in such a state.

Anyway, the spectral woman terrified me. It wasn't until Maisie stepped into her path that she finally gave up and left me alone. My gratitude was so immense that I forgot to be afraid. Maisie was intelligent and aware enough not to try and touch me; instead we sat down together on a small patch of balding grass and started to chat. My father found us there almost an hour later.

Maisie and I bonded because of our ages; I was barely nine to her sixteen but her gentle manner won me over. It was like having an older sister, not one who bullied and taunted and teased or hogged the bathroom and made me wear her hand-me-downs, but one who listened and giggled and became a real friend. Until that is, I kept getting older while Maisie stayed the same. She is trapped forever as a teenage girl.

It was a sobering realisation for me at the time, filled as I was with a belief in my own indestructibility. The day after I turned seventeen, I came to find her – and she simply wasn't here. I returned several times, but I never saw her again and I assumed that she'd finally found peace. Not long after that, I said goodbye to my own father for good. His soul didn't linger; I'm sad to see that hers has.

'Hello, Maisie.'

She's holding a rose in her hands. Unfortunately it's seen better days. Its few remaining petals are tinged with black and curling at the edges. Nonetheless, she smiles shyly and offers it to me. I give her a smile of both gratitude and friendship in return.

'You are different now.'

'I am,' I tell her solemnly.

'You are older.' She stretches out a long thin finger and points to my eyes. 'I can see it. There are shadows now where before there were none.'

'Much has happened. Where did you go, Maisie?'

She doesn't answer my question. Instead she looks troubled. 'You have joined the walkers of the night.'

As much as I would like to deny it, I can't. 'Yes.'

'They are not good people.'

'I did not choose this life.'

As soon as the words are out of my mouth, I regret them. It's not like poor Maisie chose her life either. I'd bet my own soul that I've had it easier than her. She doesn't seem to register the unintended slur, however, she just reaches towards me and lightly brushes my cheek. I feel nothing more than a frisson of ice on my skin that vanishes the moment she withdraws her hand.

'You are unhappy.'

'Have you,' I swallow, 'heard of anyone who changed? Who was a nightwalker and then went back?'

She shakes her head. O'Shea walks up. 'Are you talking to a ghost? And is that what this is about, Bo? You're trying to find a cure?'

I give an uncomfortable shrug. 'Not exactly.'

'There isn't one,' he says.

'So everyone keeps telling me.'

'I mean it.' He's very earnest. 'I know a bit about spells, remember?'

I bite my tongue to avoid snapping that it was his use of spells that landed me in this mess in the first place. I turn away from him. 'Maisie,' I say, 'I'm looking for Mother. Is he around?'

'He's at the shrine,' she murmurs.

I start to thank her and ask her to wait but she's already gone, melting into the rain.

'Who's Mother?' O'Shea asks.

'The guy with all the answers.' I don't look at him; I just stare at the spot where Maisie was. 'Stay here.'

'Confucius said to respect ghosts but to keep away from them,' he shouts at me. I ignore him.

The gate is festooned with paper, material and colourful flotsam and jetsam left by well-meaning humans. Many of the scraps include names of the departed; they hang soggily and are difficult to read. It's a much more impressive sight on a sunny day with a slight breeze blowing. The gate yields at my touch, although it still lets out a rusty squeal in protest. Several ghostly shapes turn in my direction, curiosity on their worn faces. When I stride in, hands reach out to me in supplication.

Whatever it is they're looking for, I don't have it in me to give. Tentacles of cold wrap round my flesh. A flowery dress and a leather jacket are no protection against the touch of the dead.

I try not to flinch and incline my head in acknowledgment at each one. Some are faded versions of their human selves, wearing patched, old-fashioned clothes that advertise the date of their death. Others are more terrible to look at: ruined faces and caved-in skulls. Rather than diminishing with time and experience, it feels like my empathy for their situation has grown. I'm relieved when they finally move aside and I spot the familiar shape of Mother beside the oddest collection of bricks and knicks-knacks that ever made up a shrine. I walk up and stand beside him.

He nudges a plastic skull with his toe. A circle of bricks lies to his side, enclosing a cross. We're surrounded by carefully laid, intersecting paths, banks of poppies long since in bloom and a jungle of vertiginous weeds. The overall effect should be that of a junkyard; instead there's a rustic charm which seems more fitting than a perfectly manicured graveyard.

Observing propriety, I wait for Mother to address me. 'You have not visited us for some years,' he says finally in a grating raspy whisper.

'I have no excuse.' I bow my head.

'You have life.' His eyes flick towards me. They are neither benign nor malevolent. 'Even vampires have life.'

Mother knows and understands a great deal. 'I'm seeking a newly departed soul,' I say. My voice echoes around the walled space. 'His name was Samuel Lewis.'

'More than 250 people pass every day in this city,' he intones. 'Why should I know this one?'

'He was young. And healthy. His death was not natural.'

Mother raises his head. 'There are no longer many stars,' he comments, apropos of nothing. Then he looks directly at me. An involuntary shudder shakes me but I hold my ground. 'I know of this one,' Mother says. 'He has gone.'

'He is blessed,' I murmur. 'Did he speak with anyone before his passing?'

'Why should I talk to you? The living lands are not my concern.'

I have nothing to offer Mother in return for information. I rack my brains. 'Life and death are balanced on the edge of a razor. Someone is trying to unbalance the blade.'

Mother touches the wall and traces the faint lines of old graffiti with his finger. 'Someone is always seeking to unbalance the blade.'

I twist Maisie's rose in my hands. A single petal falls off and drifts to the ground. The rain distorts its heavy shape almost immediately.

'She likes you.'

'Who?' I ask, surprised.

'Maisie.' He cricks his neck as if easing his aching muscles although that's impossible for a ghost. 'She was sad when you didn't return.'

I'm confused. 'I lost her. I looked for her many times but I never found her. I thought she'd passed on.'

'She was hiding. She did not want you to feel beholden to her, to continue visiting until it became a chore. Sometimes we are afraid of the things we want most.'

A heavy weight settles on my chest. I crane my neck round, trying to spot her slender shape again.

'Visit,' Mother says suddenly.

'Pardon?'

'Visit. Regularly. She needs a friend.'

'I will.'

He nods his head. 'You speak the truth,' he rasps. 'Do not be afraid of it.'

I'm still trying to make sense of his words when he whispers, 'Janus.'

'Pardon?'

'That's what he said. Janus. Do not ask me about the dead again, Bo Blackman.' Mother turns away and it's clear I'm being dismissed.

'I don't know what that means!'

There's no answer. Just like Maisie, he's becoming ethereal as the last of the night swallows him up. I stay where I am, staring at the stone circle. Then I bend down and carefully brush off the wet leaves and fallen twigs until it's cleared. It's a small gesture; there are many who look after this place diligently. It feels appropriate though. I stand back and look around. The remaining icy ghosts are quiet; all I can hear is the patter of raindrops. I leave, picking my way back carefully. This time no spectre reaches forward and I'm granted access to the gate. I close it behind me, re-arranging a few of the names and scraps of material, taking my time in case Maisie shows her face again.

When I can wait no longer, I turn back to the car. O'Shea is already inside, having closed all the doors and windows as if he needs protection from a ghostly assault. The windows are fogged up. I get in and start the engine.

'Did you find out which morgue to go to?' he asks.

'It's a bust,' I tell him. 'His spirit has already gone to the other side. I thought we might get lucky and he'd still be here.' I think of Maisie and abruptly regret my words.

'Is he a secret too?'

'No.' I tell him about my encounter in Fingertips and Frolics, along with the green feathers and Samuel Lewis's untimely demise.

'This isn't about some petty thief,' he says. 'You really think that this woman gave you that feather because she would give you information about a cure in return for meeting whatever challenge she set?'

'No,' I snap. 'It's about someone having the temerity to waltz into a sodding police station, kill a suspect and steal a bloody feather.'

'Lying to yourself is still lying.'

I scowl at him in the mirror, Mother's words about not being afraid of the truth come back to me. I don't argue.

O'Shea leans back in his seat. 'We should go. It's almost dawn.'

I drop the handbrake and move into first gear, giving the gates of Crossbones Graveyard one final look before I drive off. It seems I'm spending every night running from the sun these days.

CHAPTER 10

STREETS OF FIRE

I'm sitting on my hands on O'Shea's leatherette sofa, waiting for the sky to darken again, when there's a soft rap at the door. O'Shea is in the shower, singing loudly out of tune, so I get up and answer it. Connor is standing there with an older vampire in tow.

'Hi, Bo!' he beams.

I'm started to feel an odd fondness for his freckled face. 'Uh, hi Connor,' I say. 'How did you know I was here?'

He looks puzzled. 'The daemon called, of course.'

I curse O'Shea under my breath. For a moment, Connor looks worried then he smiles at me with sudden understanding. 'You're hungry. That's why you're annoyed.' He pushes past me and settles on the sofa, pulling up his sleeve. 'Breakfast of champions!'

'Actually, I drank from you yesterday, so I don't think…'

He shakes his head and tuts. 'Lord Montserrat said you'd do this. You have to drink every day.'

As soon as I've kicked O'Shea into oblivion for constantly giving away all my secrets, I'm going to send Lord freaking Montserrat after him. Bile rises in my throat. The vampire outside gives a little cough. I glance in his direction and he waves. Until O'Shea gets out the shower and invites him in, he's stuck there.

'Who's your friend?'

'Doctor,' Connor says, practically thrusting his wrist into my mouth. I gag, then let my teeth do the work.

When I'm finished, I wipe my mouth with the back of my hand. The bathroom door opens and O'Shea struts out, wearing a tiny towel around his waist. I look him up and down. For someone who puts on a good show of being a lazy good-for-nothing, he certainly works out. Unfortunately he knows it because when he clocks both Connor and the waiting doc, he grins and takes his time going to the fridge. He pulls out a carton of orange juice and stretches upwards to flex his pecs. Then he starts to drink. All of us watch him; there's no doubt he's achieving his desired effect. In my case, however, it's because concentrating on something other than my troubled stomach will keep the blood down.

Once O'Shea's finished, I stand up. 'There's some doctor at the door you should invite in.'

'Oh yeah. Lord Montserrat said he'd be coming.' He flicks his fingers airily upwards. 'You're invited.'

I blow my cheeks out in exasperation. Bloody hell. If there's a circle of trust surrounding the Montserrat Family members and hangers-on, it appears that I'm not part of it. I'm painfully aware of the doctor's scrutiny so, in a bid to not come across like a raging lunatic, I paste on a smile. I'll save my useless death stare for when O'Shea and I are alone.

'Your desire to avoid blood is clearly an important symptom of your trauma, Ms Blackman,' the doctor says, shaking my hand.

'It's nice to meet you,' I murmur, not bothering to tell him that my blood avoidance is a symptom of not wanting to be a damn vampire. It has nothing to do with my alleged PTSD. 'You have me at a disadvantage though. You know my name but I don't know yours.'

'Love,' he says.

I blink, not sure I heard him correctly. 'You want me to call you love?'

He chuckles. 'Doctor Love will do. And before you say anything else, I've already heard all the jokes.' He glances around. 'Is there somewhere we can talk?'

Given that I spent the night on O'Shea's lumpy sofa, not really. Connor realises my dilemma and departs, giving me a wide, reassuring grin. I look at O'Shea.

It takes him a moment. 'Oh. You want me to hide out in the bedroom of my own apartment?'

'Well, you do need to get dressed,' I point out.

He glances down at himself as if surprised. Then he offers me an arch grin and disappears into his room. The doctor settles on the sofa and pats the seat next to him. Feeling like a child, I sit down.

'So,' he says, 'tell me what the problem is.'

I suspect that the good doctor is in Michael's circle and knows every detail but I describe the hallucinations anyway.

He nods. 'And this has happened twice?'

'Yes.'

He frowns. 'The best cure for PTSD is to receive counselling immediately after the event. Several weeks later makes it more complicated.'

'It's not debilitating. I can still function normally most of the time.'

'Hmmm.' He scratches his head. 'But you've had mood swings.'

It's not a question. That confirms he's already been fully briefed about my situation. I sigh. 'Yes. A bit.'

'Well,' he says, 'there are several different approaches we can take. The most effective would be regular sessions of cognitive behavioural therapy.'

'That sounds nasty,' I interject with a nervous laugh.

He doesn't smile back. 'There's no guarantee of success but I can assure you it's completely painless. We can start straight away. It's a good thing you're still entirely nocturnal as my schedule is free in the evenings.'

I stare at him. 'How many evenings are we talking about?'

'Oh, I think every day to begin with.'

'I don't have time to sit down with you every day!'

'What else are you doing?'

Finding a cure for vampirism that no one in the triber world has ever heard of and tracking down a kidnapped woman so that my friend's heart doesn't get smashed into smithereens for a second time, I want to say. 'You mentioned there were other approaches?'

'There's medication. I don't think…'

I nod vigorously. 'Yes. Medication sounds good.' It'll take me all of two seconds to pop a pill. I don't have time for anything else at the moment.

'Until we've fully diagnosed your issues, I don't believe drugs are a good idea.'

'What's to diagnose? I've got post-traumatic stress disorder. Load me up with the drugs.'

He's unimpressed by my attitude. 'Four sessions a week and medication.'

'One session a week.'

He shakes his head. 'Three.'

'Two.'

'Done.' He snaps his fingers. I have the feeling that I've just been conned. He reaches into his briefcase and pulls out a small white container. 'This is topiramate.' I move to take it but he pulls it away. 'You may experience some side effects.'

'Like what?'

'Aggression. Nausea. Hypersensitivity.'

'So all the things it's supposed to cure, then.'

'Constipation. Alopecia. Amnesia.'

I take a deep breath. 'And a few more thrown in besides.'

'Anaemia...'

'What in hell is a vampire with anaemia like?'

He opens his mouth to answer but I hold up a hand. 'I get it. There are a lot of potential side effects. Therapy good. Drugs bad.' He nods. 'Give me the drugs.'

He hands them over. 'Tomorrow night at nine o'clock.'

'I'm not...'

I receive a hard look. 'Okay, Doc. Tomorrow night.'

'We'll meet in the atrium.' He stands up and walks to the door as I register what he just said.

'Wait! We can't meet there! I can't go back to the Montserrat mansion after...'

It's too late – he's already gone. I grit my teeth in irritation. I may be back on speaking terms with Michael but showing my sorry arse at the mansion after stalking out is not going to go down well with the rest of the Montserrat Family. I'm still frowning when O'Shea comes back in.

'The doctor's gone?' he says, disappointed.

'Yeah.' I scoop up my car keys and phone. 'I'm going out.'

'Can I come?'

'No. I'm going back to do the secret stuff.' I waggle a finger in his direction. 'You're right, you know.'

He smiles. 'I'm always right. Although in this context, you're referring to...?'

'Keeping secrets. You have a big mouth.'

He grins at me disarmingly. I roll my eyes, leaving him to

whatever nefarious plans he's putting in place to recoup his losses from the previous night. I'd prefer not to know.

LESS THAN AN HOUR later I pull up outside the offices of Streets of Fire. The company obviously demands a lot from its employees because, despite the late hour, there's still a lot of traffic coming to and from the building. I use my camera phone to photograph as many of the people as I can, then compare them to printouts I have from the company website. Experience dictates that the newbies trying to put on a show of competence will be the ones who leave last, so when the faces change from those listed as middle managers to others who aren't important enough to be named on the employee pages, I know it's time to head in.

Streets of Fire, as a technology-based company, is more concerned about protection from human rather than triber security threats. Most of the big tech firms don't bother with the sort of intrusion spells that the police or companies like Magix worry about. They probably spend a lot more time fretting about people like Rogu3 than vampires like me. I still need to be canny about how I'm going to get inside, though. I wait until I spy the right person: a skinny twenty-something wearing a T-shirt emblazoned with the photo of a cat. Underneath, in block capitals, are the words 'Lost. Please return dead and alive to Erwin Schrodinger'. He stumbles slightly as he comes out of the revolving doors and glances down at the offending pavement as if expecting to see a banana skin. He's perfect. As soon as he starts ambling down the street, I get out of my car and follow him.

Weaving in and out of the path of other late-night workers, I walk briskly until I'm barely a metre behind him. I can hear him humming a variation of the Star Wars theme. I keep my head down and my hands by my sides on the off-chance that he glances back. I don't need to worry. When he reaches the first intersection, he waits for the lights to change. I stand beside him, pulling my phone out as I come to a halt. My keys fall, crashing down to the pavement. Letting out a hiss of exasperation, I bend down to pick them up. My unfortunate target does the same and our heads bang together.

'Ouch!' I rub my forehead while he curses. Then I straighten up and smile ruefully. 'Thank you.'

He starts to grin at me, then abruptly spots the red in my eyes. He coughs and stammers. 'S-sorry.'

'That's alright. It was my fault.' I hold up my dangling keys with one finger. 'I hope you're not hurt.'

He trembles slightly and turns to face the traffic. The second the cars stop, he dashes off in an effort to put as much distance between me and him as possible. I spin round, my hands – and his wallet – stuffed in my pockets, and move away quickly, hoping he doesn't notice that his pocket has just been picked. I'm about twenty feet away when I pull out his wallet and flick through it. His company ID card is proudly displayed, along with his grinning photo and the number seventeen. I palm it.

When I return to the Streets of Fire office, I'm too taken with my own skills to notice the woman ahead handing out flyers and trying to stop pedestrians until it's too late. She beams at me.

'Hi! I'm Robin Gefen and today I'd like to take five minutes of your time to...' Her eyes widen when she realizes I'm a vampire. Without warning, she lets out an ear-piercing shriek. I think she's about to run away but her flight instincts seem to have completely shut down and she freezes.

I ignore the alarmed looks from other passers-by. 'I'm not going to hurt you,' I say softly.

She stares at me like I'm about to eat her. I'm tempted to

stay and plead my case. Perhaps take her out for a coffee and prove that, despite what the press and various protest groups are currently saying, we vampires are really not so bad. Unfortunately I don't have the time. I sigh and give her a half smile. She doesn't respond.

'Good luck,' I tell her. Then I walk on before I draw any more attention to myself. Vampires used to be admired by many humans, they had celebrity status. Now we're seen as worse than Jack the sodding Ripper by almost everyone.

I time my entry through the door with that of a group of interns who are just leaving. I walk briskly to the bank of elevators situated away from the main desk, then use Cat Guy's card to unlock the nearest one. I step in, keeping my face angled away from the security camera, press for the seventeenth floor and wait. I don't have to hang around for long. It's one of those 'blink and you'll miss it' lift rides. Clearly no expense has been spared in setting up of Streets of Fire's flagship office.

As I venture out onto Cat Guy's floor, I pause in case there's an alarm system my research didn't tell me about. Unless it's a sneaky silent alarm, however, I'm still in the clear – maybe because some people are hanging around and working. You can't lock down a building when people are still inside. Maybe there's something to be said for this working late lark after all.

Although it delays me, I spend several minutes wandering around searching for Cat Guy's cubicle. For once my lack of height is an advantage; if I were any taller I'd draw attention from the hangers-on sitting in front of their illuminated screens. The office manager has helpfully provided labels next to each space with the names of the employees and the Streets of Fire logo. When I locate Cat Guy's, I drop his wallet in the top drawer, alongside what seems to be a lifetime supply of Snickers bars. With any luck, he'll think he left it here by accident.

I head back out and look for the cleaners' closet. As I'd hoped, there's a cart inside, filled with sprays and disinfecting accoutrements. I search carefully, hoping for a discarded card for the service lift but I'm not that lucky. I pull the cart out, keep it in front of me and move slowly down the corridor. I bend down and wipe the skirting board in a few places to make my slow progress look more natural. As soon as I see a woman pressing the lift button though, I speed up so I can wait with her. She doesn't even bother to glance in my direction.

When the lift door pings open, I rudely push my cart in first, getting in her way. I stand as close to the buttons as I can while still leaving the woman enough room. She squeezes in and swipes her card. Before she can press the button for the ground floor, I swoop in and hit twenty. She has more access than Cat Guy and, to her audible annoyance, the lift sets off upwards rather than down. I flash her a smile when the doors re-open, and keep my fingers crossed that she's more focused on her irritation than the fact that I'm oddly dressed for a cleaner.

Once the doors close behind me, I twist round and watch the LED numbers carefully. The lift drops to the ground floor. I smile grimly. Unless she mentions my presence to the security team at the entrance, I'm in the clear. Templeton's guy is on the twenty-fourth floor, just one below the CEO. I'm getting closer.

I push the cleaning cart to the end of the corridor, noting thankfully that this floor is empty, then search through the cleaning contents, eventually deciding on glass spray. Singing loudly, I go back towards the lift, pausing every few seconds to spray the fluid on greasy smudges on the glass wall separating the corridor from the offices. When I'm in front of the lift – and directly underneath the security camera – I start spraying more liberally. As soon as the camera's vision is sufficiently obscured, I drop the spray bottle and twist round.

My fingers scrabble at the lift doors. I finally create a tiny gap so that I can push them apart. I glance swiftly down before the safety feature kicks in and the doors close automatically again. The lift is nowhere in sight. I take a swift breath to acknowledge the flutter of nerves in my stomach, then jump into the gaping shaft. I lose a few metres in the leap but as soon as I grab hold of the biting steel cable, I know I'm solid. I grin. Rogu3 would be horrified at my low-tech ways of circumventing expensive CCTV systems but as long as they work, I have no issue with going old school. The lift doors slide shut and I'm plunged into darkness. I start hoisting myself upwards, hand after hand. I can't see a thing so I'll have to judge the distance as best as I can.

My biceps are just starting to protest when I think I'm past the doors leading to the twenty-fourth floor. I kick out with one foot to test my theory and hit metal rather than cement. Concentrating carefully, I manoeuvre so that I'm hanging on the cable about a foot above the doors and cross my ankles tightly round the steel rope. Then I twist round until my back is to the doors and throw myself out so I can reach them with my hands. It's considerably harder forcing them apart now that I'm hanging upside down and can't see what I'm doing. Every so often, there's an odd groaning noise which sends me into spasms of fear that the lift is about to start climbing in my direction again. If that happens I will quickly become Vamp à la Squish. Fortunately, I manage to prise the doors apart, loosen my ankles, slide down two feet and somersault out, landing easily on the soft carpet. I smile, bow and wave to an invisible audience while the doors snap shut. Then I turn round and get to work.

It must take considerable authority for anyone to reach this far up the Streets of Fire building whether they're the innovations director, like Templeton's fake daemon, or a lowly cleaner. I think that I've been careful to ensure that none of the myriad of cameras have captured my face, so my identity will be hidden – but I bet my proud little backflip is already making headlines. That leaves me with one last resort: I shuffle over, bend my elbow and smash it into the fire alarm. There's a second of silence before it starts screaming. I pull out the earplugs I bought especially for this occasion and stuff them into my ears. If the security staff didn't know I was here before, they do now. The lift will be automatically put into lockdown but I'm on the twenty-fourth floor and that's a long way up if you're a security guard who spends most of the day sitting staring at screens for the minimum wage. I reckon I've got at least fifteen minutes. Not only that, D'Argneau is ready if my exit strategy fails.

I jog down the corridor, searching for the right office. It's at the end. Unlike the others, there's no name on the door: just the title Director of Innovations. I take a deep breath and push it open. There's no one inside. Relieved, I flick on the lights. Whoever this guy is, he's obviously valued highly. Not only does he have a much-coveted corner office, his furniture is antique.

I turn on the computer. It flickers into life and asks for a password. Given that this is a technology company, the likelihood of the nameless executive keeping the password scribbled down nearby is pretty small. I search, though, lifting up the large blotting pad on the desk. There's nothing there. I pick up a small framed photo of a beaming family and pull out the back. There's no password there either but it still gives me pause. It's not a real photo inside –just one of the generic shots used by shops as backing when you buy a picture frame. A trickle of doubt runs down my spine.

I could call Rogu3 and ask him to help me break into the computer. Unfortunately, I know from my daytime research that Streets of Fire runs off a closed network that's virtually unhackable. With time, he could probably find a way in but I'm not about to risk him on the Templetons' behalf. I abandon the spotlessly clean desk top and computer and pull open drawers. When I spot the notepad, I pick it up and hide it in a pocket inside my jacket. Then I keep rooting around. There's nothing else.

I examine the wastepaper basket. There's an empty jar of Marmite and a single ball of crumpled paper. I smooth it out. There's nothing on it. I'm about to add it to the notepad in my pocket when I feel a slight vibration. As I watch, inked letters start to appear. My mouth goes dry as, one by one, they become visible. The innovations director must be a witch – and a damned powerful one at that. No wonder he was able to fool Templeton into thinking he was a daemon.

T.I.M.E.'.S.U.P.

I drop the paper and extricate myself from under the desk. In my haste, I bang my head and screw up my face in pain. When I open my eyes I see the shoes. I stand up very, very slowly, my eyes travelling upwards. When I see his face, I freeze.

The Kakos daemon in front of me cocks his head and leans down. 'And who might you be?' he mouths.

CHAPTER 11

I pull out my earplugs and back up until I feel the window pressing against my spine. The fire alarm continues to shriek; it's almost appropriate. I'm not dead yet though. No one's ever escaped a confrontation with a Kakos daemon but that doesn't mean I'm not going to try.

If I grab the fake photo frame perhaps I can fling it at his face and blind him for long enough to make my escape.

He quirks an eyebrow. 'It won't work.' Can he read my mind? 'I have faster reflexes than a vampire could ever hope for,' he continues mildly. 'I'll dodge and you'll be dead.' He folds his arms and rocks back slightly on his heels, as if he's waiting for me to come up with another plan. There's an unnatural stillness about him, as if he's barely breathing. His skin ripples with tattoos, not dissimilar to those of a Maori. His tattoos appear and vanish every few seconds, however, twisting their shapes and reforming in different patterns.

I consider smashing the pane of glass behind me with my elbows. It's a long way down and it's unlikely that I'd make it to the ground; the sides of the building are glass and steel and there's nothing to aid my descent. But a tiny chance is still a chance.

'The glass is reinforced. You won't manage it.'

Sweet Jesus. Stephen Templeton's face flashes into my mind. I can't believe I'm going to be dead because of him. The daemon's black eyes narrow fractionally but it's impossible to tell what he's thinking. I take a deep breath and close my eyes, filling my thoughts with the Stars Wars theme that Cat Guy was humming out on the street. It's the first thing that comes to mind. I allow the tune to take over my thoughts. Then I run.

Unbelievably, I make it round the open door. My speed is such that I'm forced to vault off the far wall of the corridor so I can continue without losing ground. I won't have time to get into the lift but perhaps the fire escape...

I slam into a hot, hard body and fall backwards. The daemon is standing in front of me, a vaguely perplexed expression on his dark face. All down one side, where my body collided with his, I feel the painful pricks of pins and needles. Slowly, I get to my feet and look into his glittering eyes. I bow my head. Make it quick, I think. Please, make it quick.

There's a sudden vibration in my pocket. Half a beat later, my phone starts to ring.

'You should get that.' His voice is deep and mellifluous. Surely such a creature of death and destruction should speak in a grating, harsh tone, not like Louis Armstrong singing 'What a Wonderful World'.

Trembling, I dig out the phone and answer it.

'Sorry,' Rogu3 says. 'It shouldn't have taken me this long to get back in touch but you wouldn't believe the set-up these guys have. I've had to track the signal across half of Europe! It bounces off at least twelve satellites. Triber companies don't normally know that much about tech but these guys...' He whistles.

'Uh, this isn't a very good time.' I do everything I can to keep my thoughts away from Rogu3's identity. I'm glad I never took the time to find out his real name.

'Are you okay?'

'Mmm.'

'You're about to sink your fangs into someone's neck, aren't you? Feed on their blood.'

I sneak a look at the Kakos daemon's face. He seems amused, if that's possible. 'No,' I squeak. 'That's definitely not what I'm about to do.'

'You know I've picked this week's word based on you,' Rogu3 adds.

'Oh?' I say, trying to sound disinterested and wishing he'd get off the phone.

'Yeah. *Ketsuekigata*. It's Japanese.'

'Defining personality through your blood type,' the daemon informs me.

Rogu3's voice is cheerful. 'It means...'

'I know what it means,' I interrupt. I need to get rid of him before my thoughts betray him.

'Well, there's no need to be snarky,' he huffs. 'I suppose you want to know where that camera's transmitting to?'

'Mm.'

'You know, Bo, I'm the one who's supposed to be a hormonal teenager with an attitude problem, not you.'

'You'll be paid for your services,' I tell him. If the daemon thinks he's nothing more than an employee, he might leave Rogu3 alone.

Rogu3 snorts. 'Eventually. Anyway, the signal's going to that company Magix. The same one that was trying to drive the shop out of business.'

'Thank you.'

'You're welcome.' He sounds stiff. Better that he's annoyed at me rather than a corpse at the hands of a homicidal daemon.

'Goodbye.' I hang up. The phone dangles uselessly in my hand. I could try to call or text someone for help but there's no point. I'll be dead before they even walk out of their door.

'I won't go near the kid. And I've not decided if I'll kill you yet.'

Death might be the preferable option. Sometimes Kakos daemons turn their victims insane until they become babbling versions of their former selves. I met one once and it wasn't pretty.

'Just kill me,' I mutter. I've had enough of a taste of insanity from the PTSD hallucinations to know that anything's better than going crazy. 'Eat my heart and feast on my entrails.' At least I won't end up in the cold, hard ground.

My phone rings again. Without looking at the display, I lift it to my ear. 'Rogu3, you need to stop...'

'Who the hell is Rogu3?' Michael growls. Sodding hell. Why does everyone suddenly want to get in touch?

'No one you know.' I can't disguise the fear in my voice.

'Bo?' He's alarmed. 'What's wrong?'

I watch the daemon, who watches me. 'Nothing.'

'You slept with the daemon.'

For a moment I'm utterly thrown. Then I realise he's referring to O'Shea. 'Uh, yes. No. I stayed on his sofa.' O'Shea's gay. Michael knows that.

'I thought you'd stay at your grandfather's.'

'I had things to do.' Please, please go away.

'You're still looking for the cure.' His voice is flat.

'Not exactly.'

'Are you in town?' he demands.

For now. My corpse will probably be cremated in the 'burbs. 'Yes.'

'Come to my apartment when you're done. You can spend the day there.' There's a pause as if he's expecting me to argue. 'It makes sense. I can drive you to the mansion to meet Doctor Love. Arzo will be there as well. He wants to discuss the plans for the new agency.'

The tattoos on the daemon's face are mesmerising. 'Okay.' There's a palpable lack of enthusiasm in my voice.

'Bo, promise me you'll come.'

'I can't,' I whisper. Then I hang up.

Almost immediately the phone starts ringing again. I drop and stamp on it, crushing it. Even a vampire of Michael's strength and experience is no match for a Kakos daemon.

Ignoring the fact that I'm shaking, I step forward. 'He has nothing to do with this. I'm here on my own.'

'I think the vampire Heads have enough problems right now,' the daemon says. He copies my movement and comes closer until we're barely an inch apart. 'They're close to becoming as feared and hated as my own kin.'

I rediscover the last vestiges of my spirit. 'Vampires don't destroy every person they come across,' I snap.

'And yet,' the daemon says with velvety softness, 'you're desperate not to be one.' A smile plays round his lips. 'There is a cure, no matter what others tell you.'

He's playing with me like a cat plays with its prey, letting it escape time and time again before finally getting bored and killing it. 'I'm not lying,' he says, amicably.

Much good a cure is going to do me now. I shiver while he licks his lips as if in anticipation.

'So,' he continues, 'you're here because of the accountant.'

I feel a flash of guilt that quickly dissipates. The daemon already has Dahlia Templeton; I'm not giving away anything he doesn't already know.

'Actually,' he says, 'I don't have her. I've never met her.'

'Bullshit,' I whisper.

He starts to smile. 'You're challenging a Kakos daemon? Ms Blackman, you are either incredibly brave or incredibly foolhardy.'

Damn it. He must have plucked my name out of my mind. I feel violated – it's like he's gained absolute control. I'll never learn what he's called but he already knows everything about me.

'X.' The tattoos continue to snake around his skin. 'You may call me X.'

'Catchy,' I mutter.

He smirks. 'The truth is I have a certain admiration for Mr Templeton. We have never met in person but he knows what I am and he was still brave enough to steal from me. Some humans just can't stop themselves from playing with fire.' His black eyes gleam. 'Some vampires too.'

I stand my ground. 'Is Dahlia dead?'

He tuts. 'I told you, I don't have her. I don't know where she is and I don't care.'

'You don't care that her husband was stealing from you?'

'I expect a certain amount of underhandedness. It's useful. It means I know where I stand. Besides, money doesn't interest me. We have far grander plans and, as long as Stephen Templeton doesn't involve himself in those, I will allow him to do what he wishes.'

I wonder about his use of the word 'we'. The Kakos daemons must be planning something. The thought of what that might be is beyond frightening.

'The thought of big, bad scary monsters crawling out of the shadows disturbs you.'

'It would disturb anyone.'

He gazes at me with interest. 'Really? We've decided to re-enter your society and act in a manner which you would describe as civilised and you think that's disturbing?'

'Civilised? You're homicidal maniacs!'

'Perhaps. However, I'm not the one illegally breaking into a private office building.'

I stare at him mutely. The alarm continues to peal while, far below, there's the siren of a fire engine. X lifts a hand and inspects his fingernails. 'Do you know what Google's motto is?'

'Don't Be Evil.'

The corners of his mouth rise. 'Indeed. It's virtually a challenge. Especially when you consider the vast opportunities for sin provided by the internet.'

'So that's why you're working for Streets of Fire? You want to manipulate the internet?'

He laughs. 'I don't work for Streets of Fire. I *am* Streets of Fire.'

'The CEO...'

'Is the palatable human face. His history and identity are known and accepted. His strings, however, are pulled elsewhere.'

I may be uncovering the greatest conspiracy the world has ever seen. It's a damn shame I'll never be able to tell anyone about it.

'The other people in this building. They're human. And they're okay working for you?'

'Watch.' His features twist, melding into a benign, respectable human face. The tattoos vanish and his eyes, while still dark, look benevolent.

'They don't know,' I whisper. 'You mask your true self.' How many more Kakos daemons are posing as humans right under our noses?

He gives a little bow. 'Most people have the sixth sense

when something isn't quite right.' His face returns to its original form. 'They can't work out what it is though.'

'Why does Stephen Templeton know the truth?'

I receive an unpleasant smile in return. 'I wanted to see how he'd react. He was planning to steal and I was interested in finding out if he still would when he knew I was a demon.'

Stephen Templeton is a sodding idiot.

'Yes,' X says, 'he is.' He looks at me thoughtfully. 'You are not. How were you planning to get out?'

'Excuse me?'

'You broke in. In about sixty seconds' time, security will burst through that door. How were you going to avoid them?'

'I wasn't,' I say shortly. 'I just had a good excuse for being here.'

He reads it in my thoughts. 'The right to be forgotten?'

'It's a new thing. Maybe you've not heard of it.' It's a stupid jab, but I make it anyway. Anyone in the tech industry – even a Kakos daemon – will know about it. I put on a slightly patronising tone for effect. What else do I have to lose? 'People can make a legal challenge to have their name wiped from search engines. Vampires cherish anonymity once recruitment is over. Erasing their virtual presence is the next logical step.'

'It's a reasonable excuse, I suppose. But it does beg the question of why not make a legal challenge? Why break in illegally?'

'Because approaching the courts makes the petitioner more famous. I was going to let myself get caught and use the right to be forgotten law as an excuse.'

He nods. 'If you couldn't persuade in-house security to let you go then the police would. It's not yet public knowledge that you've left the safety and immunity of the Families.'

'And when it is, the press will believe I've gone rogue so the Families won't be censured for my actions.'

'You know,' he says slowly, 'I rather think you'll be wasted on the Lord of the Montserrat Family.'

I stare at him wide-eyed while shouts and the sound of a slamming door echo down the corridor. Several security guards burst in from the fire escape. X smiles at me, his face again re-forming into its human version. Then he turns. 'Everything's fine,' he calls out.

'Sir...'

His gaze hardens. 'Leave us.' Even as a human, he's intim-idating.

The security guards mutter but do as they're told. The daemon turns back to me, tattoos flickering their return.

'I have decided,' he announces.

'A wooden box or a padded cell?' I ask bitterly.

He smiles, reaches out with his fingertips and touches my temples lightly. 'Hold still. This will only hurt for a second.'

There's a blinding attack of pain. My mouth drops and I scream in both pain and terror. I collapse to my knees and he pulls away.

'If you tell anyone about this meeting, I will change my mind.' The darkness in his eyes sucks me in. 'And not just about you. About the child. The vampire Lord. Your grandfather...' His voice drifts away, although the threat remains in the air. 'Come back and see me when you learn about the cure, Bo Blackman. And throw away those pills.'

Suddenly I'm alone in the corridor with the lingering pain in my head and the continuing shriek of the fire alarm. I touch my forehead gingerly. I'm still alive and I don't feel insane. My thoughts are tinged with clarity. The weight inside me that's been growing since the day I pulled O'Shea's fading body from a blood-soaked room in the suburbs of London seems to have disappeared. I feel lighter. The sadness and anger remain – perhaps they always will – but they no longer possess my soul.

Unconsciously, my hand reaches into my pocket and I pull out the topiramate which Doctor Love gave me. I gaze down at the innocuous white bottle. X is right: I won't be needing it any more.

I have no idea why the daemon did what he did; I'm just glad to be alive.

I stumble out of the building, taking the lift down this time. The narrowed eyes of the security guards in the lobby follow my every move. A fire engine sits by the revolving doors, its red bodywork muted by the night shadows. I'm tempted to knock on the window and tell the firefighter inside to get his buddies and go home but I'd probably land myself in more trouble. I'm sure they've worked out it's a false alarm by now.

I drag myself across the street to the car. There's no clamp or parking ticket, but someone with too much time on their hands has drawn a crude penis in the dust coating the side door. I stare at it for a moment, shrug and get in. For once, I have hours to go until dawn breaks, but I'm completely drained. I don't know if it's because of the adrenaline leaving my system or if it's a side-effect of X's Jedi mind-trick. Either way, I don't have the energy to keep going for much longer. I didn't promise Michael I'd stay at his place but he'll be worried after what I said on the phone. Not only that, but his massive bed is more comfortable than O'Shea's sofa. I drive to Michael's, almost running three red lights along the way.

The apartment is too close to the inner city for me to get away with more illegal parking, especially as both my car and I will be stuck here during daylight hours, and it takes time to locate the entrance to the underground car park. The guard on duty must have a high definition camera and be able to see the red in my eyes because the automatic barrier lifts and I drive in. Annoyingly, however, once I park and get out, I can't open the door into the building. Like the front entrance, it's protected by a thumb sensor. I try it anyway, on the off-chance that Michael has had it keyed to me, but it buzzes an angry red. I sigh. There's not much point in demanding I stay where he can see me when I can't even get inside. Thank goodness for the car park. I'm not sure I'd survive if I had to drive anywhere else to find shelter. I unlock the car again, clamber into the back seat, curl up and fall asleep.

CHAPTER 12

PLAYING WITH FIRE

A loud noise wakes me some time later. My body clock seems to know instinctively that it's daylight outside, even though the car park remains dark. I dimly register raised voices and open one eye. I can't see a damn thing from my position but to open both eyes and sit up would take too much energy.

Words drift over. 'Are you sure she's not with the lawyer?'

'Positive.'

'Have you been to his house?'

'My Lord, she's not with him.'

'What about Soho? The daemon said they were there yesterday.'

'We've got people out looking.'

'Goddamnit!' There's a slam. 'What about this Templeton guy that keeps phoning?'

'He wants to talk to her too.'

I think about getting up but my brain isn't sending the right signals to the rest of my body and my limbs won't comply. I hear a door close. I've missed my chance. My eye droops and slumber reclaims me.

When I come round again, I feel more refreshed. I sit up and yawn, rubbing my eyes. It feels much later and I wonder how long I've been asleep. I kick open the door and ease myself out, then stretch to shake off my grogginess. I feel grimy. There are spots of oil all down my dress, probably from my antics in the Streets of Fire lift shaft. I wipe my palms down the front of it. I really need a sodding shower.

An engine rumbles and I see an expensive sports car drive in. Its owner parks it neatly next to my rusting heap. I glance from the gleaming bodywork on one side to the filth on the other and it's hard not to giggle at the contrast. I'm still amused when the driver gets out without looking in my direction and struts towards the inner door. He presses his thumb against the keypad and enters. I scoot up, my fingers grabbing the door before it closes again, and squeeze in, then follow him to the lift.

Once the doors shut, his eyes flick in my direction. He side-steps away from me. It's a bloody lift; it's not like he can actually escape. If I wanted to sink my fangs into his stupid neck, I would. When we reach his floor and the doors open, he sprints out. I roll my eyes heavenward. The other inhabitants of this building must know they share the space with the Lord of the Montserrat Family. It doesn't make sense for the guy to be so spooked by one little girl vampire.

Shrugging to myself, I dismiss him. I step out onto Michael's penthouse floor and knock loudly on his door. There's no answer. I press my ear against it. Silence. I knock again. When the door still doesn't open, I eye it speculatively. The allure of fluffy towels and hot water is strong. He'll be pissed off but, to be fair, he *did* invite me. I stop prevaricating, take a step then leap up and kick, aiming for the lock. Unfortunately, the door opens at exactly the wrong moment and my foot connects with Michael's chest instead of solid wood.

There's a snarl and, before I can react, I'm thrown backwards against the far wall. A fist comes flying towards my face. Rather than smashing into my nose, however, it lands just to the side of my head, sending bits of plaster flying in all directions. Another arm shoots out on my other side, hitting the wall and effectively trapping me. Michael's face looms over me.

A muscle jerks in his cheek. I stare back. He's shirtless, his broad chest and winged tattoos bared. The red mark where I struck him is already fading. I hope I'm not about to be done for treason.

'Bo,' he grates.

'My Lord.' My voice has an unusual breathy quality.

He slowly licks his lips. 'Where have you been?'

'Er…' I can't tell him about X. 'Working,' I say finally.

'Where?'

'We've already had this conversation. If I'm going to be your independent bridge with the humans then it's better if I don't tell you everything that I do.'

'If you're looking for a damn cure that doesn't exist, then it's nothing to do with the humans and I should know about it. If it's the Arzo thing, then you said it had nothing to do with vampires so you can tell me about it anyway.'

'*Probably*,' I say. 'It *probably* has nothing to do with vampires.' I aim for insouciance. 'You didn't mind not knowing before.'

He leans in closer. 'That was before.' His eyes drop to my mouth.

I swallow. 'Before what?'

His shoulders tense and a shadow crosses his face. He pulls back, freeing me. 'There was an attack.'

'What? What kind of attack? Where?'

'Gully. A group of their vampires were set upon by some humans.' His jaw hardens. 'There were some casualties.'

My stomach drops. Oh, shit. 'Human?'

'And vampire.' He folds his arms and gazes at me. 'Tempers are flaring, Bo. It's not safe to be out on the streets alone.'

'I'm fine. I'm not about to get into an argument with a bunch of pissed-off humans.'

His eyes harden. 'You were frightened. When I spoke to you on the phone, you were fucking scared. And then your phone was dead.'

Guilt floods me. 'It broke. I dropped it.'

'You're lying.' He lowers his voice until it's dangerously soft. 'Who were you with?'

'I'm sorry. I can't tell you.'

He snarls and punches the wall, then turns and stalks back inside. I stare after him, wide-eyed. I've never seen him so tense, not even when Nicky was weaving her Machiavellian magic. Relations with the humans must be far worse than I thought.

'Can I come in?' I call after him.

For a moment I think he's not going to answer. Then he growls, 'It looks like you were going to anyway. Were you seriously trying to break down my door?'

'Um...' I step gingerly in. 'I need a shower.' I'm aware of how pathetic that sounds.

'The door is reinforced steel, Bo. About the only thing you'd have broken is your foot.' He walks to the window and stares out at the skyline. 'At least tell me where you spent the day.'

I relax slightly. 'Here.'

'I was here. You were not.'

'I was downstairs. In my car,' I explain. 'I couldn't get in because of the keypad.'

He turns to face me. His face is blank. 'You're kidding me?'

'Uh, no.'

Comprehension dawns. 'Hold on. You mean that rusty piece of...'

'Don't,' I interrupt. 'Don't you dare denigrate my car.'

'Does it even work?'

'I'm not going to deign to answer that. Can I use your shower or can't I? I've got things to do.'

He waves a hand towards his bedroom. 'Feel free. The doctor will be at the mansion soon, so be quick.'

Except that, thanks to X, I no longer require his services. 'The thing is...'

Michael's eyes narrow. 'What?'

I think better of it. 'Nothing,' I say hastily. 'I can't wait to get started with the therapy.'

He growls something under his breath.

'What was that?' I ask innocently.

'Nothing.'

I shrug and head for some heavenly scrubbing bliss.

'By the way, I got you some clean clothes,' he calls out after me.

I pause. 'I can't wear the Montserrat uniform. I'm not with the Family any more.'

'As you say.' There's the faintest hint of amusement in his tone.

I frown suspiciously, but don't turn round. My nostrils are assailed by the deep masculine scent of his bedroom. I glance towards the bed. It doesn't look slept in.

'Stop it, Bo,' I whisper to myself.

I go into the bathroom and stare at myself in the mirror. I don't look any different. I prod my temples. There's no visible sign that a Kakos daemon has been messing with my mind. X's face swims into my mind and I shiver. I wish I could tell someone what happened. I think of Michael's tense frame and sigh. Life seems to become more complicated, not less.

I TAKE my time getting clean, standing with my back to the searing spray and letting it hit my neck and cascade down. The heat turns my skin lobster red but it definitely makes me feel better. When I finally step out, I feel renewed. Then my eyes fall on the clothes hanging on the back of the door. I'm sure they weren't there when I came in. I look around as if I expect Michael to be standing there, leering at my naked body. Chance would be a fine thing.

I take down the clothes and gape. There's a short, fitted black dress made of heavy, expensive material. It allows for movement so my actions won't be restricted if I do something stupid and end up in a fight. It's also a perfect match for my trusty leather jacket. It's not the dress itself that makes my stomach squirm though – it's the lacy underwear next to it. Both the bra and panties are my size. I can't imagine Michael Montserrat picking out the set for me in La Perla. No, he must have asked Ria or someone to do it.

I get dressed quickly, towelling off my hair. When I pick up my jacket I realise it feels rather bulky. I pat it down and pull out a notepad from the inner pocket. I frown for a moment then remember it belongs to X. I look at the first page; there's an odd indentation in the middle. As far as I can tell, it's a diamond shape with a weird squiggle inside. Much good that'll do me. I shove it back into my pocket. I'll have to dispose of it later. The further away I stay from the Kakos daemon and his belongings the better.

When I leave the bedroom, Michael is also fully clothed, wearing another immaculately tailored suit in midnight blue. Does he ever get bored with that colour? He looks up as I enter the room. I feel uncomfortable, as if he's suddenly developed X-ray vision and is staring through the dress to the underwear below. Then he turns away.

'Let's go,' he says tersely. 'The car's waiting.'

'I need my own car.'

He throws an impatient look over his shoulder.

'I'm not planning to spend all night hanging around the Montserrat mansion,' I explain patiently. 'I've got things to do.'

'And you're still not going to tell me what these things are?'

I purse my lips then shrug. 'Nope.'

'You're not going out alone.'

I want to argue but, in light of the Gully attack, I realise he's probably being sensible. I've already established that I can't trust O'Shea enough to take him, not while I'm still on Dahlia Templeton's trail. Arzo is out, naturally. 'You said you were going to release Matt from his fledgling training so he can join the new agency. Did you mean that?'

'After Nicky's spell, he won't cope with the demands of being an independent vampire. You and Arzo can help him more than the others.'

'It won't piss off the other Heads too much to have another Montserrat fledgling fly the coop before they're supposedly ready?'

Michael is silent for a moment. 'They've got other things to worry about.'

I suppose they have. 'Well,' I say cautiously, 'I'll take Matt with me. Give him a taste of what it'll be like.' As long as we don't run into any more Kakos daemons, we'll be fine.

'You're both fledgling so you're both weak. He will do whatever anyone tells him, no matter who they are, and you're suffering from trauma. I don't think Matt on his own is going to cut it.'

I frown. I could ask D'Argneau but although I'm sure the

lawyer would jump at the chance to strut around town with a vampire, I suspect Michael won't be too keen about that suggestion. He seems to have taken umbrage against D'Argneau, no doubt for involving himself in Montserrat matters.

'Look,' I say patiently, as we get into the lift. 'I understand that safety is an issue. Technically, though, you're not my boss any more. I need someone I can trust not to blab about what I'm doing. Right now, the only person I can think of is Matt. I don't want to put him in danger but it's either him and me, or just me. Any other Montserrat vampire, even Beth and Nell, will tell you what I've been up to. O'Shea will tell you what I've been up to.'

'*You* could just tell me what you're up to.'

'No.' I shake my head firmly.

He scowls. 'This solo thing will only carry you so far.'

I smile disarmingly. 'One of my more endearing qualities is that when I make a decision, I stick to it.'

'Unless it's joining my Family as a vampire.'

My smile falters. 'Okay. But that's a one-off. And you goaded me into leaving.' The lift opens at the car park. I face him. 'I'm trying to meet you halfway.'

'I suppose Arzo is out of the question?'

I nod.

'Fine,' he growls. 'Take Matt. But you will damn well call me every two hours, no matter what is going on. I also want you back here by 4.30am. We still have your fingerprints on file. I'll make sure you're not locked out again.'

I put my hands on my hips. 'You do remember the "you're not my boss" part, right?' He looks at me. I throw my hands up in the air. 'Fine.'

Michael smiles. I smile back. 'Thank you,' I say awkwardly. 'For Matt. And the shower. And the clothes.'

'You're welcome,' he murmurs. There's an odd light in his eyes.

I look away and walk to my car. 'Would you like me to drive you to the mansion?'

He takes in the lack of passenger seat, rusty metal and dust-etched penis. 'You really drive this?'

'Hey,' I say lightly, 'I sleep in it too. But if you want to give me an advance on my salary, I can take it to a garage and get it fixed up.'

'What salary?'

'For the agency. The bridge that will smooth over issues between the humans and the vampires.' I'm patient, but confused.

Michael laughs. 'But Bo, if I pay you, you're not independent.'

I stare at him.

'To maintain your integrity you're not going to tell me about your investigations, so I can't have a financial hand in what you're doing. And when you make a decision, you stick to it.' His grin broadens. 'It's one of your many *endearing* qualities.'

Bastard.

'I am, however, not getting in that death trap. And neither are you.'

I start to protest but he holds up a hand. 'I've still got Ursus's bike. I'm sure he won't mind if you hang onto it a little longer.'

'I don't think a motorbike is any safer than a car,' I grumble. Secretly, of course, I'm thrilled. As fond as I am of my car, I'll take Ursus's gleaming machine over it any day.

'Compared to that thing?' He jerks his head at my car. I wrinkle my nose in his direction and he laughs again. 'Let's get going.'

IT'S STILL FAIRLY EARLY when we pull up outside the familiar gates of the Montserrat mansion. Michael strides up the steps. I don't bother hurrying to keep up with him; I know he must be busy with Family business. I try to ignore the looks I receive when I enter, which run from outright hatred to mere curiosity. I swear I even spot a touch of envy from one or two of the milling Montserrat minions.

I'm barely out of the lobby when the good doctor approaches. 'Ms Blackman!' he says, clasping my hands in a manner that makes me think I'm an invalid in a dusty Victorian novel. 'I'm so glad you made it. We weren't sure you would.'

I mutter something about being tied up with other things. It's annoying that I have to waste time pretending I'm still under the dark shadow of PTSD. Given that I'm in no position to tell anyone the truth, though, I have to go along with the pretence.

'Let's get going, Doc. I've got things to do.'

He nods briskly. 'Of course, of course. Any more hallucinations?' His tone is akin to that of someone inquiring about where I've been on my holidays.

'No.'

'Good.' He claps his hands together. 'The drugs are helping then?'

'Mm.'

'You're not exceeding the dosage.'

'No,' I answer truthfully. 'Definitely not.'

'I'm pleased to hear it.'

I force a smile and prepare for a long, painful hour. When I finally escape, Connor and Arzo are waiting for me. I push away the familiar sinking feeling and drink while Connor stands placidly and Arzo watches, unblinking. Apparently I'm still not trusted to take care of my dietary needs. When I'm done, Connor smiles and leaves. I scan Arzo's face, worried that he somehow knows what the majority of my nocturnal activities involve these days, but he gives me an easy grin.

'How'd it go with Doctor Love?'

'Great. I don't think I'll need many sessions. I feel much better already.'

'You can't rush these things, Bo. It takes time to recover from that kind of trauma. If you ever do recover.'

I curse inwardly but paste on a smile. 'You're right.' He relaxes. 'How's the hunt going for an office?'

'Getting there. I've found a suitable place on Harbour Road and another on Link Street. I'm negotiating with the landlords. Hopefully we can sign the papers on the cheapest one and move in not long after the announcement is made.'

'Michael said he wasn't going to involve himself financially.' I manage to keep the rancour out of my voice.

'Indeed. That's a good idea of his to keep out of it.' I narrow my eyes in suspicion - is he having a dig at me? He winks from his wheelchair. 'I've got some savings to get us started,' he says, patting my hand. 'We'll be fine.'

'We still need a human,' I tell him. 'A proper investigator, not a drinks dispenser like Connor.' My mind drifts back to X telling me about the human face of the Streets of Fire CEO. I don't want to work for a puppet. 'Someone with enough experience to help out the rest of us rookies.' Then I hastily amend my words. 'Not you, of course.'

'I'm a better office manager than investigator,' Arzo says, not taking offence. 'Especially these days. I have a few ideas. Once things get firmed up, I'll run them by you.'

'Okay.' I trust him implicitly.

He shifts uncomfortably in his chair. 'There is one thing...'

'Yes?'

'There'll be you, me, Matthew, Connor and whichever human joins us.' I nod, not sure what he's getting at. 'We could probably do with another body in the office to help out.'

I shrug. 'You're the expert, Arzo. And it's your money starting up this whole thing anyway. Do what you think is right.'

He won't meet my eyes. 'I was thinking that Peter would be a good addition.'

I start. 'Peter as in Sanguine Peter?'

He nods. I've not seen Peter since before the events that overtook me at Big Ben. Both of us were recruited as vampires at the same time. I'd wanted desperately not to complete the turning process so I could become Sanguine like Arzo. Peter hadn't cared. Unfortunately things didn't turn out quite the way I'd expected.

'That's cool. I like him.'

'I thought that maybe...'

'Working with two Sanguines when I'm a vampire would be too much for me?'

Arzo nods. I smile. 'Peter didn't have anything to do with what happened.'

'I know. But...'

'Thanks for checking. It's fine though, Arzo. Ask him.'

'I'm not sure he'll say yes. He's rather troubled.'

I sigh. 'He always is.'

'That's why I think having something to do will help him.'

I laugh. 'This agency is going to be full of waifs and strays. It's better than a bunch of criminals though.' As soon as the words are out of my mouth, I realise what I've said. Embarrassment overcomes me and I choke.

'You probably shouldn't go around advertising that fact, Bo. It's not public knowledge.'

I stare down at my shoes. 'Sorry,' I mumble. I mentally kick myself.

My blushes are interrupted by a clamour from outside. There's a screech of speeding tyres and a lot of shouting. Alarmed, I run through the lobby and out the front doors. A huge wooden cross has been shoved into one of the flowerbeds that line the edge of the property. It's on fire, lighting up the night with stark orange flames, and it reeks of petrol. Several Montserrat vampires push past me, carrying buckets of water.

'Fuck.' Arzo wheels up next to me. Together, we watch the cross burn, the heat burning our skin even from this distance.

'Maybe you should hurry along those rent negotiations,' I mutter.

His troubled eyes blink in acknowledgment.

CHAPTER 13

FINGERTIP'S DEID

I hover around the front long after the flames are doused and Arzo has disappeared. Montserrat vampires cluster together, speaking in hushed voices, and Michael emerges rigid with rage. It's not until Beth and Nell appear that anyone talks to me. I definitely have the aura of a pariah clinging to me.

'Smeg, Bo. Did you see who did this?' Beth breathes, staring at the blackened cross.

I shake my head.

'It was probably just kids,' Nell dismisses. 'Some kind of prank.'

'A prank?' Beth rounds on her. 'It's what the Ku Klux Klan does!'

'The Ku Klux Klan don't worry about getting drained of every drop of blood in their system. We catch one or two of the pricks who did this and they won't dare come near us again.'

'You'd kill them, Nell? Even if they're just kids?' I say it quietly but I'm appalled by her words. Obviously tensions are running equally high on both human and vampire sides.

'What the hell would you know about it, Bo? It's not as if

you're a real vampire!' Nell strides off, joining another group and gesticulating wildly in the cross's direction.

Beth watches me carefully. 'Nell just feels hurt that you left. She wasn't aware of everything that was going on with you before.'

'If I'm not a real vampire and I'm not a real human, what am I?'

'She didn't mean it.'

'I think she did.' Pushing away my own problems, I change the subject. 'How's training going?'

Beth beams. 'It's fantastic! Every day I feel stronger. Last night, Ursus had us climbing up to the roof of the atrium. Can you believe it? The atrium!'

I don't burst her bubble by telling her about my own rooftop adventures. She mistakes the expression on my face. 'I mean, there's a lot of boring PowerPoints too,' she adds hastily. 'You know Ursus.'

I smile reassuringly, then glance up as I sense Michael's gaze on me. Another vampire is next to him, speaking earnestly about placing a permanent guard outside the mansion.

'What is with you and our sexy Lord?'

'Huh?'

'You arrived together, Bo. You're not making the beast with two backs, are you? Engaging with the one-eyed snake?'

'Jeez, Beth.' I scrunch up my face.

'You should be careful,' she warns. 'You've broken with the Family and that's fine, but it'll only end in tears if you fall for him.'

'Nothing's going on.'

'Yeah, right,' she scoffs. 'Why is he looking at you in the same way a lion looks at a juicy buffalo?'

She's right. He's still watching me and there is definitely a tinge of the predator about him. 'Because I think he's about to come over and forbid me to go out on the streets without an armed guard.'

'You're not Montserrat any more. He can't do that.'

'Exactly.' I change the subject. 'I need to find Matt.'

'Birdbrain? What do you need him for?'

'Don't call him that, Beth. It's not his fault he's the way he is.'

'I called him that before Nicky forced that stupid spell on him. Admittedly, he's fractionally less annoying now than he was then.'

I throw her a look and she holds up her palms in submission. 'I think he's in the gym. Ursus told him to work out about five hours ago. Until he's told otherwise, he'll still be there.'

'Great,' I mutter. He'll be tired and sweaty. It'll be like wandering around the streets with a heavy ball and chain attached to my leg. Still, I promised I'd take him with me. 'I'm going to fetch him then he and I are going for a little jaunt.'

Her mouth drops open. 'What? That's not fair! I'm smegging stronger than he is. He drank blood hours after his turning. I lasted much longer.'

'I know, Beth,' I say softly, 'but I can make sure he won't go blabbing to anyone about what I'm doing.' Before she can protest, I add, 'Not that I don't trust you. Of course I do. But you're Montserrat.'

'So's he.'

'Yeah, but you're not suffering from the effects of a spell that makes you do whatever you're told. You're also not allowed out.'

'Matt is?'

'Matt's chances of surviving as a vampire are tiny. He can't do what you're doing. And while you *are* stronger, he *looks* like he is.'

'He spends five hours in the gym every day.'

'People believe what they see. Even if what they see is a lie.'

'I can't believe Lord Montserrat is breaking his own laws for Matt as well as you.'

I glance at the cross. 'Winds of change.'

'And not necessarily good ones.'

I don't disagree; my own situation aside, she may be right. 'Look, when I come out with Matt, I need you to do me a favour.'

'I might not be strong enough.'

'Beth…'

'Fine. But only because I like you. Plus you're short. Standing next to you makes me look like an Amazonian warrior.'

I snort. 'It's only thanks to your shoes.'

She grins. 'I think Ursus secretly covets them.'

I try – and fail – to imagine the large senior vampire as a cross-dresser. We exchange a glance and giggle.

'What do you need me to do?'

'Just keep him busy so Matt and I can get away.' I don't need to specify who I'm referring to; Beth understands. I can't deal with Michael changing his mind because of one burning cross.

'Okay. But you'll smegging owe me.'

'I'll add it to my ledger.' I smile gratefully.

'Bo?'

'Yes?'

'Be careful,' she says. 'You don't want to end up as another statistic.'

I nod. 'Thanks, Beth.'

'THIS IS EXCITING!' Matt shouts in my ear, when we're finally speeding away from the mansion.

'Kidnapping is not exciting. We're not in a movie, Matt. You need to be more serious.'

'What?'

'I said, you need to be more serious.'

'Oh.' He's silent for a moment then yells again. 'The financial markets are recovering well, don't you think?'

'Matt?'

'Yes, Bo?'

'Shut up.'

I accelerate out of the corner, keeping my eyes peeled for anyone who may have perpetrated the attack on the Montserrat Family. Unless I pass someone carrying a cross and a jerrycan, it's unlikely I'll be successful but I still try.

We finally pull up outside a dilapidated block of flats on the outskirts of the city. I park the bike then turn to Matt. 'Whatever happens when you're with me, you don't tell a soul about any of it. Got that?'

'Yes, Bo.'

'And don't speak unless I give you permission.'

'Yes, Bo.'

'You're here as back-up. That means I need you to watch my back in case anyone tries anything sneaky.'

He immediately scoots behind me. I twist round. Matt's eyes are fixed on my spine. I sigh. Matt and I did not exactly gel when we first met but his total lack of self-awareness now is pathetic. I wonder whether I could find X again and ask him to do his freaky mind stuff to help Matt out. Then I dismiss the thought. If I never see another Kakos daemon again it will be too soon. Even if he purports to know something about a cure for vampirism.

We walk inside the open door to a tiled space that reeks of urine. There's the frame of a wheel-less bicycle propped to one side and numerous black bags. One of them rustles and I shudder and move away. It's probably just a cockroach or a rat but that doesn't mean I want to get any closer. The dull grey walls are decorated with meaningless graffiti: *Rab woz here* and the like. This is the address for the last name on Templeton's list – the leader of a small coven of white witches. In stark contrast to Cheung and X, this person's bank accounts have clearly seen better days. It seems strange that someone who lives here would need an accountant but if they're desperate for money then they have the motive to kidnap Dahlia.

The lifts are, unsurprisingly, out of order. Despite my enhanced vampire physicality, I don't fancy climbing thirteen flights of stairs but we don't have much choice.

Matt and I are barely past the second floor when we pass a youngish man heading in the opposite direction. I pause to let him pass; Matt, meanwhile, snarls. I'm disturbed to see a drop of drool hanging from the corner of his mouth.

'Have you drunk today?' I ask, as soon as the man is out of sight.

He bobs his head. 'Three times.'

I'm aghast. 'Three times?'

'I get hungry a lot.'

'Are you hungry now?'

Matt frowns as he thinks about it. 'No,' he says finally, 'I'm good.'

Thank goodness for small mercies. 'Please don't act aggressive towards everyone we meet. A lot of people don't like vampires at the moment and it would be a good idea if we did something to stop that.'

'Okay.' A huge smile spreads across his face.

I eye him suspiciously. 'What?'

'You said please. Most people don't. They just tell me what to do.'

I feel a wave of empathy. I guess Matt isn't as brain dead as everyone thinks. I pat him on the shoulder and we continue upwards. We're almost at the right floor when Matt nudges me. 'Someone is following us,' he whispers dramatically.

'They're probably on their way home to their own flat.'

He shakes his head. 'No. When we stopped on the seventh floor, they stopped too. They're copying what we're doing.'

Interesting. I gesture to Matt to pick up speed. Instead of stopping on thirteen, we continue up one more flight, then curve round the corner so we're out of sight. I flatten my body against the wall and listen. Matt copies me.

I realise he's right. There are heavy footsteps behind us and I can hear panting. Someone is on our tail. I'm irked at myself for not noticing; maybe having Matt in tow will be a good thing. I give him a nod of approval and he beams.

'I was in the army. It was important to know when someone was after you.'

I shush him and refrain from pointing out that I'm a PI who should know that. I'll praise him later; right now I need to find out who is following us. I flex my muscles and wait. As soon as the footsteps pause and a head pokes out into the corridor, I send my fist flying in its direction. I just manage to change course at the last minute when I see who it is.

'What are you doing?' Stephen Templeton yells.

I wince. 'Jeez, keep quiet. It's already gone ten o'clock. Some of these people will be sleeping.'

His pale face is unhappy. 'I guess you don't believe in asking questions first.'

'You were following us. Someone friendly would shout a cheery hello instead of lurking in the shadows.'

'I came here to find out if the witches took Dahlia. When I saw you, I thought I'd check what you were doing.' He folds his arms. 'I'm paying you a lot of money and you won't even return my calls.'

There's a rumble of anger from Matt. I place a reassuring hand on his arm and he subsides, although he still glares malevolently at Templeton.

'It's all about money with you, isn't it? My phone broke while I was busy getting myself almost killed on your behalf. I'll call you when I have some concrete information about where your wife is. All I can do so far is tell you where she's not.'

'You've been to Cheung?'

'And Streets of Fire.'

Templeton's eyes widen and his voice drops to a whisper. 'Did you meet the daemon?'

'I can't talk about it. Suffice to say, neither are responsible for what's happened to Dahlia.' I give him a hard look. 'Is this your first port of call? Because if you think these people are the most likely ones to have nabbed her, you should have mentioned that before.'

He looks away. 'I didn't think that.'

I laugh. 'Right. You've come here because they're the least dangerous, not the prime suspects. You don't want to get hurt.'

'I'm paying you for that!' He realises what he's just said and tries to backtrack. 'I mean, I'm not paying you to get hurt. I don't want that. I don't want anyone to get hurt.' He subsides into a mumble. 'I'm just worried about her.'

Sympathy and irritation war inside me. Sympathy wins, but only just. 'I understand but I don't think you're doing any good by being here. You're better off letting me do the job you keep reminding me you're paying for.' He still looks troubled. 'What is it?' I ask.

'Well, you're a vampire.'

I stare at him. 'Congratulations. Yes I am.'

He shuffles his feet. 'There's been some stuff on the television lately. About vampires. How they can't be trusted. They're evil.' He starts to stammer. 'I don't mean that *you're* evil. I trust you. I do. But maybe you're only doing this because you know that Arzo took her after all. Not anyone else. Maybe it's a smokescreen.'

'You came to me. Besides, I'm here, aren't I? I wouldn't be following your list if I knew where she was.' I chew the inside of my cheek, thinking about what he said. 'Don't you trust your wife, Mr Templeton?'

'Of course I do,' he answers stiffly. 'Maybe I just don't trust vampires.'

I shrug. 'Okay. I've spent several days on this so far and, by my tally, you owe me about another hundred quid for the hours I've put in. But I'm prepared to call it quits. The witches and the search for the lovely Mrs Templeton are all yours.' I nod to Matt who's hovering anxiously next to me and the pair of us start to leave.

'W-wait!'

I ignore him. Frankly, I'm thrilled to be shot of this entire mess.

'Ms Blackman! Please! If you're going to leave me stranded like this then at least give me Arzo's phone number so I can contact him.'

Arse. I stop in my tracks and turn around. 'I told you. Arzo isn't around.'

He digs into his pocket, pulls out a wallet and thrusts some notes in my direction. 'Here, I'll pay you more.'

I look down at the money then back up at him. With the new agency being set up, some cash would come in handy but something about Templeton's sweaty offering and constant financial references turn my stomach.

'I don't want your money.'

'Please! You have to help me.'

I give him my death stare. For once it works and he takes a half step backwards. 'I have been helping.' I move towards him and am immensely satisfied when he tries to sidle away. 'I will continue to help if you promise to stop getting in my way. I don't want any more of your not-very-hard-earned money. In return for my work, you will promise to remain in whatever hole it is you're currently staying in. You will not call the Montserrat Family again. You will not try to take matters into your own hands again. This is not Vigilantes-R-Us, Mr Temple-ton. I will contact you when I either reach a dead end or find out where your wife is.' I think about it a little more. 'Or you can call the police and let them deal with this. I'm okay with that too.'

His eyelids flutter rapidly. 'No! No police! I'll stay out of your way, Ms Blackman, I promise. Please.' He takes my hands. I struggle not to flinch. 'Just find her.'

'I'll do my best,' I growl at him. 'Where are you staying?'

'Holiday Inn near Marble Arch.'

'Wonderful.' I wait then, when he doesn't move, snarl as viciously as I can. 'Go on then – get out of here!'

He stumbles away. Once I'm sure he's gone, I relax my shoulders and sigh.

Matt looks at me curiously. 'You don't like that human. He's annoying, I get that, but you really don't like him.'

'A long time ago he was very shitty to Arzo.'

'We've all done things we regret, Bo. Some mistakes might be more conscious than others but we should be allowed to make amends.'

I lapse into silence.

'What?' he asks.

'I just can't believe Beth called you bird-brain.'

He puts on a goofy smile. 'Beth's pretty. And she has big breasts.'

I shake my head. 'And you were doing so well.'

'What?' I start walking back down the stairs. 'What, Bo? What did I say?'

I place my finger on my lips, encouraging him into silence. At least I know he'll do what he's told.

I LOCATE the head witch's door fairly easily as it's one of the few that has a number on it. Admittedly, the grubby plastic 4 is upside down and about to fall off but the fact it's still there should be applauded, considering the state of the rest of these flats. I knock loudly. After my previous epic failures at sneaking around, it makes more sense to try the direct approach.

There's a lot of shuffling inside, then the sound of several locks being undone. Finally the door opens fractionally and an eye blinks out at me.

'Whaddayawant?'

It takes a moment to decipher the words. 'Uh, I'm Bo Blackman. I'm here to ask you a few questions about your accountant.'

The eye narrows. 'Polis?'

I'm struck by the fact that the witch can't tell I'm a vampire until I realise how dingy the corridor is. I move out of the darkest shadows.

'No,' I say, calmly, keeping my fingers crossed that, as a triber, this white witch is not one of the many who have taken against vampires.

'Ain't no Family called Blackman.'

'There's not,' I agree cheerfully. 'I was Montserrat. I left.'

'Bloodguzzlers don't leave.'

'I did.'

The eye stares at me suspiciously. 'Yougonnagetmadoshback?'

'Pardon?'

'She asked if you're going to retrieve her money for her,' Matt whispers helpfully.

'Who that?'

I step aside so she can see Matt. 'He's my colleague.'

'Traitor too?'

I sigh. 'I'm not a traitor. I just left. He's still with them.'

'Mon'serrat?'

'Yes.'

'Better'an Medici.'

I can't argue with that. Further down the corridor, a door opens and a curious face pokes out to stare at me. I guess there aren't many house callers in this neck of the woods. 'Look, you obviously know that Stephen Templeton was skimming money from your account, Mrs Jackson. It is Mrs Jackson, right? Could we talk about what he did inside?'

The eye blinks, then there's a rattle as Mrs Jackson undoes the chain. She opens the door; she's a rake-thin woman wearing a nondescript black dress. Her white witch tattoo on her cheek is the brightest thing about her. She smiles, baring a row of yellowing teeth.

'Try, vampire. Try an' enter.'

'If you prefer discussing your finances in the hallway, that's fine with me.'

She scowls. 'Yer invited.'

I incline my head and indicate to Matt that he should wait outside to keep an eye out for anyone else arriving, then I step in. The door slams shut behind me, making me jump. Mrs Jackson hacks out a laugh, lights a cigarette and stumbles to a grubby sofa that may once have been covered in a floral fabric. To be honest, it's difficult to tell. I sit gingerly beside her.

'Can you tell me how you got involved with Mr Templeton?' I ask, trying to sound as if I'm investigating him rather than her.

'Yello' pages.'

'Why?'

'Lots of accountants in there.' She roots around in the cushions then pulls out a copy of the directory, throwing it in my lap. 'See for yersel'.'

'I mean, why did you need an accountant?'

She snorts. 'Think I dunno 'at's what ye meant? Jes' cos I live 'ere now doesna' mean I always did.' She hawks up some phlegm in her throat then rolls it around her mouth as if chewing. ''Ard times.'

'What happened?'

She spits out a greenish glob onto the carpet. I try to avoid looking at it. 'Magix' appened.'

I blink. 'The company?'

'Nah,' she says sarcastically, 'the cuddly toy. Course the bleedin' company. Moneygrabbingbastards.' She scratches at a scab on her chin. 'Vampires don' know wha's like. Ye've all got dosh. Loads o'dosh. Livin' in lap o' luxury in yer mansions.' She shakes her head. 'S'no like 'at fer witches.'

I can feel my atoms firing. I lean forward. 'What did Magix do?'

She raises her eyebrows at the Yellow Pages. 'Open it.'

There is a crumpled letter inside the cover. I glance at her and she nods. Carefully unfolding it, I read.

'*Dear Mrs Jackson, It has come to our attention that the series of spells called Tracker that you claim to have developed, and which you are using to help owners locate missing objects, infringes on our own patent. You will cease and desist all activities involving this spell immediately or face prosecution.*' I look up. 'Tracker? That's *your* spell?' I don't mean to sound so surprised but I'm genuinely astonished. At Dire Straits we did steady business in finding lost items until Tracker came on the market. All that business disappeared virtually overnight. These days, advertisements for it run on a nightly basis. The jingle is particularly annoying.

'Yeah. Tracker was mine. They took it. Tried to fight 'em,' she mumbles. 'Too damn big. Too damn powerful. Fuckin' Magix.' She spits again. 'Offered me a job afterwards, they did. Like I'd work for those feckers.'

Stephen Templeton is clearly not the only prick with sticky fingers in several pots. All roads are starting to lead to Magix.

'Do you know Frolic?' I ask, doing my best to keep the excitement out of my voice. 'From the shop – Fingertips and Frolics?'

'Fingertip's deid. They killed' im.'

'I thought he died of a heart attack. Natural causes.'

'Yeah,'at's what they wan'ye ta believe.'

'The shop's closed,' I say softly.

Mrs Jackson nods distractedly.

'Do you know where she's gone? Do you know where Frolic is?'

A knowing look crosses her face she licks her lips. 'Mebbe.' She rubs her finger and thumb together.

I curse myself for not taking more of Templeton's money. I reach into my pocket and pull out what remains – less than fifty quid. I hope it's enough. When I hold it out, the witch grabs it. As soon as she touches the notes they disappear, magicked into wherever she keeps her valuables.

'Where is she, Mrs Jackson?'

''Yde Park.'

She has to be kidding me. Hyde Park is directly opposite the Montserrat mansion. 'Are you sure?' I demand.

'I ain't a liar.'

My mind races. Why there of all places? It's too sodding close and too sodding pat for it to be a coincidence. I stand up. 'Thank you, Mrs Jackson. You've been a great help.'

'Wha' 'bout accountant?'

I realise I'd forgotten why I was here in the first place. Abruptly I sit back down.

'Magix tole me 'bout him,' she confides.

I hold my breath. Is it possible that somehow Magix is responsible for the disappearance of Dahlia Templeton?

'Sent someone roun'. Tole me I was stupid. Tole me I couldn't be trusted if I can't look after me own money.' Her face takes on a sour expression. 'Wanted ta rub it in.'

'Who did they send? What was his name?'

'Dunno. They all look the same.'

'Black or white?'

'Huh?'

'Was it a black or a white witch?'

She laughs humourlessly. ''Uman. They're all 'uman.'

I try to look like I'm not surprised. 'Do you feel angry towards Mr Templeton for what he did?' I watch her reaction carefully just to be sure.

''E ain't the reason I'm 'ere. Why?' she asks. 'Is 'e in trouble fer nicking?'

'No,' I say. I stand up and reach out to shake her hand. She looks at my palm for a second then shrugs and clasps it. 'Thank you for your time, Mrs Jackson.'

'Thank ye for yer money,' she returns.

I walk to the door then pause and turn back as if I've forgotten something. 'Did you ever meet Mr Templeton's wife?'

She looks at me like I'm crazy. 'Who'd wanna marry that bugger?'

I smile at her. 'Indeed,' I reply. 'Who would?'

I open the door and walk out.

CHAPTER 14

PLAYING DIRTY

'It's Magix,' I tell Matt, when we pull up outside Hyde Park. I leave the bike outside the Montserrat mansion, noting that the burnt skeleton of the cross has already been removed. 'It's got to be. Magix killed Fingertip and put Frolic and Mrs Jackson out of business – and goodness knows how many others.'

Matt's eyes are round. 'You're so clever, Bo.'

I snort although I can't help feeling pleased with myself. I suck a deep breath into my lungs, savouring the fresh night air.

'So why did Magix kidnap Dolly?' He's watching me with Labrador-like eyes, as if waiting for his mistress to provide him with a chewy treat.

'Dahlia.'

'Oh.' He nods his head sagely. 'Why did Magix take her?'

'Templeton probably screwed them over too.'

Except he didn't include them on his list of potentially disgruntled clients, and the firm probably has its own accountants to do its dirty work. Considering the state of its business practices, it's unlikely to trust an outsider with such a delicate job. I had looked around when we left Mrs Jackson's place, on the off-chance that Templeton was still hanging about so I could ask him but, other than a few teenagers, the wasteland of a car park in front of the flats was empty. There could be other reasons why the company is involved with the Templetons, though. There's one way to be sure.

'Come on,' I tell my faithful companion. 'We need to get a move on. Keep your eyes peeled for a woman communing with nature.'

I jog across the road. I'm about to hop over the fence when I realise Matt's not behind me. Frowning, I turn round. He's standing smack bang in the middle of the road and scrabbling at his eyes.

'What are you doing?'

'I can't do it, Bo!' His voice is anguished.

I'm alarmed. Perhaps Mrs Jackson cast a hex on him when I wasn't paying attention. 'Can't do what? What's wrong?'

I run back to him and grab his wrists while his fingers flail uselessly in the air. His eyes are already bloodshot. 'I can't peel them! I don't know how!'

Momentarily baffled, I stare at him. Then the penny drops. 'It's an expression, Matt. I didn't mean to literally peel your eyes.'

'I didn't know that!' he wails, beginning to cry.

There's something heartbreakingly pathetic about the musclebound vampire in front of me bawling out his eyes in frustration. The Matt of old was full of misplaced machismo; this version is like a child. I pat his arm awkwardly, wondering whether bringing him along was a good idea. At this rate, I'm likely to say something thoughtless that'll cost him his life.

'There, there. It's alright. It was my fault. I should be more careful with my words. Don't peel your eyes, just keep a look out. That's all.'

He sniffs loudly. I reach up towards his face, wiping away

the tears. 'If I ask you to do something that hurts, you have to tell me.'

''Kay.'

'I mean it, Matt.'

He nods. I smile cautiously in return. 'Do you want to go back home?'

He shakes his head vigorously. 'No! It's awful there. People are mean to me.'

'Who? Who's mean?'

He reels off a list of names. By the tenth one, I shush him. No wonder Michael is prepared to break his own laws for Matt. He's become an easy victim for a bunch of bored, cooped-up vampires. I'll have words with Beth again. Matt may have been an arrogant prick but he doesn't deserve this. I guess the minders assigned to him at the Montserrat mansion only care about protecting others from him, not vice-versa. I force down my anger.

'Okay,' I soothe. 'I will deal with this. Right now, however, I need to find Frolic. Can you help?'

'Yes.'

'Okay, then.' I take his arm and we walk to the pavement. I vault over the fence and wait for him to do the same. Then I turn and grin. 'Let's stretch our legs. I mean,' I backtrack hastily before Matt moves into a yoga pose, 'let's go for a run.'

He beams at me. Overhead an owl hoots loudly, as if in agreement, and we take off.

Hyde Park covers a vast area. While it's certainly not the largest public park in the world, and Matt and I have useful vampiric speed to help us cover a lot of ground, it's still 350 acres. I'm hoping that my suspicions are right and that Frolic is here because it's close to the Montserrat mansion and she wants to be found. We've barely gone half a mile when I hear shouting and realise I'm right.

'You promised me!' It's a woman's voice, raised in anger.

'You only collect when you return the feather.'

'I don't have the fucking feather! Some kid stole it.'

'Then our bargain is null and void.'

I gesture to Matt, silently instructing him to take up position nearby while I pad forward to get a better idea of what's going on.

'You can't do this to me. I risked my life...'

'We are all risking our lives,' Frolic responds.

'This isn't my fight!'

'We didn't force you to get involved.'

I peer out from behind a tree. As far as I can tell, there's only two of them. Unfortunately I didn't see enough of the woman Michael rescued from the mugger but I'm sure that this is her. Frolic appears unchanged from our last meeting, an implacable and immoveable woman.

'It's just a feather. I'll get you another one.'

Frolic shakes her head. 'It's proof of purchase. A receipt, if you like. You know it needs to be the same one. Unless you return it, I can't do anything. I'd like to help you, I really would, but my hands are tied.'

The woman rushes towards the so-called neo-druid. A man appears from out of nowhere, hauling her back before her flailing fists connect with Frolic's face. He seems familiar but the shadows swallow him up again before I get a clear look. He drags the yelling woman away and I hear him tell her to get the hell away if she knows what's good for her.

'You may as well come out, Ms Montserrat,' Frolic calls in my direction.

I stiffen before shrugging and stepping into the moonlight. 'It's Blackman now,' I tell her.

A tiny smile plays around Frolic's mouth. 'Is it? Well now, that's interesting.'

'That was a bit harsh,' I say, gesturing in the direction of the departed – and still yelling – woman.

She shrugs. 'I'm not a charity. You wouldn't return an item to a shop without a receipt, would you?'

'Yes, but still...' I wonder if Michael still has my green feather. Perhaps I could give it to the woman and she can get whatever she was promised.

'Every feather is unique,' Frolic replies, as if reading my thoughts. I think of X and shiver. 'Without her specific one, there's nothing I can do. Rules are rules.' She leans forward. 'Unless, apparently, they are fledgling vampire rules.'

I shift uncomfortably. I don't want this conversation to be about me and my place – or lack of it – in the Montserrat Family. Now that Frolic is standing in front of me, I have more important things to question her about. 'Why did you make me take a feather?'

She ignores my question. 'I wasn't sure you were going to turn up. I was under the impression you were vaguely intelligent for a vampire, yet it's taken days for you to come and speak to me. I was beginning to think you wouldn't come at all. Vampires don't tend to do much without their Head's permission – and yet here you are.' She glances behind my shoulder in the direction of Matt. 'Is there some kind of vampire exodus going on?'

'You can read about it in the papers next week.' I fold my arms. 'I didn't know where you were.'

'I'm a neo-druid,' she answers calmly. 'I like nature. It's hardly surprising that I'm in the largest park London has to offer.'

I think of my grandfather. 'There's no such thing as a neo-druid.'

She laughs. 'I'm here, aren't I? I'm not a figment of your imagination.'

I'm getting tired of her prevarication. 'What in the hell is going here? Is this about a cure?' I demand.

'It's about Magix.'

'That much I know,' I growl.

'Then you'll know that Magix ran me out of business.' Her expression turns cold. 'And others like me. The company is creating a monopoly. Soon witches, black or white, will have no choice but to get all their materials from it. Magix is developing a stranglehold over every magic user in the country. Imagine what it can do with that kind of power.' She plucks a leaf off a nearby branch and examines it carefully before tossing it away. 'Maybe you want to develop a new spell, something to help sick children with congenital heart problems. Except Magix makes a deal with the pharmaceutical company that creates the medicine for that illness. Magix doesn't want the spell. It pulls the necessary ingredients from its shelves and,' she snaps her fingers, 'just like that, innocent children suffer and die as a result of Magix's need to make more money.'

'Why would it do something like that? I'm sorry that its executives saw you as competition and you had to shut down your business but that doesn't mean they're going to be complicit in killing people.'

'They're not complicit. They're the perpetrators! The masterminds! They need to be stopped.'

'Did Magix kill your husband?' I ask softly.

Frolic's jaw tenses. 'He was a good man. He didn't deserve what they did.'

'I'm sorry,' I say, 'I really am, but this still doesn't explain what's going on with the feathers.'

'Didn't your grandfather work it out?'

I start, surprised.

'I'm not an idiot,' she tells me. 'I know who you are – and who he is.' She looks at me pointedly. 'There was a time when he would have prevented a company like Magix from getting away with all this.' Her face becomes ugly and twisted. 'From taking away all my hard-earned profit.'

I doubt that. Back then, Grandfather had little to do with humans, even humans who were trying to dip their toes into triber pools. I don't rise to the bait, however. 'Tell me why. Why me and why the feather?'

'Magix needs to be stopped.' She raises her eyebrows in my direction. 'Call the feather an IOU of sorts.'

I try not to hold my breath. 'An IOU for what?'

Frolic smiles. 'You already know the answer to that.'

I watch her. 'The cure.'

'Just so.'

'You said it was too dangerous to go looking for it. Even if it did exist.'

She rolls her eyes. 'There was a Family Head about fifty feet away at the time. What else was I going to say?'

'So there *is* a cure?'

'I have absolutely no idea. But you help me bring down Magix and I promise I will find out either way.'

'As long as I give you the feather back.'

She smiles. 'Those are the terms.'

'Did Magix kidnap Dahlia Templeton?'

'Who's that?' She frowns at me. 'Magix doesn't waste time bundling people into cars. There would be a too much of a trail. Why kidnap when you can murder?'

'So much for that theory,' I mutter. I dig into my pocket, searching for the card the policeman gave me. When I find it, I pull it out and pass it to Frolic. 'Have you seen this hex before?'

Her face clouds over. 'It's a Magix speciality. Black magic. Very similar to what killed Fingertip.'

I sigh, pressing my fingertips to my temples. The policeman

had been convinced it was white magic. 'What do you want me to do?'

I spot a flicker of triumph before she answers. 'There's a new line coming out. Glamour spells, distasteful things if you ask me, but there's a market for them. The woman who was here before you stole the recipe for us. All you have to do is break into the factory and alter one of the ingredients. Then, when Magix's big new product is released and goes wrong, the company's reputation will be ruined.'

I don't even need to think about it. 'No.'

She starts. 'What do you mean no?'

'You can't mess with spells.' I point at Matt. 'You see him? He's fucked because of a spell created with good intentions.' I pause, then amend my words. 'Okay, with semi-good intentions. People died. I won't do it and you shouldn't either.'

She doesn't bother to hide her fury. 'No one will die.'

'You're not a witch,' I say. 'You're not even a triber. How do you know?'

'I've worked in the magic business for years. I know when a spell is true or not! My husband was a white witch. He taught me what to look for. The spell is clean.'

'It doesn't matter.' I shake my head. For once, I'm immoveable. 'I wouldn't be in the mess I'm in now if it wasn't for that spell. I'm not going to twist another one just so that I can be cured.'

'It's not just about you,' she hisses. 'Magix is...'

'Evil. I know.' Regret fills me. 'I'm sorry.'

Frolic stares at me. 'Fair enough. There is an alternative. It's more dangerous but our terms can remain the same.'

'Go on.'

'The Magix executives know we're after them. We need to know what they're planning. Find whatever files they have on us so we can be sure we're one step ahead.'

I think of my failed attempt at breaching Streets of Fire. 'I'm not a thief. I don't have the skills to…'

Frolic interrupts me. 'I'm sure you'll think of something.' She shrugs. 'Otherwise we are done.' She may appear benign and friendly but there's an edge of steel to her.

'I'll consider it,' I say finally.

'You know,' she replies slowly, 'my husband would have liked you. He also had a strongly defined sense of what was right and wrong.' She stares at me. 'He was going to change the world. Are you?'

I ignore her question. 'What makes you think Magix killed him?'

'Because I begged him to meet with them. To do something to reverse our failing fortunes. He didn't want to go but I was adamant.' Her mouth tightens. 'The last thing I said to him was to get our money back.' Her shoulders fall. 'I never saw him again. When his body turned up and the police wanted me to identify him, I refused. I couldn't face them trying to convince me that he'd died of nothing more than a heart attack. Magix killed him. I know it did. And now that Magix has acquired my shop I have nothing left.'

'I'm sorry.'

'Do you know, I rather think you are.' Her tongue wets her lips. 'I'll be here waiting when you finish your task.'

The man who escorted away the previous supplicant emerges from the shadows. I look at him hard but I still can't work out who he is. He doesn't glance in my direction, just murmurs something in Frolic's ear. I watch them for a few moments but it's clear that the shopkeeper is done with me. I'm tempted to rush them both. I could grab Frolic and haul her plump arse to the Montserrat mansion and do whatever is necessary to make her find out if there's a cure or not. I realise that my fingers have curled into tight fists. I force myself to relax. I'm desperate, but not that desperate.

Twenty minutes later, I drop Matt back at the mansion. To my surprise, Harry D'Argneau is outside. When he sees me, his face clears.

'Bo! Where have you been?' He glances up at the imposing building. 'I thought Montserrat might have done something to you.'

Exasperated, I say, 'Like what?'

'I don't know. You can't trust bloodguzzlers. Not these days.'

'I'm a bloodguzzler.'

'You're different.'

I sigh. 'Not you too. Harry, you need to stop believing everything you read. Vampires aren't evil. They're not out for world domination and they're not even angry about what I did.' I'm tempted to tell him that Michael engineered the whole thing then I decide against it. D'Argneau already has an unhealthy obsession with the Families. 'They're the good guys,' I say eventually.

'You've not gone back to them, have you? Is that why you're here?'

I smile. 'No. Not exactly.'

'Good. Although...'

'What?'

'Well, I wondered if there might be chance for some more negotiation. You know, about what happens now, that kind of thing. You lost your flat when you were recruited, didn't you? And all your belongings?'

I nod slowly, unsure what he's getting at.

'I could sue them. Get you some compensation. We can make it public and then you'll be more likely to make a killing. Their reputation has already taken a hammering, they'll want to settle quietly and out of the court. I can make an appointment and discuss it with Lord Montserrat. In fact,' he licks his lips, 'it might be better if all the Family Heads attend. We can set up new guidelines for other vampires who are in a similar situation.'

'You're not in this for the commission or the glory, are you?'

'Huh?'

I lean in and drop my voice. 'You want access to the Heads. That's what this is about.'

He stares at me meaningfully. 'Bo, the Families keep to themselves. They've got all those secrets and all those laws. I can help them. Give them a direct line to the human world.'

I stretch up on my tiptoes and try to match his height. It doesn't work but it makes me feel better. 'You mean *you* want a direct line to them.'

He lowers his head. 'Everyone wants something.'

Suddenly there's a crash from the direction of the mansion. Both D'Argneau and I jump. He grabs my arm and I turn to see Michael standing on the threshold, glowering at us. It occurs to me that I'm standing compromisingly close to the lawyer. I pull my arm away and step back.

'Don't touch her,' Michael snarls.

I hold up both my palms. 'He's my lawyer. He's just checking everything's okay.'

'Get inside, Bo.' Michael strides towards us.

I move in front of D'Argneau. 'Again, Lord Montserrat,' I say, attempting to keep my tone light, 'you're not my boss.'

'Lord Montserrat,' D'Argneau interrupts. 'We should discuss this inside. I understand you're angry that Ms Blackman left…'

'I'm not angry.'

No, I think you're bloody furious. 'Harry,' I say nervously, 'you should go now.'

'But...'

'Please.' My voice is strained. 'I'll talk to him about a meeting. Right now, you need to leave.'

'I should stay. I don't want you to get hurt.'

'I won't. Just go.'

Michael's face is thunderous.

'Perhaps you're right,' D'Argneau says hastily. 'Give me a call in a day or two, Bo.'

I hear his footsteps as he leaves but I keep my eyes trained on Michael, where the danger lies.

'You can't do this.'

His shoulders tense and I watch him track D'Argneau's figure as the lawyer gets into his car.

'Michael, he's not done anything wrong.'

'You called him Harry,' he snaps

'So?'

'Are you fucking him?'

'Bloody hell! No, I'm not.'

He towers over me. 'You almost did before.'

'Key word,' I tell him. 'Almost. And I was under a lot of stress then.'

'You're under a lot of stress now. You've got PTSD. He could be taking advantage of you.'

Goddamnit. 'He's not.' I put my hands on my hips. 'You can't tell me what to do because I am no longer one of your vampires. And I'm not some weak little girl who needs you to step in and act like my bloody father!'

He stills. 'Your father?'

'It's like I've been out on a date and you're waiting up!'

He steps towards me. 'Is that how you think of me?' he asks quietly. 'Like I'm your father?'

'No, but you need to stop acting as if you are. I don't need you to look after me!'

His eyes gleam. 'Because you're a big strong vampire girl now?'

'Exactly!'

'Then let's see about that.'

I blink. 'Excuse me?'

He points behind me in the direction of Hyde Park. 'You and me, girlie girl. Right there.'

'You want to fight?'

He circles me like a predator. 'Damn right, I do.'

My mouth is dry. 'Then let's do it in the sparring room.' Where you're less likely to kill me because there'll be witnesses.

'The sparring room is for Montserrat vampires.' He stops and bends down to my ear. 'You're not Montserrat.'

I clench my teeth, realising there's now an audience watching us from across the road: several Montserrat faces are staring, wide-eyed. Perhaps he's right.

'Fine,' I snap. 'Let's go.' I vault back into the park and stride towards a clearing. I take off my leather jacket and hike up the dress so it's around my hips and I can manoeuvre more easily. Michael joins me, pulling his T-shirt over his head and baring his torso. He cocks his head and smiles, without humour.

'Let's dance, little girl.'

I don't waste time and launch myself at him, aiming high. He sidesteps neatly. 'Too easy,' he growls.

'Oh yeah?' I kick, snapping my heel into his shin. I'm rewarded with a groan. He throws a punch, connecting with my chest and sending me flying backwards onto the grass. I spring up. 'Is this how you get your kicks, my Lord? Beating up weak little fledglings?'

He snarls and tries again but this time I block him and swipe my elbow into his side.

'I thought you said you weren't weak,' he says, grabbing my shoulder and twisting me forward.

I use my feet to launch off his hard body and flip backwards, somersaulting away from his grip. I punch again but he catches my fist in mid-flight.

'I seem to recall the last time we did this, I had you in about two seconds flat,' he informs me.

I wrench away. 'You mean in the hospital when I was still human. You're forgetting I body-slammed you in your own office.'

He snatches hold of my arms. I try to kick but, when that doesn't work, I use my knee instead, jerking it upwards towards his groin. I think I've missed and hit his thigh but he moans in pain and collapses. Alarmed, I bend over. 'Are you…?'

He pulls the collar of my dress, yanking me on top of him. Then he rolls so we switch places. My back is on the ground while he manoeuvres his legs on either side of mine. I try to pummel him but he catches my hands easily and pushes them down.

'Classic mistake,' he whispers. 'Don't let your opponent fool you into thinking they're down.'

I kick upwards so I can free myself but I'm trapped. 'You play dirty.'

He lowers his face. 'You bet I do, Bo. Do you want to know the real reason why I was so keen for you to leave the Family?'

I stare into his glittering eyes. 'You couldn't stand the competition?'

He laughs. 'Hardly. I didn't want you to feel like you had to obey me in all things. Because when I do this, I want to know that you respond of your own free will.'

'Do what?'

'This,' he breathes. Then he kisses me.

Heat flickers in my belly. Without thinking, I twine my fingers into his hair and moan. He groans in return and deepens the kiss. His mouth is hot and tastes faintly of brandy. I feel my heart thudding while his body presses into mine. Releasing one hand, he cups my face and lifts himself up half a foot.

'Do you still think me of as your father now?'

I don't answer. Instead, I trace the tattoo on his chest, brushing his nipple with a feather-light touch. He sucks in a breath. Then there's a loud cough from behind us. Michael swears. He gets to his feet, pulling me with him, and clears his throat.

'What is it?'

I step away, flushed and hot. Ria emerges, avoiding looking directly at us. 'My Lord, there's a problem.'

'Go on.' There's an undercurrent of frustration in his voice.

'It's one of the vampette clubs. There was a fight and the police got involved.'

'I'll be right there,' he snarls.

She bows her head then almost runs back towards the mansion.

'I have to deal with this,' Michael tells me.

'I know.'

He retrieves his T-shirt and puts it back on. 'Will you go to my apartment? Can you wait for me there, Bo?'

I nod mutely. He gives me a half-smile in return. He lowers his head and plants another quick kiss on my lips. 'This isn't over,' he promises. Before I can reply, he vanishes into the night.

CHAPTER 15
CUFFED

I'm painfully aware of Michael asleep in the bed next to me. He didn't come home until some point during the day when I was out for the count. I woke up briefly when he curved an arm round my waist and pulled me against him. Unfortunately I can't sleep like that and at some point I moved away. I'm wide awake now but I can't decide whether to stay until he wakes up or get up. The knock at the door makes up my mind for me.

Gingerly, I pull myself free from the sheets, trying to stay as quiet as possible. I slept in one of Michael's shirts. It reaches almost to my knees so, after a quick check in the mirror to make sure I'm decent, I tiptoe to the door.

Connor's grinning face greets me. 'I thought you'd be here!' he says loudly.

I shush him. He winks and holds out his arm. Eyeing it as if it's an unexploded grenade, I eventually sigh and drink my fill. Nausea overtakes me and I'm unsure if I will keep down the precious blood. I dash to the kitchen sink. Damn it. This is supposed to get easier, not harder.

'Are you okay?' Connor asks, concerned.

I take a deep breath, not trusting myself to speak, and nod. After several more deep breaths, I turn to him. 'Why do you do this?' He looks puzzled. 'Offer yourself up as food. Why do you do it? What do you get out of it?'

'I told you before. I want to.'

I shake my head. I'm not going to let him get away that easily. Not this time. 'I'm not buying it,' I tell him.

'It's true. I get a kick out of it. Plus, I get paid for helping out. If I didn't do this, I'd be on the dole. Not,' he says in a rush, 'that I'm doing it just for the money. Medici offered me a lot more money.'

'Really?'

'Yeah. Lord Medici approached me,' he says cheerfully. 'He was very persuasive. Wanted me to come and join him. I'd have said yes if I wasn't already with you guys.'

I wonder if there's something special in Connor's blood. It doesn't make sense for Medici to go after a Montserrat vampette. I'm about to ask him more questions when he says, 'Some bad shit today.'

I look at him questioningly. He passes over his phone, pointing at a news article. Five Montserrat vampires got into a fight with a group of humans. Tragically it turned nasty and two of the humans died from their injuries on their way to hospital. The police released the vampires into Montserrat custody and a spokesperson made it clear that the assailants would feel the full weight of vampire law. My stomach twists. I know what that means. I wonder if Michael will dole out the sentences himself.

I rub my forehead. Why can nothing ever be cut and dried? From what I saw of the human protestors in Soho, I can imagine how things got out of hand – though that's no excuse for murdering anyone. But the thought of the resulting executions horrifies me. On the one hand, those vampires could be ex-criminals who should have known better than to get into a fight with humans. On the other... I sigh. Things were a damn sight easier when I was human.

I pass back Connor's phone. 'I've got a message for you,' he says. 'Someone called Frolic? She called the mansion and asked for it to be passed on. She's decided that time is a factor and you either bring the documents to her before dawn or she'll find someone else.'

I curse silently. She's trying to push me into making up my mind. I'm annoyed. I also fail to see what the hurry is.

'Thanks,' I tell him.

He beams. 'Should I go back to the mansion and tell Matt to wait for you?'

I think about it. I can't cope with Frolic's demands just yet. Since all the names on Templeton's list are apparently not involved in Dahlia's disappearance, I should get on with talking to her neighbours. It's already after seven in the evening. If I wait much longer they won't open their doors to answer questions. Especially when they see two vampires standing on the doorstep. It'll be faster and easier if I do it on my own. Matt's not all that strong as a vampire; he'll be safer where he is. I don't need anyone to feel threatened by his presence and be provoked into an attack, especially after the events earlier today. Sometimes there are benefits to being only five foot tall. Even as a bloodguzzler, people are less likely to view me as dangerous.

'No,' I tell him, 'it's okay. I don't need him today.'

His face clouds over. 'Are you sure?'

I nod, lead him to the door and gently push him out. Then I go back to the bedroom. Michael hasn't stirred. I grab my clothes, take them to the living room and dress. Less than five minutes later, I'm out of the door.

When I arrive in the Templetons' neighbourhood, I check their house. It still seems undisturbed since my last visit so I head to the well-lit home on the left. A child's bike is propped against the wall, pink streamers tied to the handles. I don't know if having kids inside will make the occupants more or less likely to talk to me. I ring their doorbell to find out. A harassed looking mother opens the door. 'Yes?'

I do my best to look friendly. 'My name is Bo Blackman. I'm investigating the disappearance of Dahlia Templeton from next door.'

There are several squawks from inside and a child's yell, 'Mum! Derek hit me!'

The woman takes a deep breath, wiping her hands on her apron. She's so distracted by her children that I don't think she's noticed I'm not human. 'Are you police?' she inquires.

'No. I'm a private investigator.'

There's another barrage of shouts from within. She half turns and yells back, 'Stop fighting and get your homework done!' Then she sighs. 'Do you have kids?'

She's definitely not spotted I'm a vampire. I shake my head.

'Well, count yourself lucky.'

Even though I know she doesn't really mean it, I feel a bit sad. I stick to the topic, however. 'Did you know Dahlia?'

'Sure. We met up at least once a week for coffee. You know, when she wasn't...' her voice trails off.

When it's clear she's not going to complete her sentence, I prompt her. 'When she wasn't what?'

'Out.'

There's more to this than meets the eye. 'Out doing what?'

'Look, it's really none of my business,' she begins.

'Dahlia might be in danger,' I say softly.

She snorts. 'The only danger Dahlia Templeton is in is not remembering which hotel she's left her knickers in.'

'She was having an affair?'

The woman lowers her voice. 'They were at it like rabbits. I can't believe her husband never caught on.'

'Do you know who the man is?'

'Simon someone.'

'Can you remember his last name?'

There's a scream. Her face twists. 'I'm sorry, I have to go.'

'Wait! His name?'

She shrugs. 'All I know is he's a copper who works out of Belgrave. Now, I really do have to go.'

'Thank you,' I start to say, but she's already closing the door.

I rub my chin thoughtfully. Despite Stephen Templeton's dodgy dealings, perhaps Dahlia's kidnap is the result of her own actions. A jealous wife maybe? Or this Simon guy himself? It could even be Stephen Templeton: he might have found about the affair, killed her and made it look like an abduction. But why would he not tell the police if that was the case? It would make his story far more plausible.

I switch to the house on the right, hoping I'll be able to talk to someone who knows more about Dahlia's extra-marital affairs. When this door opens, however, it's a perky looking kid who answers. 'Yes?' Her mouth drops. 'You're a vampire! That's so cool! I want to be a vampire when I grow up.'

'Stella! What did I tell you about answering the door to strangers?' A man appears, drying his hands with a towel. When he sees me he drops it. 'Stella, go back into the house.'

'But Dad...'

'Now.' She puts on a face but does as she's told.

I guess I'm no longer incognito. 'Hi. I'm Bo Blackman. I'm here to investigate...'

'You're not welcome.' He slams the door in my face.

I grit my teeth and knock again. He opens it a crack. 'We've got children! You need to get out of here before I call the police!'

'I can't come in unless you invite me, sir.'

'I'm not fucking well inviting you!' he hisses.

'What I meant,' I explain patiently, 'is that even if I wanted to hurt you, I couldn't because I can't come in until you invite me.'

His face pales. 'Hurt us? What have we done to you?'

'No, I...'

He shuts the door again. Through the window I see him go to the phone and pick it up, and realise he's making good on his threat. Arse. The police won't arrest me but they'll make damned sure I do nothing else to bother the good people of this neighbourhood. I wonder how they'll react when they spot Templeton's fake crime scene tape.

There's nothing else I can do here for now so I make myself scarce. I keep thinking about the look on Stella's dad's face when he realised that I was a vampire. Revulsion. Hatred. Fear. All the things I feel about myself.

I remember that the Magix headquarters are between here and Belgrave police station. Maybe it wouldn't hurt to make a short stop, just in case.

When I reach the imposing building, I take several minutes to walk round it. It's a gleaming edifice of steel and glass, not dissimilar to where Streets of Fire is housed. The difference between the two is that the internet company purports to be run by humans, when in fact it's run by the most terrifying of triber species, whereas Magix pretends it's a triber corporation and, as far as I've uncovered so far, is actually wholly human. Ironically, the only group that's honest about who they are and what they're doing is the vampires – and they're the ones who are attacked for being evil.

I'm tempted to try another covert entry. After all, the more I do, the better I'll become. With Frolic's unrealistic deadline looming over me, however, I decide against it. If she wants the information by dawn then she can damn well live with the methods by which I obtain it. I grin at the thought of her face if she knew what I was up to.

I stride back to the front doors. The first five floors are given up to the Magix emporium and, unsurprisingly by this hour, they're dark and closed. The floors higher up are still well lit, presumably occupied by another company that demands that its employees work late. It makes my life easier. I bang loudly and continuously on the reinforced glass door, startling several passers-by. I keep thumping my fist until a security guard appears, peering at me from the other side.

'We're shut,' he mouths.

My grin widens and I bare my teeth, allowing my fangs to grow. He jumps back.

'I want to speak to the boss,' I yell.

He gestures rudely so I run my tongue over the sharp edges of my teeth as if promising further action. The guard disappears. I lift my fist and continue banging.

It takes less than ten minutes. Eventually the guard returns with a buddy by his side – and a woman wearing a blush-pink trouser suit. On anyone else it would look ridiculous but her olive skin allows her to carry it off. She says something to the guards and they scowl, then one of them mutters into a radio. I hear a click as the front door is unlocked.

I incline my head in acknowledgement. The woman pulls the door open; apparently she's braver than the goons by her side. 'May I help you?'

I retract my fangs. 'I would like to speak to whoever's in charge.'

'You can make an appointment for later in the week and I'm sure Mr Connell will be able to free up some time.'

'I'm under time constraints. It's imperative that I meet with him now.'

'He's not here.'

I smile. 'Really? Then whose limousine is parked round the back? The one with the rather distinctive number plate?' I frown as if trying to recall, then snap my fingers. 'MAG1X. That's it.'

Her mouth tightens. 'Which Family are you from?'

I look her in the eyes. 'I'm not with a Family.'

The only indication that she's surprised is the slight furrow that appears on her forehead. She looks me up and down. 'So you're the one. I thought you'd be taller.'

It's my turn to be startled. Outside of the five Families, no one is supposed to know about my defection; the announcement isn't taking place until next week. The thought that Magix has somehow penetrated the inner workings of the Families is disturbing.

'We know more than you think, Ms Blackman.'

Somehow I doubt that. I raise my chin. 'I need to meet with Mr Connell in private. Right now.'

'To what does the meeting pertain?'

'That's between me and him. But he'll want to hear what I've got to say.'

She gazes at me thoughtfully. 'I can allow that.'

'Ms Swanson, I don't think that's a very good idea,' the first guard interrupts.

She throws him such a quashing look that I'm impressed. I could learn something from this woman. 'It's the perfect opportunity to field test our latest item. If you're going to enter, Ms Blackman, we need to take precautions.' She holds up a set of handcuffs. They appear simple enough but I can sense the magic clinging to them. The fact that she brought them with her, however, suggests she was prepared to let me to enter all along.

I'm wary but prepared to submit to her demands. 'No problem,' I state confidently.

Swanson jerks her head and the two guards walk forward, neither of them looking happy. They take the handcuffs and I hold out my wrists helpfully. The guards snap them on, the slightest tremor visible in their hands as they do so.

The second the cold metal touches my skin, I feel it. I touch my fangs with my tongue again and realise that I can no longer make them grow. I try to lift my hands but my movements feel slow and sluggish. Swanson watches me carefully.

'How do you feel?' she inquires. I give her a dirty look. She claps her hands together. 'Excellent! Our spell techs promised they'd work but it's not easy to find test subjects.'

I find my voice. 'What the hell are these?'

'Vampire inhibitors.' She holds up a hand. 'I know, I know, the name isn't very catchy. We've been toying with the idea of calling them Bloodguzzler Bonds. Or perhaps something more generic, to promote more of a sense of safety and well-being. What do you think of "Protectors"?'

'Why?'

She laughs. 'Because they'll protect humans from nasty vampires, of course. Now we know they work, we can put them into mass production almost immediately. They'll fly off the shelves.' She gives me a wink. 'Thanks to the current climate of fear.'

Bloody hell. I stare at her wide-eyed. There's been little in the past to restrain vampires. The thought of what these things could do if they land in the hands of the Families' enemies is terrifying.

'Don't look so worried, Ms Blackman. After all,' she smiles, 'people still have to get close enough to put them on to their would-be vampire attackers.'

Until the Magix techs work out a way to make the spell attach itself to a weapon as well as to restraints, I think to myself. It's probably only a matter of time. Assuming that is, they've not already managed it.

'How did you make these?' I ask. I need to find out as much as I can about them so I can pass on the information to the Families.

Swanson laughs. 'Oh, they've taken years of development. We don't let any products onto the street until we are convinced of their efficacy. Usually we spend considerable time trialling them, often on ourselves and own employees. Of course, it's harder with products that target vampires. There aren't any bloodguzzlers working here.' She arches an eyebrow in my direction. 'Mr O'Connell urged us to find suitable test subjects. He wants to make the world a safer place for everyone. He's a true idealist.'

I swallow my nausea at her fawning tone. She moves away from the entrance and gestures me inside. I can still move but I feel as if I have a ton of bricks weighing me down. Flanked by the two guards, I shuffle forward. Despite Swanson's words, I doubt I'm the first vampire these bloody things have been tried on but I'm damned if I'm going to let anyone see just how much they affect me.

It takes us a long time to reach the lifts. Swanson swipes her card while I stare at the lift doors. One side is painted with a huge black-magic symbol, while the other side is emblazoned with a white-magic sign. They look incongruous together.

The doors open and Swanson walks into the lift. The guards are taking no chances: they grip my arms in case the spell on the cuffs fails. If the magic starts to fade, I could probably take them out in about three seconds flat but I play the role of meek little vampire and don't react. I sense that, given the chance, guard number one would be more than happy to slap me around for a few hours.

We finally emerge on the top floor where the carpets are deep and expensive and the walls are filled with familiar looking pieces of art. Profits must be high. Then again, it's no wonder when the company is so adept at putting the competition out of business.

I'm dropped on a stylish but remarkably uncomfortable sofa in the waiting area. A large television screen flickers into life. At first I think it's showing an art-house film, then I realise it's not a film at all but the CCTV footage of me inside Fingertips and Frolics. It starts with my first foray, with Frolic moving towards me. I'm thankful there's no sound and the camera is positioned in such a way that our lips can't be read. The people here already know too much about me as it is; I don't need them to realise how desperate I am to find a cure for vampirism. Even if they knew where to find one, it would give them too strong a hold over me.

The screen flips to my illegal entry into the now-empty store. My movements are tracked, up to the point where my face looms into the camera and is distorted by its proximity. Then the screen goes dark as I successfully cover the lens with the disposable coffee cup. Watching myself is uncomfortable.

'We've had some issues with the proprietor of that shop,' a deep voice says. There's no rancour in his tone. If anything, he sounds pleased by the fact that Magix is important enough to have 'issues' with other magic businesses.

I try to stand up but I'm foiled by whatever it is the cuffs are doing to my system. Their effect seems to be growing stronger.

'Stay seated.' The man smiles. 'I understand how overpowering the spell can be.'

'Mr O'Connell?' I ask.

He sits opposite me. 'Indeed.' He puts his palms together as if in prayer and gazes at me speculatively. 'Are you working for this woman? Frolic?'

I consider my answer. 'Let's just say I'm doing her a small favour.'

'You know, it's not our fault her business had to shut down.'

'Really?' I say, disbelief in my voice.

'It's true. Internet sales, the recent recession, consumer habits.' He shrugs. 'Many factors are responsible. Not to mention her own poor management. I feel for her, though. How is she doing?' He seems eager for information about her.

'Fine,' I answer shortly. 'Did you kill her husband?' I keep my tone free from accusation but I watch his reaction carefully.

'Is he dead?' There's the oddest flicker of amusement in his eyes. 'Goodness, no. Whatever gave you that idea?' I can't tell whether he's lying or not. He leans towards me. 'Is that why you're here?'

I shake my head. 'No. I'm here for a little *quid pro quo.*'

I can tell I've piqued his interest although he tries to keep his expression bland. 'Go on.'

'One of your spells is about to be compromised.'

I leave my words hanging in the air, eventually forcing him to fill the silence. His eyes shift. 'Which one?'

'Give me fifteen minutes' full access to your files on Frolic and I'll tell you.'

He looks at me as if I've suddenly sprouted green horns. 'Absolutely not.'

I shrug. 'It's your funeral. I hope you have decent liability insurance.'

O'Connell's face twists. 'How do I know you're telling the truth?'

'You don't.' My gaze is open.

'Does Frolic know you're doing this?'

I smile and cock my head. 'She asked me to get the files for her. She didn't give me any pointers as to how to go about it.'

'She doesn't know you're here, talking directly to me?'

'No.'

A muscle jerks in his cheek. 'So why are you doing this? Why not break in and steal the files?'

'I'll be honest with you, I've not had much success in that area lately. But while I don't like you, Mr O'Connell, and I don't like Magix, I have no desire to see thousands of people suffer thanks to corporate espionage.'

'What makes you think we won't find the compromised spell now that we know about it?'

'Go ahead,' I say softly. 'Be my guest. Try and find it on your own.' I link my fingers together, giving the impression that I'm relaxed and uncaring. 'How many spelled items do you sell, by the way?'

He frowns. 'Our files are electronic. I'm not giving you access to our system.'

'I can assure, Mr O'Connell, I'm no computer genius. You can stand over my shoulder and watch if you wish.'

'For all I know you could send a virus to attack our entire system.'

'I don't have the knowhow.'

'Perhaps not. But you may have others at your disposal who do.'

I think of Rogu3. I'm glad I didn't involve him in this. 'Those are my terms.'

He mulls it over. 'No. It's too dangerous. I'll print out the files for you.'

'How do I know you'll give me full disclosure?'

He smiles. 'You don't.'

I sense that this is far as I'm going to get with him. I give an almost imperceptible nod. 'Okay then. Give me the files and I'll tell you where to look for the duff spell.'

O'Connell rises. I watch him vanish into a nearby office. This might actually work. I close my eyes for a moment. Something brushes past my cheek. I jump, snapping my eyes open. When I see who it is, I let out a quiet snarl.

'Bloodguzzler,' whispers the security guard.

'What do you want?'

He reaches out stubby fingers and trails them down my cheek. I flinch and try to move away but my energy has been sapped to the point where my efforts are feeble. The guard fingers a loose curl.

'Your boss is right over there,' I tell him.

The guard's eyes gleam. 'He won't mind.'

I have the horrible feeling he's probably right. 'You like your women tied up and helpless? Does that make you feel like a man?' I taunt.

He ignores me. 'I always wanted to fuck a vampire.' He forces his index finger inside my mouth while his other hand travels to my breast and squeezes it painfully. 'I've heard the turning makes your pussy tight, like a virgin's.'

I open my mouth a little more and bite down as hard as I can on his finger. He screams like a stuck pig. 'I might not have the use of my fangs, you prick,' I spit, 'but I can still bite.'

He pulls back a hand to punch me in the face. I prepare myself for the pain but O'Connell appears from behind and grabs his fist. 'She's only in those cuffs while she's in our building. The moment she steps outside she'll be free,' he says to the guard. 'Unless you want to spend the rest of your life hiding behind these four walls, I suggest you rethink your actions.'

The guard sags. 'Yes sir,' he mumbles. He stumbles away.

O'Connell bows. 'I apologise. That shouldn't have happened.'

I'm spitting fire. 'Some great company this is. Is sexual assault always on the menu?'

'I'll have him removed immediately.' From the expression in his eyes, he's not just talking about giving the guard the sack.

'And people worry about vampires,' I hiss.

'Don't be so naïve, Ms Blackman. We humans may lack your physical superiority but we can be far more dangerous.'

Despite my revulsion, I pull the shreds of my dignity together. 'I'm not a fucking monster. Fire him and hand him over to the police so they can make sure he doesn't try this kind of thing on anyone else.'

O'Connell purses his lips. 'If that's what you want.'

I want to rip the guard's throat out and watch him bleed to death. That's the reason why victims should never be responsible for doling out punishment. Unable to trust myself, I glare at O'Connell.

He nods. 'So be it.' He tosses a manila folder into my lap. 'Here are your files.' There's a glimmer of satisfaction in his face. 'I've added in a little something extra, just for you.'

'What do you mean?' I ask warily.

'We don't just keep files on wannabe witches, Ms Blackman. There's a sample in there of what else we have on offer. Information can be a valuable currency. If you wish for more, come and visit us again.'

'You're not giving it away for free.'

His smile doesn't reach his eyes. 'This taster, so to speak, is gratis. I'm sure we can come to an arrangement if you want more.'

'Unlikely.' I struggle to my feet, just avoiding toppling over.

'Never say never. You were recruited by Montserrat, were you not?'

I look him directly in the eyes. I've had enough of this place. 'You have a new line coming out.' I look down at the handcuffs.

'Other than your vampire inhibitors that is. Something to do with glamour spells?'

'Yes. They're more popular with men than women these days. Everyone wants to look,' he pauses as if searching for the right word, 'buff.'

'There is going to be a problem with it,' I say.

'What's the problem?'

'Frolic has the ingredients. She's trying to recruit someone to break in and subvert one of them.'

'Thank you,' O'Connell says, after a long moment. 'Ms Swanson?' he calls over my shoulder.

She moves up soundlessly. 'Yes, sir?'

'Free Ms Blackman. I believe she can be trusted to make her own way out.'

She passes a wand across my wrists and the cuffs unclasp and fall to the carpet. I rub my wrists. The sensation is rather like when X did his mind-sucking thing. I stretch my limbs and flex them carefully. There seem to be no side-effects; once the cuffs are removed, recovery is instantaneous.

'Thank you,' I mutter.

'Please deliver a message to Frolic from me. Tell her that this is for the best. Her obsession with her little shop was unhealthy. She's free now. She can do whatever she wants.'

'What if she wants is to destroy you.'

He looks away. 'She probably does,' he says softly. 'I'm not – we're not – the bad guys, however. We're making the world a safer place.' There's an appeal in his expression. 'A better place.'

'You're making me feel all warm and fuzzy.' I give him a false smile then, without another glance, turn and walk back to the lift. The guard who assaulted me is standing there, visibly shaking. I knee him swiftly in the groin. He screams in pain and collapses. Then I leave.

CHAPTER 16

TATTOO TALES

I'm still trembling when I pull up several streets away. The anger I feel at the guard's actions is almost overwhelming. I rub furiously at my cheek where he touched me. I'm a goddamn vampire – how does he treat human women? I make a note to check up on whether O'Connell makes good on his promise to hand the guard over to the police. If he doesn't, this won't be our only encounter. I calm down as best as I can, then walk into the twenty-four hour newsagents on the corner and use their photocopier to make a copy of the files on Frolic.

While I wait, I flick through the extra papers that O'Connell gave me. I stare in shock at the top sheet: it appears to be a printout of the Montserrat accounts. Not only am I aghast that anyone could access such information, let alone a dodgy place like Magix, but I'm stunned by the figures. The Montserrat Family has close to nine hundred million pounds in its coffers. I knew they are rich but that amount is staggering. If Magix chooses to release this information to the rest of the world, it's hardly going to appease the masses.

Deciding not to look through the rest of the Montserrat papers, I roll them up and stuff them inside my leather jacket.

I'll pass them to Michael later and he can decide what to do; it's not really my call. I buy an envelope and stamps, and mail the copy of Frolic's files to my grandfather's house. A little insurance never hurts.

Five minutes later, I paste a smile on my face and stroll into Belgrave police station. 'Hi!' I say cheerily. 'Is Simon in?'

I receive a shocked look.

'Yes,' I say, without missing a beat, 'I'm a vampire. I'm looking for Simon. I'm helping him with some inquiries.' Well, technically he's helping me, but what's a misplaced pronoun or two?

'Simon Beauvoit or Simon Raval?'

Bugger it. 'The good-looking one.' I wink, keeping my fingers crossed that I'm right. 'In his forties perhaps?'

The sergeant glares at me suspiciously. Unfortunately for me he knows how to do his job properly. 'Sergeant Raval or Inspector Beauvoit?'

I have a fifty-fifty shot. I take a stab in the dark and guess. 'Sergeant Raval.'

'I'll see if he's available. What's your name?'

'Bo Blackman.'

His head jerks. 'Blackman?'

'That's what I said.'

His eyes narrow but he doesn't comment on my lack of a Family name. I'm getting a bit tired of this routine. Maybe I should just abbreviate my name to Bo. If it works for Madonna and Prince, why can't it work for me?

'Please take a seat,' he says finally.

I can feel the policeman's eyes on my back as I turn. He definitely doesn't trust me. The small room is almost identical to the one I was in with Michael when we handed over Samuel Lewis, aka Slick, the feather mugger. I wondering if there are particular guidelines for the premises, like McDonald's, and the government is aiming for reassuring conformity. There's a rack of shiny leaflets on one side of the wall, filled with recruitment pleas for special constables and tips on how to avoid being burgled. On the other side, there's the desk sergeant's spot and to the left of that a keypad-locked door leading into the station itself. As I stare at the door, something tugs at my memory and I frown.

The door opens and a kindly face appears. The wires in my brain connect and my insides turn to ice.

'Ms Blackman? I'm Sergeant Raval.'

I know instinctively that this isn't Dahlia's Simon. He's too old and too damned nice. At this point in time, however, I don't care. I stand up and shake his hand. 'I'm sorry. I've made a mistake.'

He looks confused but I don't have time for niceties. I spin round and walk straight back out again. I remember now where I saw Frolic's henchman from Hyde Park: he was in the police station when we brought in Samuel Lewis. He was leaving while we were scuffling around with Lewis and the helpful offi-cer. He'd come out from the secure door then saw us and made an abrupt return inside – meaning he works for the police too. I dig through my memory, trying to remember everything from that night and think of the scrawled hex the other copper showed me during my second visit. He also told me where Samuel Lewis lives. Or rather lived.

I pat my jacket, making sure the original files are still there. It's barely eleven o'clock; I've got bags of time before dawn and Easthouse Road is only a couple of miles away. I look back at the police station, feeling a trickle of guilt that I'm not putting more effort into Dahlia's case. I can't help thinking she's prob-ably safe and sound, and wrapped up between the legs of Inspector Simon Beauvoit rather than in danger. Besides, the faster I can sort out this mess with Frolic, the better.

I glance up and down the street to check I'm safe. There's no one close. I swallow hard, wondering if I'm getting paranoid. The trouble is that I don't think I am.

I MAKE it to Easthouse Road in record time. Parking Ursus's bike, I pocket the keys, sprint up to the fifth floor and hammer on the door. From within, I hear a baby's cry. A tired looking girl barely out of her teens opens the door and stares out. Her hair is limp and there are dark circles under her eyes.

'You woke my baby! Who the hell are you? Who the fuck...' She pales and takes a step back as she registers that I'm a vampire.

'I need to talk you about Samuel,' I say urgently. For a moment she looks confused. 'Slick!' I amend. 'Slick! I need to talk to you about Slick!'

'He's dead.' Her voice is flat.

'I know. Please, hear me out.' The baby continues to wail. 'Are you his wife?'

'What if I am?'

'Did he talk to you about what he was doing the night he died?'

'No.' She starts to close the door.

'Wait! Please. Did he say anything at all? Were there any clues about what he was doing?'

'He was on a job, alright?'

'What kind of job?'

'Look, he wasn't an angel. I know that. Just go away,' she mutters.

I shake my head. 'I can't do that.' I take a deep breath and try to slow down. 'What's your name?' She stares at me. 'I'm not going to hurt you. I can't even come in.' I wave my hand at the threshold as if to prove it. 'But I think I know who killed him.'

Her eyes are despondent. 'What does it matter? He's dead. Knowing who did it isn't going to bring him back.'

'No,' I say softly. 'But it might stop them from hurting anyone else.'

'Suzanne,' she says, 'my name is Suzanne. Slick liked to call me Suze.' Her eyes well up. 'He wasn't all that bad. He was a good father. He looked after us. He was just trying to make some extra money, that's all.'

A knot of sympathy rises in my chest. 'How?'

'There was a woman. He was supposed to go after her and take some feather from her. He wouldn't have hurt her. He wouldn't have done that.' Her hands tense by her sides. 'It was just a shitty feather,' she says quietly.

'Who asked him to do it?'

'I dunno. Slick said it was someone with a stupid name. I can't remember. I'm not sure he even told me.'

'Frolic?' I scan her face, searching it for the truth. 'Was it Frolic?'

'If you know then why did you ask?'

'I'm sorry.' I reach out to touch her, then remember that she's still behind the threshold of her home and I can't. 'I'm sorry,' I repeat. 'I had to be sure.'

She shrugs. 'Whatever.'

The door closes and I'm left in the corridor. A pain shoots through my stomach and I bend double. Samuel Lewis, Slick, whatever he was called, wasn't an innocent. But he's still dead because of me. Frolic gave that woman a green feather like mine as an IOU for obtaining the recipe for Magix's glamour spell. Then Frolic paid Slick to steal the feather so she wouldn't have to pay the woman. Considering what she theoretically owes me for these files, she could have promised anything as payment. A bit of money thrown in Slick's direction would have been easy in comparison. Frolic probably didn't plan to have him killed but when he ended up in custody it would have been the easy choice. Especially when she already had an insider to do the job. Who needs a spell to magic away a vital piece of evidence or to draw a hex on the wall of a cell when you have your own policeman on the inside prepared to do it for you? And now that I have the files Frolic wants, she'll be sending someone after me.

I straighten my shoulders. She can send whoever she damn well wants. I'll be ready.

UNFORTUNATELY FOR ME the attack comes sooner rather than later. I speed out of Easthouse, intent on getting back to the Montserrat mansion to retrieve the feather before I contact Frolic. I zip through the darkened streets, paying little attention to anything other than the late night traffic and the bundle of papers stuffed away in my jacket. That's probably why I don't notice the wire stretching across the road a few blocks away from Hyde Park until it's almost too late. It's only thanks to the owl hooting in a nearby tree, and my automatic glance towards it, that I spot the glint of steel. My reactions overtake coherent thought and I leap upwards in the split second before the wire cuts through my body and I end up in two halves, sprawled across the road. The bike spins away, crashing into a parked car, while I land several feet away in an ungainly heap.

As I stagger to my feet, something sharp skims by, cutting the side of my face before embedding itself into a tree. I leap backwards, using the tree to block any more attacks, and examine the object. It's a bloody shuriken, stuck fast into the bark, its lethal spiky edges still on display round one side. I shiver. This doesn't look good.

There's another whirring sound and I just manage to pull my exposed fingers away before they're sliced by another spinning weapon. I can't get a visual on my assailant; at this point all I can think is that it's a sodding ninja warrior - though as we are not on the streets of seventeenth-century Tokyo, that's an unlikely conclusion.

Not knowing who I'm up against puts me at a disadvantage. I look at the tree then I leap, grabbing a low branch. I swing up, doing everything I can to keep the thickest part of the trunk between me and my assailant. I may be a vampire but I'm still a fledgling; I heal quickly but I remain vulnerable. The wrong shot and it'll be curtains.

I scoot up as far as I can and peek out from the branches. There's a dark figure about thirty metres away. It's unlikely that Frolic will send a human after me – she'll pay someone more skilled at triber action. I wonder whether their intention is to maim or to kill. When another shuriken flies past my exposed face, I get my answer.

I twist round to the other side of the tree. I get lucky and a passing car with headlights on full beam swings across the road and highlights my attacker. Clad in black and with most of their face covered, they are indeed wearing what appears to be traditional ninja garb. I'm fairly certain it's nothing more than an ill-fitting costume, however, as I can just make out the edge of a tattoo on their right cheek where the dark material is slightly loose. I suck in a breath. Another damn black witch. The fact that I'm a Blackman is probably a bonus for them.

I have little defence against magic. I can dodge what is thrown my way but that's about it. What I need now is to be on the offensive. That thought solidifies when there's a sudden crackling sound from underneath me and I realise that the tree is on fire. Cursing, I somersault backwards, landing on my feet. There's scant other cover so, keeping my head down, I run towards the car into which the bike smashed. I start to unscrew the cap on the fuel tank as quickly as I can. Two can play the fire game. My fingers fumble and I hear footsteps getting closer. I grit my teeth and try harder.

'Little Blackman,' a voice coos. 'I only want the files. Give them to me and you can go.'

I roll my eyes. Yeah, right. I finish unscrewing the cap and toss it into the witch's path. He throws another shuriken in the direction of the cap and it explodes in a hail of sparks. Great. Spelled ninja weapons. I keep my focus and unzip the top of my jacket to make sure the folder with the original papers inside is still secure. Then I grab the roll of Montserrat documents and shove them into the open fuel tank. The reek of petrol when I withdraw them tells me I've been successful. I turn round and eye the burning tree. If I sprint it'll take me about two seconds to get back to it. I get ready.

'Little Blackman,' the voice calls out again.

I don't wait for him to finish. Instead I run, head down and body low. I'm a fingertip's length from the flames when something slams into my chest and brings me down. Despite the force of the throw, the blades don't penetrate my jacket but I can feel the heat spread as the flames lick against the leather. I close my eyes and let my body go limp. Then I hope for the best.

The footsteps get nearer. I'm still clutching the roll of papers in my right hand but I make sure my grip is loose so I appear unconscious. Michael taught me well.

'Vampires are not so tough after all,' sneers my attacker.

There's a blast of pain in my chest as he kicks me. I gasp and allow my body to jolt to the side with the assault. When I hear the crackle and hiss of burning paper, I know I've hit pay dirt. I curl my fingers round the now-flaming roll and thrust it upwards, jumping to my feet at the same time. The burning brand slams into the witch's face. He screeches, blinded by the flames, and I grab his body and throw him headfirst into the tree. Loose paper and burning branches fly in several directions.

I pat furiously at the burning leather on my chest; thankfully the flames go out then I turn to grab the witch. Unfortunately it's too late and I cover my nose with my cuff as the stench of roasting flesh fills the air. The witch writhes and yells for a few seconds before falling silent and still. Sickened, I back away.

'I'm sorry,' I whisper. 'You didn't give me any choice.'

As I turn to run before anyone else shows up, my eye catches one sheet from the Montserrat roll. Only the edge is on fire so I stamp it out, then examine it. It's a photo – which is probably why it didn't burst into flames as fast as the other papers. There are five people in the frame: three of them appear to be Chinese and are very, very dead. Their clothing is old, probably 1950s, and I'm fairly certain that the one nearest to the camera has had his head severed from his body. There are two vampires to the side. The photo is black and white so it's impossible to tell what Family colours they're wearing. It doesn't matter though; I don't need colour to tell me who they are. The one on the right with the frown is Medici, while the one of the left with the well-tailored suit, easy smile and dimpled cheek is Michael Montserrat.

I can't tear my eyes away from his happy grin. He's standing next to three dead humans and he's laughing. I think about Cheung's fear when I told him I was originally Montserrat. Now I'm starting to understand why he was afraid.

I PULL myself together and hurry back to the Montserrat mansion. It's the last place on earth I want to be right now but I need to get my feather. I keep pulling out the half-burnt photo and staring at it. It's just a photo, I don't know anything about the context, but the chill down my spine won't go away. I know that Michael is scary – he wouldn't be the bloody Head of the Family if he weren't – but taking pleasure in murder is an entirely different proposition.

Until I speak to Michael, I have no way of knowing what happened. The photo suggests that he slaughtered three people. Maybe they were Triads, maybe they weren't; either way, I still don't know the full story. And am I really in a position to judge after what I just did? I think about the carnage I left behind. I snuffed out a black witch's life. I'm responsible for someone's death. Yes, it was self-defence and, yes, I took no pleasure from it, but I still did it.

I run my hands through my hair in frustration. I can't think of things in terms of black and white. There are always a million shades in between unless, of course, you're talking about magic.

I freeze in my tracks. Frolic works with white witches. Her shop only catered to white witches. Why would she hire a black witch to do her dirty work? It doesn't make any sense. Black and white witches don't mix and they never have.

My heart rate increases. The adrenaline that coursed through my system during the fight kicks back into action. I need to see that corpse. Damning myself for a fool, I sprint back in the direction I came from. As soon as I get near, I shimmy up a lamppost and spring to a low rooftop then slow my steps and run in a half crouch. When I spot the van, I know I'm too late. I snarl quietly and get closer. Three figures, also dressed ninja-style, are beside the flaming tree. Two grab hold of the dead witch's corpse, one at the feet and the other at the head, while the third raises his hands and starts to mutter, chanting a spell to extinguish the still-flickering flames. I sneak towards them. I have scant seconds left.

When I'm as close as I dare, I get down on my belly and peer over the edge of the roof. The corpse carriers struggle to maintain their grip on their companion's body and open the van's back doors at the same time. One of them says something while the other nods, and together they lower the body to the ground. The witch's body flops lifelessly, the head lolling in my direction. In the dying embers of the fire, I see that the material covering the witch's face has burnt away. His skin is blackened and charred but there's no mistaking the evidence. He has two tattoos, one on his right cheek and one on his left. He's not a black witch or a white witch. He's both.

CHAPTER 17

LIFE AND DEATH

I drum my fingers impatiently on the desk. 'I know it feels like it's the middle of the night, O'Shea, but it's almost morning. And this is important. You dabble in magic. What do you know about the differences between black and white?'

'You're kidding me, right, Bo? Everyone knows what the differences are.'

'Humour me,' I say grimly, staring at the charred and useless pages from Frolic's files. Not only did my leather jacket have a gaping hole where the witch's burning shuriken hit me, but the flames had effectively destroyed the only leverage I had.

He sighs. 'Black witches deal in black magic. Voodoo, necromancy, maleficium, that kind of thing. Modern blacks descend directly from the Knights Templar. It's thanks to the Catholic church's hatred of their actions that black magic practitioners were accused of Satanism and hunted down for years.'

'And white witches?'

'Scrying, alchemy, communing with spirits. White witches can trace their lineage back to shamans in prehistoric times.

They argue that their magic is more pure because they have a longer history.'

'You're not a witch. You made spells.'

'Anyone can create a spell. It's simple chemistry half the time. The witches' powers go beyond mere tokens and potions though.'

'The enhancement spell. Was it black or white?'

'Bo, why are dredging this all up again? I'm steering clear of magic. Lord Montserrat would have my head if I tried anything again.'

I think of the decapitated corpse in the photo then firmly push the image away. 'Was it both?'

'Eh?'

'Were you using both white and black magic?'

'That's impossible. My spell was white.'

'Why?'

'It was a form of alchemy. I've never tried black magic spells, there's no money in them unless you have enough power to match a witch. Although...'

'No,' I say impatiently, 'why is it impossible?'

'It just is. It's like oil and water. You can try to mix the two but it simply won't work.'

'What would happen if someone did?'

'Bo, what is this about?'

'Please, Devlin, just answer the question.'

He's quiet for a moment. 'You only call me that when you're worried.'

I blink. 'Excuse me?'

'Devlin. You only call me Devlin when there's bad shit around.'

I tighten my fingers round the phone. 'Devlin, what would happen if someone tried to mix black and white magic?'

'Probably nothing. They would nullify each other. Cancel each other out. I'm sure people have tried in the past.'

'What would happen if someone found a way to use both together without that happening?'

'Then the power they'd have would be unstoppable.' He sighs. 'But Bo, it can't be done.'

I swallow hard. 'What if a black witch and a white witch had children?'

'Seriously?' he scoffs derisively. 'They hate each other. That would never happen.'

'If...'

'If it happened the resulting baby would be either black or white. It would depend on whose magic was stronger. Not all witches are created equal, you know.' He laughs to himself. 'The Janus is a myth.'

I freeze. 'The what?'

'The Janus. The two-sided god.'

I clench my jaw. Or the person who, according to Mother, was named by Samuel Lewis's ghost as the one responsible for his death. Goddamnit. I hang up the phone and stare into space.

'Penny for them?'

I look up, giving Beth a half smile. 'Hey.'

'And here was me thinking you couldn't wait to get away from us.'

'Eh?'

She pulls up a chair next to me. 'Us Montserrat vampires. You keep coming back.' She arches an eyebrow. 'Are you regretting your decision to leave?'

I shake my head. 'No,' I say distantly. 'I just came to get something.'

'And run up our phone bill in the meantime.'

I think of how much money is secreted away in the Montserrat accounts and snort. 'I think the Family can cover it.'

Beth grins at me. 'Lord Montserrat is in his office. He's in a bad mood though,' she cautions. 'Although that's not surprising considering all that's going on.'

I suddenly remember he was called away to deal with more conflict. 'Was anyone hurt?'

'Not seriously. Thank goodness. Things are pretty tense around here.'

'I can imagine,' I murmur. I stand up and stretch. Dawn's getting nearer; I need to confront Frolic sooner rather than later. 'What's your opinion on witches, Beth?'

She blows out her cheeks. 'I've never really thought about them much. Witches are just ... there. Like flies. They're kind of annoying but they don't really do any harm.'

'Did you know any? Before you turned. Did you have any friends who were witches? Or,' I shift uncomfortably, 'any clients?'

Beth laughs and puts a reassuring hand on my arm. 'I'm not ashamed of what I used to be, Bo. And, yes, I had a few witchy clients. They were all white. Black witches wouldn't touch me once I'd offered my services to a white witch first.'

'What did you think of that?'

'The split between black magic and white magic?'

I nod.

She shrugs. 'It's just the way things are. There's a split between the five Families. A split between Agathos and Kakos daemons.' Her face twists. 'A split between humans and vampires.'

'You think we'd all be able to get along,' I say, as much to myself as to her.

'I don't know what hallucinogenic drugs you've been smoking lately, Bo Blackman, but that's never going to happen.'

'Why not?'

'People – and by people I mean tribers as well as humans –

will always fear what they don't understand. Not only that, they'll seek out differences wherever they can. Everyone wants to feel superior to someone else.'

'Why do you think that is?'

'It's a bully-versus-victim mentality. No one wants to feel that they're at the bottom of the social heap.'

I rub my neck awkwardly. 'What if someone tried to change that?'

Beth smiles at me kindly. 'You're too damned optimistic for your own good.'

Perhaps she's right. 'Speaking of bullies and victims…'

'Yeah?'

'Matt…'

She looks exasperated. 'Him again? What about him?'

'There's a lot of people around here who are not very nice to him.'

'He's an easy target.'

'That doesn't make it right,' I say quietly. 'Can you keep an eye on him?'

'Any time I go near him, he makes some comment about my body.' She wrinkles her nose. 'I could put up with that kind of thing when I was a hooker but I'm not going to put up with it now.'

'So educate him. Teach him to engage his inner mute button.'

'I'm not sure I have that much patience.'

'Please, Beth?'

She sighs. 'Fine. I'll see what I can do. I can't work smegging miracles though.'

I smile. 'Thank you.'

∽

I LEAVE Beth and wander down towards Michael's office. The photo is burning a metaphorical hole in my literally burnt pocket so I'm not looking forward to seeing him again, but I need to get the feather so I can take it to Frolic. Her cheeks may be free from tattoos and I know she's not a witch, but she's tied up in all this somehow.

I knock quietly on his door. There's no answer. I try knocking again, more loudly, then push it open and look inside. The office is empty. I scowl. Beth said he was in the mansion but I'm running out of time. I glance up and down the corridor; there's no sign of him. Cursing and feeling incredibly uncomfortable, I step inside. The feather damn well better be here.

The desk is tidy. There's a newspaper and a couple of books on it, as well as pot filled with writing implements, from cheap biros to what look like gold-plated fountain pens. I run my fingers across the books and folders on the bookshelves. There are lots of interesting titles but there's no bright green feather. It might not even be in this room. For all I know, he threw it into the incinerator. I bite my lip.

I move behind his desk and sit in the chair, scanning the space. If I can't find it, I'll have no choice but to search for him and demand to know where it is. Without thinking, I lean forward and pull open one of the desk drawers. Lying there, in all its emerald brilliance, is my feather. I give myself a mental high-five and take hold of it just as the door opens. Michael scowls at me.

I wave the feather in his direction, doing everything I can to avoid thinking about dead humans and his dimpled smile. 'I was looking for this.'

'You were snooping through my stuff.' His jaw is set and he seems angry.

'Er, no. I just wanted my feather.' I realise I'm in his chair, behind his desk. I stand up quickly and move away. 'I wasn't snooping,' I say softly, 'but I have to get this to Frolic, the woman who gave it to me, before dawn.'

His eyes narrow, the pinprick of red in his pupils deepening to a bright crimson. 'The cure. You're still after a fucking cure.'

'No, well, yes. Sort of. Actually it's…'

He snarls. 'You're so repulsed by being a vampire that you'll do anything, try anything, to get back to being human. I suppose I disgust you too.'

'No, you're not listening to me,' I begin.

He steps forward and grips my shoulders. For a brief moment I see his face in the photo again and I flinch. His mouth tightens and there's a flash of anguish in his face. He drops his hands immediately.

'You weren't disgusted by me when we were in the park.' His face leans dangerously close to mine. 'Quite the opposite.'

I open my mouth but no words come out. I want to explain but there's something about the murderous expression in his eyes that stops me. 'M – Michael,' I stammer, 'it's not what you think.'

The grandfather clock in the corner dings once. It's already 5am. I've got less than an hour until the sun rises. 'Can we talk about this later? I'll explain everything. I promise I will. I just have to…'

'Get out, Bo.' He says it quietly but his fists are balled up.

'Please,' I whisper. 'I need half an hour. If you can wait…'

'I'm done waiting. I should have listened to my instincts and kept our relationship strictly professional. I've done every-thing possible for you. I've broken the Family laws to give you the freedom you crave and you still despise what I am.' He looks into my eyes. 'Don't come back here, Bo. I'm spending enough time these days with humans who are terrified of me. I don't need it from vampires too.'

I want to tell him that I'm not afraid of him but right now I'd be lying. He pushes past me, sits down and picks up the phone. He won't even look at me. I can't believe how quickly things between us have imploded. There has to be a way I can sort this out. Then I glance at the clock again. Sodding hell. I don't have time for this.

'I'll come back before dawn,' I tell him firmly. 'If you can spare me five minutes, I'll explain everything.'

I don't wait for him to respond. As soon as I'm in the corridor, I start running. I have to deal with Frolic and then get back here as quickly as possible.

THE SIGNS that day is not far off are starting to creep into the park. The buzz of distant traffic is more distinct and the shadows of the trees are shortening as the sky makes its inexorable march towards the light. There are also far too many early joggers and dog walkers. I sprint past them, praying that they don't get in my way when I finally find Frolic. The last thing I need right now is well-meaning – or otherwise humans getting involved. I try to avoid thinking about Michael and focus on the task ahead. It's the only way I'll get through this.

I pick up speed until I'm almost flying down the path. I veer off in the direction where Frolic was last time, ignoring the stinging branches that whip my face. When I catch sight of her, humming quietly to herself next to a dark, towering tree, I slow down.

'You've made up your mind,' she says.

I stare at her like an idiot. 'Eh?'

'Will you retrieve the files for me or not? It's a simple choice.'

I narrow my eyes. 'You called the Montserrat mansion. You told them I had until dawn to get them for you.'

The placid expression on her face flickers. 'I can assure you, I did not.'

I growl. 'Bullshit!'

I step towards her then realise she is genuinely puzzled. I stop. Connor wouldn't lie, but it was only a phone call. He probably didn't answer it. I doubt very much that even a trusted vampette like him would be allowed to answer the Montserrat telephones. It doesn't matter who answered the damn call, though. Anyone could have said they were called Frolic and left a message for me. Yet again I've been hoodwinked.

I think quickly. There's no sign of the copper-cum-henchman. I'm betting he's around here somewhere though. I roll the dice. 'Whatever,' I say dismissively. 'I've got your files.'

Her eyes lighten. 'Already? This is fantastic news. Have you looked through them? Was there any proof that Magix murdered my husband?'

'There maybe something,' I say quietly. 'I didn't read them. I didn't think what they contained was any of my business.'

Frolic sighs. 'I'll have to hope then. Maybe if I can sue them...'

I hold up the feather. 'I have your IOU. So you can tell me what you know about the cure.'

'Yes, yes,' she nods. 'Honestly, you're the first person in ages who's not lost one of my feathers.' She tuts. 'I need them for my book-keeping. I can't fulfil my promises without them.'

'Indeed,' I murmur. 'People can be careless these days.'

'That's something Fingertip taught me,' she continues. 'Without proper accountability, those tax idiots at HMRC could easily come after us. Then we'd be in trouble.'

I refrain from pointing out that her business is pretty much dead and buried. I cross my fingers and reach inside my jacket. 'I have the files here,' I say.

Frolic's face is wreathed in smiles. I start to smile back when I hear a sudden whirring sound from behind. I drop to my feet and roll, just in time to see her choke. A dribble of blood appears at the corner of her mouth and her hands move to her chest. There is a gleaming shuriken embedded smack-bang in the centre. I scramble up and run towards her but it's already too late. Her eyes are wide and filled with pain. She collapses to her knees and pauses there for what seems like forever. Then she falls flat.

Slowly, I turn around. Her supposed henchman emerges from behind a tree. 'That wasn't supposed to happen,' he says. 'My boss will be pissed off.'

I avoid looking at Frolic's body. 'Who's your boss? Does he work for Magix?'

His hooded eyes flick to me. 'You are an annoying little bloodguzzler.'

I growl, then leap towards him. He's just a human, I'll be able to take him down easily. I'm already in mid-air, fists outstretched, when I realise my mistake. His eyes are rolled back into his head and he's muttering an incantation. There's a flash of silver in the split-second before I smash in his skull and then I fall down with a hard thump onto the grass below. My energy is sapped and it's a struggle to move. I pull my head up and stare at my wrists. There's a set of handcuffs encircling them with the Magix logo inscribed on the side.

He laughs. 'That was just too fucking easy.'

I try to get up. I make it to my feet but I feel like I'm moving through jelly. The goon kicks my knees and I fall down again. He circles me. 'O'Connell doesn't want you dead. He seems to think you'll be useful.' He kicks me again and I moan. 'Unfortunately for you, I don't give a shit what he thinks. Besides, I hear you hurt my friend.'

'The witch I burned? He shouldn't have come after me.'

He shakes his head. 'Black fucking witches. If he knew anything about magic then he would have had you.' He smirks. 'After all, *I've* got you and I didn't even have to break a sweat. No, I mean my other friend. That wasn't a smart move. His wife wants children and he won't be able to perform now for quite some time.'

I spit in his face. It's a feeble attempt but I still feel a trickle of self-satisfaction when it lands on his shoe.

He bends down towards me. I think he's about to punch me in the face when I realise he's picking up the feather. I must have dropped it when Frolic was hit. He twirls it thoughtfully, then crushes it in his large hands and discards it. 'I won't kill you though.' He smiles. 'I don't have to.'

I frown, not sure what he's getting at. He smirks and points upwards. Helplessly, I follow his finger. Over the tops of the trees, the sky is starting to change. It's no longer night.

'I reckon you've got about fifteen minutes.' He laughs. 'Enjoy, little bloodguzzler, enjoy.'

'Why?' I croak.

'Haven't you worked it out yet? We're trying to change the world. You're just collateral damage.' He looks down at me. 'See you in another life.'

I turn onto my back as he walks away. I've no time to do anything. Even if I could get back to my feet, I'd never make it back to the mansion with these handcuffs on. I watch the sky lighten and feel the first tingles of unnatural warmth cross my skin. I guess I won't be a vampire for much longer after all.

There's a sudden breeze and an odd rustle. I twist my head and watch as Frolic's ghost wavers in the light. 'Kakos daemon blood,' she whispers.

I stare at her uncomprehendingly.

'The cure. You need Kakos daemon blood.' She raises her eyes up to the sky. Her spirit flickers in growing light and she smiles. Then she winks out of existence.

I push myself towards her body, shoving her shoulder to flip her onto her back. Her eyes are wide and unseeing. I dip my fingertip into the blood that's leaking from her chest and use it to etch out a diagram on the dew-damp grass: a diamond shape with a squiggle inside. I have no idea whether it'll do any good. I'm not even sure if I really want it to work. Right now, though, it's all I can think about.

Then I close my eyes while my blood begins to boil.

CHAPTER 18
RIVERS OF BLOOD

'I must say, Ms Blackman,' X murmurs, 'you do have an uncanny ability to get yourself into trouble. Did your vampire Lord have better things to do with his time?'

I pull myself as far away from him as possible. My face feels strange. I prod at it gingerly with my fingers; the magical handcuffs have vanished.

'You've had to re-grow an entire new epidermis,' X informs me. 'Your vampiric attributes include fast regeneration. Still, you must have taken quite some time before you drank blood. Fledglings as young as you rarely recover so quickly.' He smiles slightly. 'The eyebrows, of course, will take far longer.'

I wince at his words then glance around, taking in my environment. I seem to have awakened in the 1980s, in a yuppie's bachelor pad. The place is decked out in black leather and gleaming mirrors.

'Where am I?' I croak.

X gives me a slow smile. 'In my lair, naturally. Where else would I bring such a delectable morsel?'

I squeak involuntarily. He laughs. 'You called me, Ms Blackman. Or have you conveniently forgotten that fact already?'

'Why?'

'I have absolutely no idea. I can only imagine it had something to do with the fact that you were about to burn up and contribute to the increasing issue we have with greenhouse gases.'

'No.' I cough. 'Why did you help me?'

He examines his fingernails. 'I suppose I had nothing better to do at the time. I would also like you to return my notebook.'

I'm surprised he's not taken it already.

'To rummage through your belongings without permission would be incredibly bad mannered.'

I guiltily think of my own rummage through Michael's office.

'Ah, I see. So Lord Montserrat is unimpressed that you invaded his personal space. It's for the best. If you really wish to return to humanity so desperately, an affair between the two of you will only end badly.'

I scowl. The daemon laughs. 'Of course, that's not the only thing that's ending badly for you right now, is it? You thought your devilish murderer was the woman. Frolic.' He shakes his head. 'Her bottom line was profit. Passion is far more dangerous.'

I find my voice. 'What's that supposed to mean?'

X chuckles. 'I'm not going to tell you. That would be too easy. I'm confident you can find out what you need to without my help.' He stands up. 'It'll be dark in an hour. I will leave you in peace since my presence clearly makes you nervous. Before you go, however, check the fridge.' He smiles. 'I left you a couple of little gifts.'

The amusement in his face is terrifying. I watch him leave, then sink back onto the sofa. I don't know why he's acting so out of character for a Kakos daemon. Rescuing damsels in distress is hardly their gig. Equally, I have no idea what possessed me to trace that damned symbol. Vampirism must be making me soft in the head. It occurs to me that unless he searched my burnt mess of a jacket, he didn't wait around for me to return his book. I shiver at the thought that it is still in my possession.

When I'm sure that he's gone and isn't coming back, I stand up and check myself over. As far as I can tell, X hasn't touched me. He's right about my skin healing quickly. I stare at myself in one of the many mirrors dotted around the room. Without my eyebrows, my forehead is bizarrely elongated, like one of those aliens you see in comic strips. My eyes appear impossibly wide, enhancing the tell-tale vampire red in the centre of each pupil.

I edge to the heavy curtains draped over the bay windows and lift one up an inch. The light outside is already dimming but I'm afraid of pulling the material apart any further to find out where I am. That'll have to wait. Instead, I stalk round the large room. There are several doors but they're all locked apart from one which opens into a large kitchen, replete with every modern device a cook could want, and another leads to the front door and the outside world.

I'll never have another opportunity like this again. I'm inside the den of a sodding Kakos daemon. Despite X's remarks about being too polite to search through my things, he's nuts if he thinks I'm going to pay him the same respect. He could kill me with a single touch. I need to know my enemy, even if he's not appeared aggressive towards me yet. I walk into the kitchen, pointedly ignoring the fridge and X's 'gifts', and nosy around, picking up a blender and sniffing inside it cautiously. I wonder if he brews up intestine smoothies with it, but the smell gives me no clue other than the fact that he uses lemon-scented washing-up liquid. I open a few drawers and peer inside. All in all, the room is unremarkable. There are plenty of plates and utensils but nothing to suggest I'm in the abode of a heart-eating, soulless daemon.

I pad back to the living room and place my ear against each locked door. There might be victims inside, people I should rescue from X's clutches. I knock on each one and call out, but there's not even the faintest whisper of a sound. I'm not brave enough to break the doors down to check they are unoccupied.

Eventually satisfied that I've covered every square inch, I sit down on the sofa. Other than the eighties' theme and the well-prepped kitchen, nothing gives me a clue about X's personality. There's a glass-topped coffee table in front of me, so smudge free that I can't stop myself from pressing my thumb in the middle to ruin its perfection. On one side of it sits a state of the art phone. I pick it up and frown. I'll hardly be giving away my secrets if I call the Montserrat mansion.

Taking a deep breath, I jab out the number. It rings three times before the dulcet tones of Iona, the vampire responsible for manning the mansion's communications system, answers me. 'Good evening. You have reached the Montserrat Family.' She may sound brisk and efficient, but there's a note of underlying tension in her voice.

'Hi Iona,' I begin.

'Bo? Thank goodness. I thought you were another crank caller. I'll put you right through.'

The phone clicks before I can ask her what she means. Michael's faintly accented voice fills the line. 'Are you deliberately trying to test me?'

I lick my lips. 'Er...'

'Goddamnit, Bo! When you said you'd be back in thirty minutes, I expected you to be back. The sun was rising. What the hell did you think you were doing?'

I feel a tiny thrill that, despite our last conversation, he's still worried about me. 'I'm fine. It was ... nothing.'

That's not strictly true and O'Connell can be damned sure I'll pay him a visit very, very soon. It's not going to be a friendly one, either. But right now his goons probably think I'm a frazzled pile of dust blowing around Hyde Park, so I reckon I have some time to spare before I need to confront him. The only positive he has on his side is that I believe the wanker who said O'Connell didn't want me dead. I'm taking my almost-murder a lot better than I took the security guard's assault. I guess my expectations are shifting now I'm a vampire.

'Where are you now?'

'Honestly, I have no idea.'

'Bo...'

'I'm telling the truth. Look, Michael, can we meet? Face to face?'

'How do I know you won't stand me up again?'

'I promise that unless I drop down dead or I'm indisposed thanks to some ravaging hordes, I'll be there.'

'You can't come here.'

I close my eyes briefly. 'Yeah. You already made it clear I wasn't welcome.' Before he can interrupt, I move on, naming a popular vampette restaurant. I've never been inside – I never had any call to enter such a place when I was human – but I've heard about it.

'When?' he snaps.

I'm assuming – hoping –I'm still London. 'Um, say in two hours?' Hopefully that will give me enough time to get there.

'Fine.' He hangs up.

I lean back and sigh. He may be concerned about my well-being but he's still bloody angry. I decide to tell him whatever he wants to know, even about Arzo's ex-fiancée. I owe him that much.

Picking up my leather jacket from the back of a chair, I

examine the burnt hole in the breast. I suppose I was lucky that Frolic's files acted as an extra barrier, otherwise not only would the witch's shuriken have penetrated it, but I'd be nursing charred skin as well as charred leather. I'm still pissed off about the jacket though. I need to find a way to get it fixed.

I shrug it on and re-check the window. Thankfully, the sky is dark enough for me to venture out without frying. I glance towards the kitchen, then pull my shoulders back and stride towards the front door instead. My hand is on the door handle when I curse. I don't want to see what X's gifts are, I really don't. I shake my head, turn round and go into the kitchen. I stand in front of the gleaming fridge, biting my lip. I reach out, my fingers curling round its cold steel edge. It's going to be gruesome, whatever it is, or why would he bother keeping it chilled?

'Curiosity killed the cat, Bo,' I whisper. I squeeze my eyes shut. 'And satisfaction brought it back.' I pull the door open, feeling a blast of cool air in my face. I open one eye and then the other.

The fridge is empty of food or drink. Nor is there a head on a platter, severed organs or a beating heart. There's simply a small vial and a transparent baggie. I reach for the baggie first and hold it up. It's a shuriken, covered in congealed blood. I stare at it for a second, then make a decision and take it, shoving into a side pocket.

I look at the vial. The liquid inside is unmistakably blood. It has to be from X himself. I steel myself then gingerly pick it up, as if it might bite me. It's cool to the touch. I drop it again and close the fridge door. Even if it is X's blood, it's probably poisoned; goodness only knows what drinking it will do to me. I have no reason to trust either Frolic's parting words or the daemon himself.

I spin round, take three steps, stop and growl. Damn it. I glance around, afraid someone is watching me, before returning to the fridge and opening it again. Sighing, I grab the vial and leave.

~

FORTUNATELY, as soon as I step outside I know where I am. It's less than an hour's stroll to the restaurant where I arranged to meet Michael. As I walk, I rehearse in my head what I'll say to him.

The streets are busy but no one pays me any attention. They don't look closely enough to register that I'm a vampire. When I'm waiting for one set of traffic lights to change, however, the headline outside a nearby newsagents gives me pause: GUZZLER PETITION DELIVERED TO PARLIAMENT. I feel a squirming sensation in my stomach and turn away.

At least the restaurant is welcoming and there are no protestors nearby. The windows are darkened to create a spooky atmosphere so that will spare me from any gawkers on the pavement.

I request a table by the window. A smiling waitress comes over to take my order. 'It's good of you to frequent our establishment,' she says. 'We've not had many vampires in lately.'

I smile back at her but I'm pretty sure my smile doesn't meet my eyes. She senses my discomfort, passes me two menus and leaves me in peace. With time to kill, I open one. There's a typical array of burgers, sandwiches and platters. Assuming the second menu is for drinks, I open it – then gape in horror. Happy faces beam out at me, with little bios next to each one. Adam is twenty-four years old, healthy and energetic. He's O negative and his blood has a spicy tinge thanks to his penchant for curries. Zoe is twenty-nine. She's more expensive because she's the rarer AB−. She drinks a glass of red wine every day to enhance her 'flavour'. Jeez. I don't know what I expected in a vampette establishment but it certainly wasn't this.

I shut both menus quickly. There are a few tables occupied by humans nearby and I sense them sending me sidelong glances, although every time I look in their direction they avert their eyes. No doubt they're waiting for me to drink. I feel ill. I order a glass of water, ignoring the waitress's disappointment, then stare into space and mull over everything that happened the previous evening.

'Have you ordered?' Michael is standing over me, arms folded, glowering. He's wearing another of his sharp, midnight-blue suits and there's a shadow of dark stubble across his jaw.

'Er, no.'

He frowns then gestures for the waitress and points to one of the vampettes on offer before sitting opposite me. 'Order,' he snaps.

I shake my head.

'Order now, Bo, so help me God.' He scowls at me. 'If you drink properly then I won't waste time asking what the hell happened to your face.'

I don't need another lecture on my vulnerability, so I nod randomly at one of the pictures. The waitress scribbles down our order, then turns to Michael. She's put on a pout to make her lips plumper and her chest is jutting out more prominently. My eyes narrow but Michael doesn't even notice. He gives her a distant smile and hands back the menus. Frowning, she stalks away.

'I think you've made a conquest there,' I say lightly.

'What?'

There's something in his expression that stops me. 'Nothing,' I mutter.

I look down, noting his fingers gripping the edge of the

table. Swallowing, I move my eyes to a point behind his shoulder.

'We agreed that you would take Matt with you if you went out,' he says stiffly.

'If I'd taken him with me last night, he'd be dead,' I answer. 'Besides, I thought you weren't going to ask me about what happened to my face.'

'I'm not. I'm talking about today.'

'Oh.'

He glances over his shoulder then back at me. 'Bo, what the hell are you looking at?'

'Nothing.' I twist my fingers in the tablecloth. 'I'm sorry,' I burst out. 'I shouldn't have gone through your things. But I had to get the feather and return it by dawn. I didn't have time to wait around for you to finish whatever meeting you were in.'

'So did you?'

'Return the feather? Um, sort of.'

'And your wonderful cure? The one that'll make all this awful bloodguzzler nightmare vanish in a second?' He snaps his fingers and I jump.

I can't tell him about X, I won't put him in that kind of danger, but there's no harm in repeating what Frolic said. I desperately want to be honest with him. I wet my lips. Michael's eyes follow my tongue and butterflies attack my insides.

'Kakos blood,' I whisper.

He throws back his head and laughs. The other diners turn towards him, startled. 'So there is a cure. But you'll never know if it works because you'll never get close to a Kakos daemon to find out.'

I don't reply immediately. I can't work out whether he's happy, relieved or just damn amused. 'Have you ever met one?' I ask finally.

'A Kakos daemon? Nobody meets one and lives to tell the tale. I thought you'd know that.' His eyes scan my face. 'For what it's worth, I'm sorry.'

'Are you?' I snap. 'You don't seem very fucking sorry.'

He glares at me. 'I knew it wouldn't work. So did you but you needed to accept it. I *am* sorry for you, Bo. I know how hard this has been.'

'No,' I say softly, 'you don't. You've been more supportive than I expected and I appreciate how far out on a limb you've gone for me. But you don't know what this is like for me. You can't know.'

A muscle jerks in his cheek. 'I know you're afraid of me. I know there's a part of you that's disgusted not only by your own vampirism but mine.'

I start to shake my head. 'No, I'm not...'

'I saw the look in your eyes, Bo. You're fooling yourself if you think otherwise.'

The waitress appears with our orders in tow. I flinch, then damn myself for the action. 'This is Anna,' she says to Michael with a flirty grin. Her smile dims slightly when she turns to me. 'And this is Jack.'

'Thank you,' Michael murmurs, although he doesn't take his eyes off me. 'Go on then, Bo. Prove you're not repelled. Drink your fill.'

Damn him. My stomach rumbles and my fangs lengthen but I can't stop myself from wanting to vomit. Anna pulls up a chair and holds back her hair, exposing her jugular. Michael licks his lips, baring his brilliant white teeth. Still watching me, he slowly sinks his fangs into her skin. Bile rises in my throat. The vampette closes her eyes and moans slightly. Michael pulls away for a moment. His mouth is smeared with blood. 'Come on, Bo,' he urges. 'Drink.'

I look at my willing victim and think about the Soho prostitute I ran away from. This situation doesn't seem any different; it's just more expensive. I take a deep breath. I've been doing okay with Connor; I can do this too. I grab Jack's wrist but Michael shakes his head. 'Not there.'

I snarl softly. Jack gives me a nervous smile. I drop his wrist. 'It's fine,' I say, not sure whether I'm attempting to reassure the vampette or myself.

Jack sits down and stretches out his neck. I stare at the tiny throbbing pulse. Michael's still watching me. I grit my teeth and lean over, my teeth nipping into Jack's skin. Warm blood fills my mouth and I gag. I force myself to swallow but I barely manage a few slugs before I'm pushing him away.

'Go,' I whisper, 'just go.'

Jack backs away, the chair falling with a loud crash as he stands up. Anna, Michael's vampette, looks at him questioningly and he nods. 'Go.'

He folds his arms and leans back. 'Of course you're not disgusted,' he says sarcastically.

The waitress starts to come over, seemingly worried. Michael holds up a hand, forcing her back.

'I'm disgusted by blood,' I protest. 'By drinking blood. I'm not disgusted by myself or by you.'

'You can pretend to yourself all you like. It's not going to change the truth.' He looks away. 'Your PTSD is probably as much a result of being a vampire as because of what happened with Nicky.'

'I don't have PTSD!'

'You see?' he says quietly. 'You're lying to yourself.' Frustrated, I ball my fists. He holds my gaze and sighs. 'I should be the one apologising. I shouldn't have got so angry yesterday. You've got no idea what you do to me. You're under my skin, Bo. You're in my dreams.' His eyes don't waver. 'I think we might have something here and I know you feel the same. I've seen the way you look at me. But if we do this now, you'll end up hating me and despising yourself. You need to come to terms with what you are first.'

'I...' I shake my head to clear away my turbulent emotions. 'I...'

'You don't need to say anything.' He passes me a piece of paper with an address scribbled on it. 'Arzo thinks he's found some suitable offices. There's a flat above where you can stay. Work with him. Set up this business. Goodness knows, we need it. Then, when you're ready, we'll talk again.'

He gestures to the waitress for the bill and she almost sprints to our table. He signs the check without looking at it and glances back at me. His mouth twists. 'Just do me a favour and don't get hurt. And don't lie to yourself. It'll make things harder.' A ghost of a smile crosses his face. 'Ursus came across his rather mangled bike this morning so I've taken the liberty of getting you one of your own. It's a gift, not payment.'

He tosses a set of keys towards me and stands up, then moves round the table and bends down, his lips brushing lightly against mine. 'I'll be seeing you, Bo.'

He walks out. I touch my lips with my fingers. 'Count on it,' I whisper.

My hands drop to the table. I realise I've still not confronted him about the photo. I don't think that the person who spoke with such honesty and displayed such altruism could be the monster the picture suggests. I'll get rid of the thing as soon as I can.

What I'll do about the vial of X's blood is another matter. I'll make up my mind later.

~

WHEN I STUMBLE out of the restaurant, every pair of eyes in the place follows me. I'm in such a rush to depart that don't give Michael's present the attention it deserves. I simply climb on and quickly head to the address he gave me. Although it's on a busy thoroughfare close to Covent Garden, the building itself is nondescript; it could definitely do with a coat of paint. There's a dentist on the ground floor but the offices higher up seem to be unoccupied. Thus far, I'm not impressed.

I climb a set of winding stone stairs to the first floor and peer round the corner. Arzo is in the middle of the room, directing a sweating Connor to move a desk further back; Matt is scrubbing a grimy window as if his life depended on it. Not wanting to be drafted into the relocation process, I'm tempted to tiptoe back down and return later but Arzo is far too canny not to notice me.

'Bo!' he barks. 'Where have you been?'

'Um...'

'Honestly, between you and Peter, I feel like I'm herding cats. We've got very little time before the official announcement. These walls need to be painted, the furniture needs to be sorted out. Connor needs to stop taking a break every five seconds...'

'That's not fair!' Connor protests. 'I'm only human. I don't have super strength.'

Arzo's lips purse. 'You're right. Swap places with Matthew.'

Matt grins, waving frantically in my direction before swooping over and picking the desk up as if it's made out of matchsticks. Connor stares at him, his mouth dropping open. When he doesn't immediately move to the window, Matt helpfully drops the desk then picks Connor up, throwing him over his shoulder and depositing him in place. He hands Connor the cleaning rag and spray bottle. Connor still hasn't managed to shut his mouth.

'Is Peter here?'

'Sure,' Arzo replies sarcastically. 'He's just using his invisibility cloak at the moment.'

'It's not beyond the realms of possibility.'

He shoots me a droll look. 'The glamour spell that can achieve that would be something to see.'

I think of Magix. 'Actually, speaking of spells, there's a company that's created some kind of binding device for vampires.'

'Another holy water trinket,' Arzo dismisses with a snort.

'No. It's the real deal.' I tell him about the handcuffs without wasting time going into too many specifics.

He looks unhappy. 'That's just what we need. Did you tell Lord Montserrat?' I shake my head. 'I thought you were meeting him.'

I scratch my neck awkwardly. 'We were, um, talking about other things.'

Arzo raises his eyebrows. 'Indeed. He's a good man, Bo.'

I nod, biting my lip. 'So, this is it then? Our new office suite.'

'It's not the Ritz but it'll do for now.'

'Mmm.'

'It's a central location. There's a lot of potential for expansion and we need people to feel comfortable. They can't walk into an atmosphere that reeks of vampire.' His eyes are serious. 'We can't screw this up, Bo. It's too important.'

'You don't think the protests are just a knee-jerk reaction? That things will settle down in a month or two?'

'You're too young to remember Enoch Powell.'

'His name rings a bell.'

'Rings a bell? He's a vital part of British history. "As I look ahead, I am filled with foreboding; like the Roman, I seem to see 'the River Tiber foaming with much blood'." He was talking about immigration, but he may as well have included tribers.

He came damn close to inciting violence and riots like this city has never seen.' Arzo's shoulders tense. 'And this city has seen a lot. Right now, the movement against us is disorganised. It consists of pockets of people who are using fear to drive their actions. The second a figurehead emerges and becomes an anti-vampire spokesperson, we're doomed. We need to dampen down the groundswell of fear before we get to that point, otherwise there really will be rivers of blood.'

His expression is filled with foreboding. I try to lighten the atmosphere. 'Well, we should get a move on then, shouldn't we?' I look round the room. 'Have you managed to find a boss for us?'

'Not yet.'

Bugger it. I open my mouth to voice my concern at the combined lack of experience of everyone apart from Arzo himself but by his posture, I realise it's unnecessary.

'You should go upstairs, Bo. Have a look at your living quarters and see if there's anything you need. Once we open our doors, there won't be time for shopping.'

'Okay.'

'Then you need to go to the East End.'

'Why?'

'It's where Simon Beauvoit lives.'

My stomach drops. I stare at him. 'W-who?' I stammer out. Arzo looks at me and I close my eyes briefly. 'How did you know?'

'Let's just say I caught sight of an old friend leaving the Montserrat mansion some days ago. It didn't take much to work out what you were up to.'

'You don't give much away. Why didn't you tell me?'

'You seemed hell-bent on keeping it a secret. The trouble is,' he says, casting an arm round the room, 'if this is going to work, we can't keep secrets.'

I swallow. 'Do you want to come with me?'

'That part of my life is over. There are echoes of it still,' he puts a hand to his heart, 'painful echoes, but I put it behind me a long time ago. Perhaps you should work on putting away your past too. But Bo?'

'Yes?'

'Thank you. The sentiment is much appreciated.' I offer a tiny smile. He smiles back, although his eyes look sad. 'By the way, your grandfather called. Something about some documents you sent him in the post? He said to tell you they were the most frank and full files on a single person he's ever seen. He wanted to know where you got them from.'

'Long story. It's related to Magix though. They gave me the files they had on a witch in return for some information. The witch is now dead. I think they might be creating some new kind of black-and-white hybrid witch.'

Arso stares at me.

'I know, I know,' I tell him. 'It's impossible.'

'Nothing's impossible.' He rubs his forehead as if he's in pain. 'The world's being turned on its head. I wonder if anything will ever be the same again.' He shakes himself. 'Now get yourself upstairs. And here,' he says, throwing me a bar of chocolate. 'A house-warming gift for you.'

I glance down at it. 'You really do know far too much.'

He winks. I clutch the chocolate, salute him and go upstairs to my new residence. It's spartan but clean, and there's already some basic furniture. I give everything a cursory examination but my mind is on what Arzo said about secrets. My life seems to be built on a shaky foundation of hidden truths. By maintaining their secrecy, the five Families may have inadvertently caused the problems they're now having with the human majority. To be a private investigator is to be absorbed into the world of secrets. Michael Montserrat thinks I'm keeping secrets from myself. And I have two objects in my half-destroyed leather jacket that may be the biggest secrets of all.

I pull out the photo first, staring at it for the umpteenth time. I touch Michael's face but avoid looking at the corpses at his feet. Then I go into the bedroom. Lifting up the mattress on the bed, I shove the photograph underneath as far as it will go and smooth over the sheets.

Next I take out X's vial. I wonder how much it would be worth on the open market. I could probably sell it and live comfortably off the proceeds for the rest of my unnaturally long life. Of course, if I drink it and it works, I'll achieve everything I've been striving for since the day Michael told me the truth about what I'd become. I'll also lose Michael forever. Vampires don't date humans. And the loss of my vampiric status will probably make me useless to the agency. I'm already regarded with suspicion by most of the vampires I meet; if I become human again, I'll really be *persona non grata*. Neither the humans nor the bloodguzzlers will trust me. And I dread to think what will happen to the anti-vampire movement if it becomes known that there is a viable cure.

With a heavy heart, I head into the kitchen and open the battered fridge. I place the vial at the back, then prop Arzo's chocolate in front of it so it's no longer visible. Out of sight, out of mind. For now at least.

LESS THAN AN HOUR LATER, I'm outside Inspector Beauvoit's house. Now that I know Arzo is aware of the truth, I'm tempted to leave Stephen and Dahlia Templeton to it. But a promise is a promise: I told Templeton I'd do what I could and I'm not about to go back on my word. Not any more.

Thankfully, Beauvoit must be off duty because there's a

light on. Either that or Dahlia Templeton is home alone. I smirk at the thought of her opening the door. I should have brought her husband along with me – it would have been entertaining to see the look on her face. Taking a deep breath, I ring the doorbell.

A rumpled, tired-looking man answers. 'Yes?'

I smile professionally. 'Can I speak to Dahlia Templeton?'

'She's not here. Why would she be here?'

Shit. He has to be lying. He's a police inspector, he's probably good at it. I try to look behind him but I can't see any signs of anyone.

I go for the direct approach. 'You're having an affair with her, Inspector, so it makes sense that she'd be here.'

He stares at me bleakly. He doesn't even look surprised. 'It wasn't an affair. We were in love. You should know that.'

'Why would I know that?' I'm confused.

'You're one of her vampire buddies, aren't you?'

'Excuse me?'

Somewhere inside a phone starts to ring. 'I have to go,' he mutters.

He shuts the door, leaving me in the porch. I slam my fist against the wall and there's a loud cracking sound. Alarmed, I pull back; I've managed to create a very visible fissure in the side of Beauvoit's house. I look from my fist to the wall and back again. I'm getting stronger.

Absently rubbing my fingers, I debate what to do next. I can't force the inspector to talk to me but I have to try again. There's something strange going on here. I hammer on the door and repeatedly press the doorbell. After about five minutes, however, it's clear that he's not going to answer. I could persist and stay here for the rest of the night, which will piss off his neighbours, but I need to tread carefully. If I act like a madwoman trying to break down a policeman's door, it's probably not going to do the vampire cause many favours.

Beauvoit spoke in the past tense. Their affair is over – or she's dead. Right now I'm more interested in what he meant by 'vampire buddies'. I decide to break my fists on Stephen Templeton's door instead.

CHAPTER 19
EPIPHANY

'Have you found her?'

'No.'

'She's dead, isn't she?'

'I don't know.'

'If you don't find a body, can I still collect her life insurance?'

I stare at him in disgust. The speculative gleam in his eyes turns my stomach. For the life of me I can't imagine why Arzo was ever friends with this man.

'Who were her friends?'

'Dahlia?' He pauses. 'She didn't have many friends.'

Like Simon Beauvoit, he's now speaking about Dahlia in the past tense. He thinks she's dead.

'She must have had some. One, even.'

'We have a next-door neighbour, Alice. I think they went for coffee sometimes.'

'Anyone else?'

He shrugs. 'There was the copper, I guess. I'm not sure you could call him a friend though.'

I stare at him. 'What do you mean?' I ask slowly.

'She was shagging him. At least once a week.'

'You knew?'

'Of course.'

'Stephen,' I say softly, watching his every move very carefully, 'were you angry that she was having an affair?'

His brow furrows as if I've just set him a complicated maths equation. 'No. She was bored. She needed something to do during the day.'

I lean forward slightly. 'What?'

'Oh,' he says, 'you think I was jealous. That's stupid.' He walks to the mini bar and pulls out a tiny bottle of vodka. I watch as he drains it in one shot.

'Stupid to think you would be jealous at your wife having sex with someone else? Screaming out someone else's name?'

He rolls his eyes. 'We're not living in the nineteenth century. Look.' He rummages around in a pile of discarded clothes on the floor by the bed and grabs hold of a laptop. A pair of boxer shorts is still attached to it when he opens it and sets it on his lap. He nonchalantly brushes them aside, then opens a video file.

It's a shot of Dahlia and Stephen's bed. On it there is a bald man, his head turned away from the camera although I'm fairly sure it's Beauvoit. A completely naked Dahlia is on top of him, rhythmically moving her hips. She opens her eyes and looks directly into the camera, licking her lips and mouthing what seems to be 'I love you, Stephen.'

I'm not quite sure where to look. 'Uh, you knew all along?'

Templeton's eyes are slightly unfocused as he watches his wife's movements gather speed. 'Mm? Oh, yes. I asked her to do it. She enjoyed it.'

She does look like she's getting a lot of pleasure from this particular request. I suppose it beats doing the ironing.

'Why didn't you tell me about this before?'

He seems surprised. 'Is it relevant?'

I resist the urge to smash the bloody laptop over his head. 'Do you think he might have harmed her?'

'Him? No way. He was in love with her. Wanted her to run away with him.' He laughs. 'Like that was going to happen.'

'Were there others like him?'

'Sure,' he says easily. 'We stuck to one at a time, though. Dahlia said she found it too hard to remember their names if she was sleeping with several guys at once.'

'Did she?' I murmur. 'How long was Beauvoit in the picture?'

'A year, maybe two. But I think she was ready for a change. We were talking about maybe mixing things up a bit, perhaps experimenting with a triber.'

'You mean like a vampire?'

'No.' He shakes his head. 'We might have run into Arzo. It could have been awkward. I was thinking witch, but Dahlia wanted to try a daemon.'

My mind flicks to X and I quickly push him away. 'Beauvoit seemed certain Dahlia was friends with some vampires.'

'Really?' He laughs. 'Well, that's Dahlia. Always walking on the wild side. She wouldn't have gone near a Montserrat though.'

He leans back and grabs the remote, turning on the television. I snatch it from him and switch it off again. 'Think, you idiot,' I hiss. 'She might still be alive. Did she ever mention anything about vampires? Or anyone else?'

'No.' He scowls at me petulantly. 'I don't see why you're here interrogating me when you should be finding out where she is.'

'I am sodding well investigating where she is! If you're not prepared to cooperate, then there's not much I can do.' I walk over to the window and stare out at the bright city lights. My frustration is building up to boiling point. After several deep breaths, I turn round and try a different tack. 'Why do you have a photo of Arzo on display in your house?'

'What? We don't.'

'Yes, you do,' I say impatiently. 'It was in the living room, smashed on the floor with the others.'

'We got rid of everything we had to do with him after he left.'

I ball my fists. 'You mean after you made him leave.'

'He got a long life and lots of power. It wasn't a bad deal for him. I might just let them recruit me, you know. In a few years' time, before it all starts to grey.' He points up to his hair. It's a flippant, throwaway remark but I still rise to the bait.

'You're already grey. And no one would have you.'

'I'm a very good accountant,' Templeton says stiffly.

'You're a cheat, a liar and a thief.' I stop. Actually, who am I kidding? The Families would probably jump at the chance to bring him into the fold. Wanker.

'The photo,' I say, returning to the topic.

'I'm telling you we don't have any photos of Arzo. Honestly, do you feel the need to question to every single thing I say?'

'Why would it be in your house?'

'How the hell should I know?'

I try to think. I pinch the bridge of my nose. Then I pick up the hotel phone.

'Hey!' Templeton protests. 'It's expensive to call from here.'

I ignore him and dial directory inquiries. When I get the number I need, I ask to be transferred. After a few rings, someone answers.

'Medici Family. How may we be of service?'

I deepen my voice to disguise it, not because the Medici receptionist will know who I am but in case the call is recorded and someone decides to trace it.

'You bloodguzzling bastards,' I snarl. 'How many children have you killed today?'

Templeton stares at me wide-eyed.

'I don't know who you think you are but we are not in the business of killing children. Or anyone,' the receptionist responds indignantly.

'Oh yeah? The whole lot of you are going down. No one's going to want to be recruited by you ever again,' I taunt. 'You'll die off and there'll be no one left.'

'Piss off!' she shrieks. 'Stop bothering us! And for your information, we recruited someone just two weeks ago so our numbers are doing fine.' She hangs up.

I slowly replace the receiver, then I look at Templeton. 'I don't think you're going to see Dahlia again.'

ARZO GRIPS the edges of his wheelchair. 'You think Medici is responsible? That doesn't make any sense.'

'It makes perfect sense. Lord Medici approached me. I turned him down and he said there would be consequences. Except those consequences were already in play because he'd already snatched Dahlia. He must have been hedging his bets. And it wasn't just me – Connor was made an offer. He turned it down. Medici left you and Peter alone because you're Montserrat Sanguine and therefore intrinsically loyal. Matt's never been alone outside so they've never had the chance to grab him. If they did...'

'Matt would be gone. He might have Montserrat loyalty but the effects of Nicky's machinations mean he'd do whatever they told him to. What's Medici's motive though? It still doesn't make any sense, Bo.'

Michael's dark eyes are hooded. 'Yes, it does. Medici doesn't want our new venture to succeed. He's the only Family Head who voted against it. He sees it as pandering to the whims of the humans and a sign of weakness. He'll do just about anything to avoid relinquishing power.'

'It's not relinquishing power! If anything, better relations with the humans will strengthen the Families.'

'We know that. He doesn't.'

'No. I still can't believe he would deliberately act against us like this. It would violate every Family law there is. If he was discovered, he'd be slaughtered. The four remaining Families would see to it.'

'If he's got Dahlia and he's turned her, then he's already got leverage against you, Arzo. That means leverage against this entire firm. Would you avoid revealing the truth about Medici to the other Families, even to Montserrat, if her life was in danger? The photo of you was left there deliberately in case you went to check on her. It would make you think she still cared for you...'

Arzo flinches.

'They made it look like a break-in. They wanted Stephen Templeton to call the police because sooner or later they'd come round asking questions and you'd be forced to get involved.' I continue. 'They would have subdued her in a heartbeat, especially if she'd made friends with them and invited them into the house already. She didn't tell her husband she suddenly had bloodguzzling besties so I'll bet they don't want us to know they have her just yet. Medici will wait until you're desperate then dangle her fledgling arse in front of you as a lure. Sabotage this firm or watch her die.'

Arzo shakes his head. 'I still don't think he'd go that far. Medici wouldn't grab someone like that, not with the way things are right now.'

'Right now is the perfect time to do it,' I argue. 'We can't accuse him because it'll put all the vampires in the country in jeopardy. If the humans have proof that someone's been recruited against their will, they have a reason to declare outright war.'

'She may have volunteered. Or she may have just left and be nowhere near the Medici Family. She might be sunning herself on a beach somewhere.'

I glance at Michael. 'There is one way to find out. We let Matt off the leash and see if they approach him. Two birds are better than one. I bet Medici jumps at the chance to create a double agent as well as pull Arzo's strings at the same time. It'll mean that this agency will never get off the ground and he'll win.'

'How do we keep Matt safe though?' Michael says grimly.

I grin. 'Matt was in the army.'

'But he's…'

'No.' I interrupt. Michael looks annoyed but falls quiet. 'Don't say it. He's not an idiot. He just needs some encouragement. In fact, he'll tell us what to do.'

'I wasn't going to call him that,' he tells me quietly. He sighs. 'You know Medici might not fall for it.'

'Let's try and see.' I look at Arzo and he gives me a brief, albeit reluctant, nod.

Michael sighs and rubs a hand over his scalp. 'Okay. I'll go and talk to Matt.'

WE BEGIN IMMEDIATELY. With no way of knowing if my theory is correct or if the Medici vampires are keeping an eye on our movements, we approach the set-up with care. If Medici takes the opportunity that's being handed to him on a plate, it's imperative that our actions remain covert. There's no point going to all this trouble and then tipping our hand – but we can't let them do anything damaging to Matt either.

'Whatever you do, Matt,' Michael says, 'don't move the chair.'

'I won't move the chair,' Matt repeats dutifully. He stands back and eyes it, folding his arms as if to prove his actions will mirror his words.

'Matt.' My voice is soft.

'Yes, Bo?'

'Can you pass me the chair please?'

His face screws up like a crumpled ball of paper. There's tension in his bulging biceps and it's clear he's undergoing an internal struggle, but within twenty seconds he follows my request. We exchange looks.

Matt is anxious. 'Did I do something wrong?'

'No, you did everything perfectly.' I smile at him reassuringly and focus on Michael. 'How many vampires like this does Medici have?'

He frowns. 'There were several.'

'Were?'

'A couple survived after Nicky's incarceration, like Matt, but Medici...' He glances at Matt and doesn't finish his sentence.

'The man's a monster,' I breathe.

'He's keeping his Family strong.'

'You agree with that?'

'Of course not,' he snaps. 'But I understand it.'

I curse under my breath. Michael frowns at me but doesn't pursue it further.

The plan is to make a midnight coffee run. Thanks to our busy central location, there are a number of twenty-four hour cafés dotted around. Each night, Matt will venture out on his own to fetch everyone a drink. We'll establish a routine, although we'll take care not to be too punctual, giving ourselves twenty minutes either side of the witching hour so his errand doesn't appear too forced. We can't bring in any Montserrat reinforcements so we need to manage on our own. Matt sets up the route himself, mapping it out carefully to create a splinter ambush. I estimate that if Medici is really going to make a move, he'll do it by the fourth night or not at all.

When I take up position on the first night, however, I immediately spot two shadows detach themselves from a darkened alleyway. I realise that with the impending announcement about the firm, Medici is more desperate than we anticipated.

'There are two vampires following him,' I whisper into my cuff, where a tiny radio is secreted.

'Colours?'

'Black.'

'So it could be Stuart.'

'The Stuart Family colour might be black, but anyone can put on black clothes.'

I skirt along the edge of the roof, keeping my distance. At the second crossroads, just as I'm judging the distance to the next set of roofs, the vampires speed up and overtake Matt's loping figure. Another vampire emerges from the corner. My heart drops. Medici doesn't have one or two bloodguzzlers out on the streets; he's got an entire team. Anxiously, I scan ahead. The last thing I need is to bang into a watcher up here but the higher ground seems clear.

'Matt,' I say softly, 'stop and tie your shoelace.'

He halts, obediently bending down and fumbling with his shoe. I focus on the figure behind him who'll have no choice other than to give themselves away by stopping too, or lose their advantage and overtake him. I arch my neck and register the figure's lips moving. I guess we're not the only ones with radios to hand. It makes sense. If Medici has set up a perimeter team, they'll be spread around the surrounding streets. I need to work out how many there are.

The tail behind Matt walks past him. I wait until he's some distance away before instructing Matt to move. As soon as he does, I spot a vampire on the roof on the opposite side of the street. I smile. There's a construction site ahead with a large gap where a building was recently demolished. In about three minutes, the vampire won't find staying up on the roofs particularly helpful.

'How many are there now?' Michael's voice interrupts.

'Four so far. Three in front of him. One's on the right, on the roof across from me.'

I wait until my opposite number has leapt over the gap where the intersection meets then I do the same thing. I land badly, my ankle turning and causing me to gasp in surprised pain.

'What's wrong?' Michael sounds alarmed.

'Nothing.'

There's a crackle in my earpiece. 'This is too dangerous. I'm coming after you. Stay where you are.'

'No. If any of those bloodguzzlers sees you, the game is up. We'll lose any advantage we could have.'

'That's better than you dead.'

'They don't know I'm here.'

'Yet.'

'Don't, Michael,' I say. 'Please.'

There's no answer. I scowl. He needs to stop sodding micromanaging. There's no way I'm going to hang around, waiting for him to show up and ruin everything. I move forward quickly, forgetting about the pain in my ankle for just long enough to lose my footing and feel my knees buckle. I put out my uninjured leg to the right to avoid falling completely and use my left hand to stop myself collapsing. Unfortunately I loosen a tile at the same time and it slides away before I can stop it. I watch, horror struck, as it disappears off the edge of the roof and smashes on the pavement below. Panicking, I swing to my left and drop down until I'm clinging onto the roof with my fingertips in an attempt to conceal myself from the vampire opposite. The only thing that saves me is that, in a bid to keep close to Matt, the vampire is twenty metres ahead; it takes him longer to turn and squint at the road and the destroyed tile, then up in my direction.

I know he's coming this way. I have to prevent him from alerting anyone else. Letting myself drop, I fall three storeys onto the pavement of the parallel street. I ignore the shooting pain in my ankle, run to the corner, press my back against the wall and shuffle silently until I can peer round. The other vampire has also dropped to the street. He's barely five metres away, standing over the splintered remnants of the roof tile.

'It might be nothing,' he mutters into his radio. 'Maybe a cat.' He looks up at the roof I just vacated. 'I can't see anything. I'll check it out to be sure.'

Arse. Michael's heading in this direction, no doubt following the same route I took. I need to stop the Medici guzzler from climbing up and recognising him. Looking around, I see a discarded soda can and pick it up. I fling it into the road and the vampire turns towards it. The second I hear his footsteps approaching, I launch myself at him. He's already on the defensive but I slam the base of my hand into his throat, forcing him to stagger backwards. If nothing else, that'll put his voice out of commission for a couple of minutes. If he can't speak, he can't use his radio to sound the alarm.

His eyes narrow and he spins round, leaping in the air and kicking at me. I dodge his foot – but only just – and roll on the ground to get away. Then I'm back on my feet, fists ready. The vampire comes forward again, this time more cautiously. I throw up my hands to block his blow and return the favour, punching him in the stomach. Unfortunately his abs are rock hard and I do more damage to my hand than to his body. He takes advantage of the break in my momentum and lunges forward, grabbing my jacket's right pocket. I slam the base of my hand into his nose. His head rocks back, his eyes spitting venom and pain in equal measures.

A low rumble emits from his chest and he springs high up in the air, then somersaults and lands behind me. Before I can move away, his elbow locks round my throat and he drags me down in a headlock. My fingers scrabble at his arm, trying to loosen his grip. He makes an odd choking sound; a corner of my brain registers that it's a laugh. His free hand smashes into the side of my head, over and over again. Blinding light flashes behind my eyelids and I yell out loud.

Forcing myself to relax, I let him continue punching me. I won't stay fully conscious unless I escape his grip soon. I manoeuvre closer to him then simultaneously knee the back of his leg and thrust my left hand into his forehead. The opposing forces of my attack force him to release me. My success unleashes another flood of adrenaline and I kick him in the chest, then slam my fists into his back. He collapses on the ground.

I back away, breathing hard, feeling like I've just been run over by a ten-ton truck. His radio crackles.

'What's your status?'

From high above us, Michael swoops down. Without taking his eyes off me, he grabs the bloodguzzler's radio. 'Nothing. False alarm,' he grunts, distorting his voice. Then he bends down, snatching a tuft of the vampire's hair and pulling upwards. Barely blinking, he slams the vampire's head onto the pavement and the last light in the bloodguzzler's eyes goes out. His eyelids close and his chest rises, but only just.

'You had him,' he says.

I feel a flicker of pride. 'I got lucky,' I mutter.

Michael raises his eyebrows. 'Take a compliment when it's given.'

'I have to go,' I whisper. 'Matt...'

He nods. 'Go. I'll sort this one out.'

I sigh in frustration. 'Because of my fucking clumsiness, Medici will know we're on to him.

'He won't.'

'Yes, he will. If this one dies, the only possible explanation is that he was killed by another vampire. He'll put two and two together.'

'I'll deal with it. Go.'

I stand there for another heartbeat then I turn and run, crossing the road and shimmying back up the roofs. I don't do anything silly like look back.

By the time I catch up with Matt, he's almost at the end of our planned route. The coffee shop is at the back of a small square. There's one road leading to it and a tiny alleyway leading away from it. The three vampires who were in front of him are already there, together with another one. They've taken up positions in each corner.

'Don't speak, Matt. If the answer's yes, scratch your ear. If it's no, lick your lips,' I whisper, keeping my voice as quiet as possible. 'Are you okay?'

He scratches.

'Can you see more than four of them?'

His tongue flicks out and I relax a little.

'Okay, go into the shop. Buy four coffees. You know what to do next.'

He scratches his ear again.

'Connor?'

'I'm here.' There's a faint tremor in his voice.

'It's fine. You won't get hurt, I promise. It's time to leave.'

'Okay.'

Arzo fills the airwaves. 'Radio silence from now on unless you're compromised.'

I nod, even though no one can see me. Then I wait. When I hear the purr of an expensive car engine, I know it's time. I crawl as close as I can without being seen. I'm still worried about will happen if someone contacts the Medici vampire I downed. I hope that Michael's plan to deal with him, whatever it is, pans out.

The car pulls into view. It stays where it is, doors closed and windows blackened. It is Lord Medici's vehicle, so I'm betting he's not leaving anything to chance and has come himself. My muscles tense. At Matt's urging we timed this before so, if Connor left on time, he should be here any second now. I can see the cashier ringing up the drinks inside the coffee shop. Connor had better hurry. Fortunately, Matt makes a show of fumbling his change, dropping coins on the floor and taking his time scooping them up. I smile grimly. He's not always lacking in initiative.

When Matt leaves the shop, balancing the cups in both hands, the car door opens and the formidable figure of Lord Medici steps out. Connor arrives in the nick of time, driving my bike past his lordship and up to Matt. He raises his visor and high-fives him.

'Hey buddy! What gives? Isn't my blood enough?'

I wince. I hope Medici doesn't register that Connor's delivery is wooden and forced..

Matt grins. 'Caffeine.'

'Did you get me one?'

He bobs his head dutifully.

'Three sugars?'

Matt's face falls. He's a much better actor than Connor. 'No.'

'You know I can't take coffee without sugar! It's not like anyone's bothered to stock up the office. You bloodguzzlers only think of yourselves.' Connor flounces into the coffee shop.

Matt shrugs and moves forward, just as Medici hails him. 'Matthew Montserrat! Come here!' Even though Medici is doing as I hoped, his imperious tone rankles. The order gives Matt no choice but to amble over. Unlike me, Matt takes no offence at the way Medici speaks; he has a goofy smile plastered over his face.

'Yes?'

Medici points to the car's interior. 'Get in.'

Matt's smile stretches wider and he moves towards the open door. Thankfully, Connor is on the ball and strides out of the coffee shop with perfect timing. 'Matt! Wait!'

Matt, inevitably, follows the last order. I watch Medici's face carefully. This is where the danger lies, although I'm counting on Medici maintaining at least some sense of responsibility. I can see the flash of cold rage on his face. As long as he stays where he is, though, his inner demons can do whatever they want. The vampires in the four corners of the square step forward, but Medici waves them back.

'I'll give you a lift,' Connor continues blithely to Matt. He glances at Medici and gives a little jump. 'Lord Medici! Hey! How's things?' Then, instead of waiting for an answer, he says quickly, 'Matt, why don't you get on the bike?'

Matt starts to turn. 'Stay where you are, Matthew,' Medici snaps. The ex-soldier freezes.

'I'm sorry, my Lord,' Connor babbles. 'You're not pissed off, are you? It was a really generous offer you made. I've been thinking about it and maybe I was a bit rash.'

Medici's cold eyes flick over him. 'If you want to see the next sunrise, you'll be wise to get out of here now.'

I grip the edges of the roof, ready to leap if this all goes tits up. It'll take me less than two seconds to make my presence known. I won't be a match for Medici, he's too old and far too powerful, but both Arzo and Michael agree that he won't attack all three of us together. Medici can get away with coercion but actual bodily harm would be too risky; if the other Families heard about it, they might ensure he feels the full weight of vampiric retribution. This is a popular square that teems with tourists during the day. There are several visible CCTV cameras to protect their pockets from criminal elements in the city. It's one of the reasons we chose this location.

'You *are* angry.' Connor is warming to his role and sounds more natural. 'Look, things aren't what I expected. Being around Bo is like tiptoeing round a freaking sleeping Kakos daemon. She snaps at the slightest thing. She doesn't like blood much either. It takes a pissing age to get her to drink. Arzo's not much better. He just mopes around because he thinks some long-lost love is going to show up at any minute.' He rolls his eyes. 'It's pathetic really.'

I think he's laying it on too thick but Medici licks his lips. I bite my tongue to prevent myself crowing in delight. He's going to fall for it.

'Who's the lucky lady?' Medici asks.

Connor's eyes widen. 'Oh. Me and my big mouth. I probably shouldn't have said anything. They told me not to...'

'Matthew,' Medici calls. 'Who is Arzo's long lost love?'

'Dolly.'

Medici looks puzzled. 'Do you mean Dahlia?'

Bingo.

'Yeah, sorry.' Matt nods. 'Dahlia.'

Medici smiles nastily. I shiver. 'Would you say he'd do anything for her?'

Before Matt can answer, Connor butts in. 'Yup!'

Medici has obviously had enough of the ginger-haired human. 'Get out of here. Matthew, get in the car.'

The nearest vampire stalks up and stands over Connor, blocking him from speaking to Matt who, again following the order he's been given, goes to the car. Unfortunately for Medici he trips, sending the hot coffee he's still clutching in a tsunami that drenches the vampire Lord from head to foot. All four vampires, including the one guarding Connor, jump forward.

'Matt, let's get out of here before Lord Medici snaps our necks,' Connor says. 'Run to the bike.' The pair take advantage of the kerfuffle. As soon as the bike's engine is revving, Connor shouts out, 'I'm sorry! It'll come out in the wash! Please don't kill us!' They disappear into the night. I want to stand up and applaud.

'You idiots!' Medici spits. 'Get off me!'

The bloodguzzlers, who are ineffectually dabbing at the coffee that's still dripping into tiny puddles around Medici's feet, spring backwards.

'I'm sorry, my Lord.'

'We can go after them…'

'Don't bother,' Medici growls. 'There'll be other times. At least we now know we did the sensible thing taking the woman. She may be an asset – when she calms down.' A dribble of coffee travels down his cheek. One of the vampires reaches forward to wipe it away. Medici lunges out and grabs him by the throat. 'I told you to get off me. Imbecile.' He lets go and the vampire drops to the ground. Medici casually aims a kick at his mid-section then gets into the waiting car. Two minutes later, the square is completely deserted.

CHAPTER 20

PLANT

Michael's spine is rigid. 'I'll kill him.'

The murderous look in his eyes makes me quake. I'm glad I'm not in the Medici Family right now.

'You can't.' Arzo is more pragmatic, despite the anguish visible on his lined face. 'My Lord, if you upset the balance of the Families, you'll set us back months. That's time we can't afford to lose.'

'His actions could destroy everything.' I gnaw on my bottom lip. 'Who knows what else he's planning?'

'We could infiltrate them.'

'How?'

Arzo shakes his head. 'I don't know.'

Michael's mouth is set in a grim line. 'The Family laws guard against that kind of action. It would be nigh on impossible.'

'Do you think he knows we're onto him?'

He shakes his head. 'He might have suspicions but he won't know for sure.'

'What about the vampire from the street that I downed?'

He doesn't meet my eyes. 'He's taken care of.'

'How?'

Arzo raises his eyebrows. 'The old time-honoured disposal technique?'

Michael nods. I put my hands on my hips. 'Which is?'

'It's a Montserrat matter, Bo.'

My shoulders tense. 'Are you suggesting I can't be trusted?'

'No. But this is on a need-to-know basis.'

'And I don't need to know? I was involved, Michael. I'm responsible for what happened.'

'No, you're not. Let it go.'

Uneasily, I search both his face and Arzo's. If I push, I'll never get a straight answer. I take the sensible – but more frustrating – approach and file it away. I'll find out the truth when emotions are less inflamed.

Arzo changes the subject. 'What about Dahlia? How do we save her?' he demands.

Michael sighs. 'We can't. It's too late. She's already a Medici fledgling.'

'Maybe she won't drink. Maybe she'll become Sanguine,' I say. Arzo and Michael stare at me. I shrug uncomfortably. 'It could happen.'

'Yeah,' Arzo spits. 'Or maybe you'll find a magical cure to reverse the process.'

I stop breathing. The vial of X's blood sitting in my fridge upstairs might turn out to be the most dangerous – or the most useful – liquid on the planet.

Thankfully Michael interrupts, although he flicks me a sardonic look. 'We used to have people trained in espionage who could infiltrate anything. The end of the Cold War has a lot to answer for. These days we leave that sort of stuff up to our American cousins. Our vampires are too damned rusty to be any use.'

'A spymaster would be handy,' I agree. Michael's eyes slide towards Arzo. 'What?' I demand.

Michael shrugs uncomfortably. 'You do need someone with experience to take charge of the firm.'

I shake my head. 'Oh no. Don't go there. Don't even say the words.'

'He knows tribers, Bo.'

'He hates tribers.'

'His beloved granddaughter is a triber.'

I hiss. 'He's retired. He won't do it.'

'There's no harm in asking.'

I glare at them both. 'He'll turn you down.'

There's the faintest of trace of a smile on Michael's lips. 'If you say so.'

I roll my eyes in disgust and grab my leather jacket. 'I'm going out for some fresh air.'

'I'll come with you,' Michael says.

'Don't bother. I've got some business to attend to.'

He stills. 'What kind of business?'

'It's personal.' I look at Arzo. 'I know you don't want any secrets, but this is nothing to do with the firm or the Family.'

'Take Matt then,' Michael says.

I point to Matt's gently snoring shape. 'I don't think he's in the mood. And I've said it before, my Lord. You're not my boss.' I shouldn't say the words but I do. 'This is on a need-to-know basis.'

Michael snarls quietly.

I sigh, softening my approach. 'I think I've proved I can take care of myself. I might be a fledgling but that doesn't mean I'm a weak little kitten. I'm stronger than Matt. Perhaps you should have a little faith in me.' I hold his gaze. I could lose myself for hours in those stormy depths. Maybe I don't need to trust him, maybe I just need him to look at me with that intense spark that somehow touches the very core of my being...

'I think that was a knock at the door,' Arzo interrupts. 'I'll just go and...'

'No, it's alright. Bo's a big girl. She's right.' A muscle jerks in Michael's cheek. 'You should go. You need to be back before dawn after all.'

'Thank you.' I reach up on my tiptoes to peck his cheek. His head turns at just the last second, however, and I kiss him on the lips. My insides tighten.

'Don't get hurt,' he says.

I smile at him while Arzo coughs awkwardly. To avoid further embarrassment, I leave as quickly as I can.

Using my newly acquired company smartphone, I call ahead. It would be better to see O'Connell's face when he learns that I'm alive but I'd barely make it across the Magix threshold before someone told him about my arrival so it would be a wasted effort. This way, at least I can catch him off guard. I'll have to use a low-tech device – my own ears – to work out if he's surprised that I'm not a burnt corpse. I'm hoping it will be news to him because then I'll find out whether he's happy or distraught. His reaction will determine whether he's made an enemy for life or merely a disgruntled acquaintance.

'Good evening. I'm calling from the *Daily Digest*. We're running a story tomorrow about Fingertips and Frolics, a store that was pushed out of the market by Magix corporation's dubious business practices. Would you like to include a quote?'

'Hold the line.'

I wait. Less than half a minute later O'Connell's voice fills the line. 'This is O'Connell. I believe you're a representative from the *Digest*?'

'Actually, no,' I say softly. 'I'm not.'

He's silent for some time before speaking. 'You're alive, Ms Blackman.'

'I am.'

'You know that it was not my desire to see you hurt. The man who attacked you has been dealt with accordingly.'

'There were two men.'

'Ah, yes. I'm told you dispatched the first one with admirable ease. Regardless, I have made it very clear to all my employees that you are not to be harmed. If you are, the consequences for them will be ... devastating.'

I shiver. O'Connell clearly doesn't appreciate dissent in the ranks. But I am satisfied that he's telling the truth. 'I was hoping that we could meet face to face,' I say evenly. 'I have a few questions.'

He laughs. 'Ah. You've uncovered my pet project, haven't you? You realise that if you really did work for the *Daily Digest*, you'd have quite a scoop.'

'I'm sure you have plenty of willing hacks who'll publicise your efforts when you want them to. After all, if you have the police moonlighting for you, why not a journalist or two?'

'I am impressed! Ms Blackman, we really should put you on the payroll. You have uncovered a great deal.'

I dangle the carrot. 'Then meet me.'

'When would suit you?'

I stop walking and gaze up at the Magix building. 'Oh, right about now sounds good.'

～

Swanson meets me at the entrance, magical handcuffs at the ready. I hold out my wrists like a good little vampire. 'It's good to see you're still in one piece,' she says. 'Mr O'Connell didn't want you killed.'

'He's all heart.'

She looks at me earnestly. 'He is. He's going to change the world, you know.'

'So I keep hearing.'

'Don't be so sceptical. It's taken a while, but he's finally aligned everything.' Her eyes shine. 'We're going to make history.'

Her adulatory tone makes me cringe but I don't want to pass up the opportunity to make a friend. You never know which contacts might prove useful in the future. I humour her. 'How long has he been in charge?'

'Since 2001. I remember the day he joined us. It was September but still very hot and sunny. He spent three days meeting every employee individually. Not every boss cares that much.'

'Mmm.'

She drops me off in the same waiting area as before. I decline the offer of a drink, even though she states proudly they have O neg on ice. I wouldn't trust anything from this place passing my lips. She leaves and I settle down on the uncomfortable sofa. Thankfully this time I'm not subjected to my own exploits on CCTV; instead, the television is playing an old interview of O'Connell's.

'There are people who say that Magix is only concerned with profit,' says the glossy interviewer. 'What do you say to that?'

'Money doesn't interest me. It won't do you any good when you're six feet under. My priority is making the world a better place.'

I clutch a cushion and stare at his smiling face. Damn. I've heard those words before.

'Ms Blackman.'

I turn in O'Connell's direction and jump to my feet. I scan his features, taking in every detail. He strides over and takes my hand. 'I would like to apologise sincerely again.'

'And yet I'm still trussed up like a criminal.'

His lips purse. 'You're right.' He releases the handcuffs. Strength and circulation return almost immediately. I murmur my thanks and pull away from his grip then raise my eyes to his.

'You've combined black and white magic.'

He bows his head. 'I'd love to take credit for it but we have some very capable techs who did all the real work.'

'Why?'

O'Connell laughs. 'Why? Are you serious?' He leans towards me, passion in his face. 'Black and white witches have been at each other's throats for hundreds of years. Thousands even. By bringing them together, I'll stop all that.'

'And double your sales overnight. If black witches buy white magic products and vice-versa...'

'That was how I persuaded the board. But think about what will happen. A new age of magic. Not black, not white. Just combined power and genuine peace.'

'You're kidding yourself.' My voice is flat. 'You can't wipe out generations of inbred mutual hatred just like that.'

'Oh, I beg to differ, Ms Blackman. We're already there.'

I snort. 'You can't even get witches to follow a simple no-kill order. The black witch who came after me first? He was one of your hybrids. He wanted to slice my throat because I'm a Blackman. Because his kind holds a grudge against my grandfather. He couldn't let go of that.'

'That's an entirely different matter,' O'Connell blusters.

'Is it? Well, take the second witch then. The one who so

deftly threw a shuriken into Frolic's chest?' I watch him flinch. 'He might have the power of black and white magic but he's still a white witch at heart. He made it clear he hates black witches and everything they stand for.'

He glares at me. 'He won't be bothering us again.'

'Two of your freaky witches and neither of them is prepared to let go of the past. You're not changing the world for the better, you're making it more dangerous.'

'There will always be non-believers,' he hisses. 'My Janus witches will prove you wrong.'

'You had Samuel Lewis killed.'

'Who?'

'Did you know he had a wife and child at home? You hired him to steal Frolic's damned feather and when he was arrested, you had him slaughtered in his own cell.'

'Some casualties are to be expected.'

'You're despicable,' I spit.

'You drink blood to survive, Ms Blackman. Who is really despicable?' His veneer of respectability is slipping.

'The witches aren't really the Janus, are they, Fingertip? You are.'

O'Connell's face drops. 'Get out.'

'You faked your own death to join Magix. Let your wife believe you were a stone-cold corpse. That's why you had such extensive files on her.'

'Have you seen a picture of this Fingertip? I can assure you I look nothing like him.'

'Your company has been developing glamour spells. I'm betting that underneath the skin you wear is a very different looking man. In fact that's probably why everyone who works here looks human. It must be a fucking good spell.' I lean my head towards him. 'But tell me, why did you do it?'

He snarls, giving in to the truth. 'We were never going to achieve anything with that shop! Here I can change the world.'

'You ran your own wife out of business.'

'She needed to get away from all that! All she cared about was making money. I thought she'd take a break if the shop shut. Think about the bigger picture. After things calmed down, I was going to talk to her…'

'Too late.' I keep my face expressionless. 'She's dead.'

'That wasn't supposed to happen.'

I shake my head. 'You set the wheels in motion.'

'Get out of here!' He fumbles towards me, arms flailing. I spin him round to avoid being hit and grab both his wrists with one hand. With the other, I reach into my jacket pocket and pull out the baggie with the blood-encrusted shuriken. It's a simple matter to transfer it to O'Connell's jacket without him noticing. I jerk him backwards. 'Your hands might not be dirty, but you're a murderer.'

'You killed a witch.'

'That was self-defence.'

'To protect yourself. I'm going to protect the world!' he shouts.

'No,' I say sadly. 'You're not.'

I release him and walk away, not looking back. I'm sure he'll be on the phone as soon as I exit the doors of Magix, sending his horde of hybrids after me. The problem for him is that I'll be on the phone too. There's a certain helpful policeman who may not be able to get enough evidence for Samuel Lewis's murder, but who might find enough to put O'Connell away for Frolic's.

I examine my conscience. I don't feel the slightest guilt. O'Connell may have had genuine motives but he's still a dirty bastard who deserves to spend the rest of his life behind bars. I'm hoping it'll make the world he's so keen to save a slightly safer place.

EPILOGUE

Stephen Templeton and I stand amongst the ruined remnants of his life. He picks up the smashed frame encasing the photograph of Dahlia, Arzo and himself and stares at it. 'I don't even remember this being taken,' he says.

I watch him silently. I'm sure that if I asked Arzo if he recalled the shot, he could expand on it in great detail. Templeton reaches down and scoops up the larger shards of glass.

'I suppose I should be careful not to cut myself,' he jokes. 'I wouldn't want you to jump on me and drain me of my blood.'

'You're in no danger from me.'

'Are you sure the other bloodguzzlers won't come after me?' He pulls at his collar. 'I could hire a bodyguard maybe. Witness protection programme even.'

'The police run witness protection. And you can't tell them what's happened. You can't tell *anyone* what's happened.' I don't change the tenor of my voice. 'Things will go very badly if you do.'

He laughs nervously. 'Is that a threat?'

'No.' I hold out my palm for the photo but he shakes his head.

'I'd like to keep this. If you don't mind,' he says.

'As you wish.' I look around. 'Will you stay here?'

'In this house?' He shudders. 'No. There are too many shadows. Too many ghosts.'

'She's not dead, Stephen.'

He stares at me balefully. 'She may as well be.'

I have nothing to say to that, nothing that wouldn't sound trite. Somehow I don't think Medici will be jumping on the 'fledglings flying the Family coop early' bandwagon.

'If you want to take anything with you, I can help you pack,' I offer.

'No. I need to start afresh.' He picks the glass out of the frame, removes the photo and places it in his wallet. It's too big to fit; it'll be creased and ruined but I don't stop him. 'I'll just keep this,' he says. 'A reminder.'

'Why did you do it?'

'What?'

'Betray Arzo like that. He was your best friend.'

'He was a naïve fool.' Templeton's tone is so dismissive it takes my breath away. I'd like to think that his callousness is the result of his grief but, sadly, I know it's not true.

'Come on,' I say finally, desperate to get away from here. 'I'll give you a lift back to the hotel.'

'No. I'll drive myself.'

I don't argue. We walk outside. Templeton lifts up the garage door. I shake my head: he should have learned to lock up by now. I cross the street, get onto my bike and start the engine. From inside the garage, I can hear Templeton revving his car. I guess it's been dormant for too long as he seems to be having some trouble. The engine turns over several times.

I'm about to take off when my eyes drift down the quiet suburban street. There's a gleaming black car parked not too far away. The driver gets out and opens the passenger door. The moment I recognise Cheung's face, I realise what's going on.

Dropping the bike, I run towards the garage, shouting at Templeton to stop. I'm still several metres away when there's an explosion and I'm thrown back by a wall of intense heat. My eyes are streaming. I scramble to my feet, using my arm to shield my exposed face. There are distressed shouts and calls as people are jolted awake in the neighbouring houses. An alarm shrieks. Templeton's garage is ablaze, flames starkly silhouetted against the dark night sky and billows of dirty smoke streaking away in every direction.

I can't watch.

Cheung strides towards me. 'I must thank you, Ms Blackman. Were it not for your visit, the accountant would probably have got away with it. You encouraged me to look a little closer.' He shrugs. 'I suppose that's what I get for out-sourcing.'

He pats me on the shoulder and turns back to his car. As he climbs inside and the chauffeur drives off, I think that it doesn't matter who you are or what ethnicity or triber faction you hail from: every group has its monsters. We might kid ourselves and think we're better, that our group is ethically and morally superior to everyone else, but there will always be daemons or witches or vampires or humans who seek to unbalance the blade. Mother is right.

I watch the flames for another moment or two and wonder whether Dahlia will be informed. Then I zip up my jacket, pick up my bike and accelerate away.

❧

I_T_'s quiet when I pull up outside Crossbones. There's a light drizzle, as if to tell me that I'll never venture anywhere near this place without suffering the effects of English weather. The walls and rusty gates are shrouded in a thin mist and I feel like I'm walking onto the set of a music video. Except I doubt that Maisie knows what a video is.

When I turn off the bike's engine, she's already there, waiting with a lopsided smile. 'Hey,' I say awkwardly.

'Good evening, Bo.' She dips a curtsey and looks at me curiously. 'You still walk in the night.'

'I do.' I swallow and meet her eyes. 'I've found a cure.'

If she's surprised, she doesn't show it. 'The allure of your new power is too strong.'

I shake my head vehemently. 'No. It's not that. There's trouble,' I explain. 'We're setting up a new agency. It's going to help the vampires, I mean, the nightwalkers. It'll help the humans too.' I think of Templeton's untimely end. 'Some of them, anyway. It's going to change things. Big things. I need to stay like this. To make it work.' I trip over my words; my staccato sentences sound thoroughly implausible.

Maisie's not fooled for a second. She cocks her head knowingly. 'That's not the real reason.'

I look away. 'It's one of them.'

'Is he terribly handsome?'

'Terribly,' I mutter.

'Is he good?'

'I think so.' My words are almost inaudible.

'You're not sure?'

I bite my lip. 'He's been good to me.'

'For some, that would be enough.'

'Yes,' I reply softly, 'for some it would.'

Maisie clasps her hands together and turns, vanishing through the walls. Being made of more solid atoms, I'm forced to take the long way round. She's still waiting inside, however. We walk down the gravelled path, past the stone circle and Mother's wraith-like figure. He raises his eyes to mine and I'm sure I see a glimmer of welcome before he turns away. Maisie breaks into a little skip. Her soul may be hundreds of years old but there will always be something of a little girl about her. I smile fondly until it occurs to me I'm being patronising. I'm not here for that.

She turns a corner and gestures towards a rickety wooden bench covered with crude graffiti. I trace over the sharp edges of a name.

'He was a sad man,' Maisie tells me.

I glance at the letters. 'Boomer?'

'I don't know his name.'

I forget that she's illiterate. 'I can teach you if you like.' I make the offer tentatively. I don't want to belabour the fact that my life in the twenty-first century is worlds away from hers.

Her face, however, breaks into a radiant smile. 'Really?'

I grin, relieved. 'Really.' I point to the first letter. 'This is a B.'

'B,' she whispers. 'Like b for blood.'

'Yes. Like b for blood.' I think for a minute. 'Or beauty.'

Maisie's eyes light up. 'Beginning?'

I lift my face up to the drizzle and gaze at the velvet black night and twinkling diamond stars. And I smile.

Press Release

We are proud to announce the opening today of New Order, a special venture to improve relations between vampires and humans. Any human who has a grievance against a vampire can be assured that their complaint will be dealt with swiftly and with the utmost professionalism. Every issue brought to our attention will be thoroughly examined and investigated by our dedicated team of vampires and humans. We will work together to provide you with the answers you seek.

Headed by former MI7 intelligence chief, Arbuthnot Blackman, New Order is striving to create a better world whereby tribers and humans can live together in harmony. We will meet the demands of the new millennium and create a more positive future for us all.

About the Author

After teaching English literature in the UK, Japan and Malaysia, Helen Harper left behind the world of education following the worldwide success of her Blood Destiny series of books. She is a professional member of the Alliance of Independent Authors and writes full time, thanking her lucky stars every day that's she lucky enough to do so!

Helen has always been a book lover, devouring science fiction and fantasy tales when she was a child growing up in Scotland.

She currently lives in Edinburgh in the UK with far too many cats – not to mention the dragons, fairies, demons, wizards and vampires that seem to keep appearing from nowhere.

OTHER TITLES

The complete *FireBrand* series

A werewolf killer. A paranormal murder. How many times can Emma Bellamy cheat death?

I'm one placement away from becoming a fully fledged London detective. It's bad enough that my last assignment before I qualify is with Supernatural Squad. But that's nothing compared to what happens next.

Brutally murdered by an unknown assailant, I wake up twelve hours later in the morgue – and I'm very much alive. I don't know how or why it happened. I don't know who killed me. All I know is that they might try again.

Werewolves are disappearing right, left and centre.

A mysterious vampire seems intent on following me everywhere I go.

And I have to solve my own vicious killing. Preferably before death comes for me again.

Book One – Brimstone Bound

Book Two – Infernal Enchantment

Book Three – Midnight Smoke

Book Four – Scorched Heart

Book Five – Dark Whispers

Book Six – A Killer's Kiss

Book Seven – Fortune's Ashes

~

A Charade of Magic complete series

The best way to live in the Mage ruled city of Glasgow is to keep your head down and your mouth closed.

That's not usually a problem for Mairi Wallace. By day she works at a small shop selling tartan and by night she studies to become an apothecary. She knows her place and her limitations. All that changes, however, when her old childhood friend sends her a desperate message seeking her help - and the Mages themselves cross Mairi's path. Suddenly, remaining unnoticed is no longer an option.

There's more to Mairi than she realises but, if she wants to fulfil her full potential, she's going to have to fight to stay alive - and only time will tell if she can beat the Mages at their own game.

From twisted wynds and tartan shops to a dangerous daemon and the magic infused City Chambers, the future of a nation might lie with one solitary woman.

Book One – Hummingbird

Book Two – Nightingale

Book Three – Red Hawk

~

The complete *Blood Destiny* series

"A spectacular and addictive series."

Mackenzie Smith has always known that she was different. Growing up as the only human in a pack of rural shapeshifters will do that to you, but then couple it with some mean fighting skills and a fiery

temper and you end up with a woman that few will dare to cross.
However, when the only father figure in her life is brutally murdered,
and the dangerous Brethren with their predatory Lord Alpha come to
investigate, Mack has to not only ensure the physical safety of her
adopted family by hiding her apparent humanity, she also has to seek
the blood-soaked vengeance that she craves.

Book One - Bloodfire

Book Two - Bloodmagic

Book Three - Bloodrage

Book Four - Blood Politics

Book Five - Bloodlust

Also

Corrigan Fire

Corrigan Magic

Corrigan Rage

Corrigan Politics

Corrigan Lust

The complete *Bo Blackman* series

A half-dead daemon, a massacre at her London based PI firm and
evidence that suggests she's the main suspect for both ... Bo Blackman
is having a very bad week.

She might be naive and inexperienced but she's determined to get to
the bottom of the crimes, even if it means involving herself with one of
London's most powerful vampire Families and their enigmatic leader.

It's pretty much going to be impossible for Bo to ever escape unscathed.

Book One - Dire Straits

Book Two - New Order

Book Three - High Stakes

Book Four - Red Angel

Book Five - Vigilante Vampire

Book Six - Dark Tomorrow

The complete *Highland Magic* series

Integrity Taylor walked away from the Sidhe when she was a child. Orphaned and bullied, she simply had no reason to stay, especially not when the sins of her father were going to remain on her shoulders. She found a new family - a group of thieves who proved that blood was less important than loyalty and love.

But the Sidhe aren't going to let Integrity stay away forever. They need her more than anyone realises - besides, there are prophecies to be fulfilled, people to be saved and hearts to be won over. If anyone can do it, Integrity can.

Book One - Gifted Thief

Book Two - Honour Bound

Book Three - Veiled Threat

Book Four - Last Wish

The complete *Dreamweaver* series

"I have special coping mechanisms for the times I need to open the front door. They're even often successful..."

Zoe Lydon knows there's often nothing logical or rational about fear. It doesn't change the fact that she's too terrified to step outside her own house, however.

What Zoe doesn't realise is that she's also a dreamweaver - able to access other people's subconscious minds. When she finds herself in the Dreamlands and up against its sinister Mayor, she'll need to use all of her wits - and overcome all of her fears - if she's ever going to come out alive.

Book One - Night Shade

Book Two - Night Terrors

Book Three - Night Lights

~

Stand alone novels

Eros

William Shakespeare once wrote that, "Cupid is a knavish lad, thus to make poor females mad." The trouble is that Cupid himself would probably agree...

As probably the last person in the world who'd appreciate hearts, flowers and romance, Coop is convinced that true love doesn't exist – which is rather unfortunate considering he's also known as Cupid, the God of Love. He'd rather spend his days drinking, womanising and generally having as much fun as he possible can. As far as he's concerned, shooting people with bolts of pure love is a waste of his time...but then his path crosses with that of shy and retiring Skye Sawyer and nothing will ever be quite the same again.

Wraith

Magic. Shadows. Adventure. Romance.

Saiya Buchanan is a wraith, able to detach her shadow from her body and send it off to do her bidding. But, unlike most of her kin, Saiya doesn't deal in death. Instead, she trades secrets - and in the goblin besieged city of Stirling in Scotland, they're a highly prized commodity. It might just be, however, that the goblins have been hiding the greatest secret of them all. When Gabriel de Florinville, a Dark Elf, is sent as royal envoy into Stirling and takes her prisoner, Saiya is not only going to uncover the sinister truth. She's also going to realise that sometimes the deepest secrets are the ones locked within your own heart.

~

The complete *Lazy Girl's Guide To Magic* series

Hard Work Will Pay Off Later. Laziness Pays Off Now.

Let's get one thing straight - Ivy Wilde is not a heroine. In fact, she's probably the last witch in the world who you'd call if you needed a magical helping hand. If it were down to Ivy, she'd spend all day every day on her sofa where she could watch TV, munch junk food and talk to her feline familiar to her heart's content.

However, when a bureaucratic disaster ends up with Ivy as the victim of a case of mistaken identity, she's yanked very unwillingly into Arcane Branch, the investigative department of the Hallowed Order of Magical Enlightenment. Her problems are quadrupled when a valuable object is stolen right from under the Order's noses.

It doesn't exactly help that she's been magically bound to Adeptus Exemptus Raphael Winter. He might have piercing sapphire eyes and a body which a cover model would be proud of but, as far as Ivy's concerned, he's a walking advertisement for the joyless perils of too much witch-work.

And if he makes her go to the gym again, she's definitely going to turn him into a frog.

Book One - Slouch Witch

Book Two - Star Witch

Book Three - Spirit Witch

Sparkle Witch (Christmas novella)

The complete *Fractured Faery* series

One corpse. Several bizarre looking attackers. Some very strange magical powers. And a severe bout of amnesia.

It's one thing to wake up outside in the middle of the night with a decapitated man for company. It's another to have no memory of how you got there - or who you are.

She might not know her own name but she knows that several people are out to get her. It could be because she has strange magical powers seemingly at her fingertips and is some kind of fabulous hero. But then why does she appear to inspire fear in so many? And who on earth is the sexy, green-eyed barman who apparently despises her? So many questions ... and so few answers.

At least one thing is for sure - the streets of Manchester have never met someone quite as mad as Madrona...

Book One - Box of Frogs

SHORTLISTED FOR THE KINDLE STORYTELLER AWARD 2018

Book Two - Quiver of Cobras

Book Three - Skulk of Foxes

The complete *City Of Magic* series

Charley is a cleaner by day and a professional gambler by night. She might be haunted by her tragic past but she's never thought of herself as anything or anyone special. Until, that is, things start to go terribly wrong all across the city of Manchester. Between plagues of rats, firestorms and the gleaming blue eyes of a sexy Scottish werewolf, she might just have landed herself in the middle of a magical apocalypse. She might also be the only person who has the ability to bring order to an utterly chaotic new world.

Book One - Shrill Dusk

Book Two - Brittle Midnight

Book Three - Furtive Dawn